HER PULSE RATE ACCELERATED

As they got out of the elevator, Madeline's heart began to pound. They came to her door, and she stood irresolutely in front of it. Something told her that this wasn't the moment to ask Chris in.

"I'm not going to pose any problems for you." Chris had sensed her indecision. Then he looked into her incredible turquoise eyes, and the passion he saw there staggered him. He drew Madeline into his arms, and their mutual yearning surfaced.

Suddenly the elevator door clanged open, and they quickly let go of each other as a portly couple passed them in the corridor.

"Saved by the gong, eh?" Chris teased. "Maybe next time you won't be so lucky."

"Really?" Madeline murmured wickedly. "I can't wait...."

ABOUT THE AUTHOR

In this spin-off of *The Forever Promise*,
Meg Hudson not only brings us back to Claire
and King Faraday's beautiful hometown of
Lakeport, New York, but also treats us to a little
of the globetrotting she is so famous for. This
prolific author takes King's best friend, Chris
Talmadge, from Aruba to Boston to New York
City, on a journey that can only lead to the heart.

Books by Meg Hudson

Don't miss any of our special offers. Write to us at the
following address for information on our newest releases.

Harlequin Reader Service
901 Fuhrmann Blvd., P.O. Box 1397, Buffalo, NY 14240
Canadian address: P.O. Box 603,
Fort Erie, Ont. L2A 5X3

Meg Hudson

A WAY TO REMEMBER

Harlequin Books

TORONTO • NEW YORK • LONDON
AMSTERDAM • PARIS • SYDNEY • HAMBURG
STOCKHOLM • ATHENS • TOKYO • MILAN

Published March 1987

First printing January 1987

ISBN 0-373-70250-7

Printed in Canada

For Don German...

who lives in our memories.
How he would have chuckled
at the idea of me dedicating
a "romance" to him. Yet, like most
true romantics, he was kind,
gentle, compassionate, sharing.
A dedicated writer...
A terrific guy.

CHAPTER ONE

THE CASINO BECKONED, tantalizing as Fate's allegorical finger. Slim-stemmed cocktail glasses, palm trees, a giant pair of dice, and a spinning roulette wheel—all fashioned from multicolored neon and strictly Deco in design—glowed above the wide entrance that opened off the spacious hotel lobby. They were an invitation to a glittering slice of nightlife, and Madeline wished it was an invitation she could accept. But she'd never been much of a gambler, and wouldn't know where to start.

She turned her attention to the hotel newsstand, and started to thumb through a magazine. But she felt as if the casino lights were winking at her.

A cheerful voice asked, "Gotten over your jet lag yet?"

Madeline looked up into the pink-cheeked face of the man who'd been her seat companion on the flight to Aruba. He'd introduced himself as Arthur Taylor, and had told her he was from Philadelphia. He was old enough to be her father and—happily—acted his age.

She smiled at him. "I still feel rather disoriented," she confessed.

"A good night's sleep and you'll be ready for everything this island has to offer," he promised.

Arthur Taylor was a widower, traveling alone. He'd just retired from a long and successful career as a land-use planner. He had a son who was an accountant in

Trenton, and a daughter, married to a lawyer in Wilmington, who'd just presented him with his first grandchild. He was a nice man, a comfortable person to be with. Someone who'd come to terms with his life.

Madeline ruefully wished she could say the same for herself.

He nodded toward the casino. "Going to try your luck?"

She laughed. "To tell you the truth, I wouldn't know how to begin!"

He chuckled. "Well, I'd say this is as good a place as any to spread your wings. As I understand it, this is one of the biggest and best casinos in the entire Caribbean, so you'd be starting right at the top." He paid for the overseas edition of the *Wall Street Journal* he had taken from the newsstand, folded it and tucked it under his arm. "Tell you what," he suggested. "Let's go in and meander around."

She smiled. "I'll chance that much!"

As she moved through the glitzy entrance with Arthur Taylor at her side, Madeline decided that the casino's designer must have been dedicated to Deco. The theme was continued in the blue-mirrored wall panels outlined by bands of shiny black glass. Even the people sitting at the roulette wheels and blackjack tables, and those standing in front of the slot machines, could have been Hollywood extras from a movie set of the post-World War I era.

Not everyone dressed up at night in Aruba's chic Palm Beach, a district comprised mainly of highrise hotels geared to the international tourist trade. But most of the clientele in the Aruban Palace Casino were fashion plates, tailored perfectly to the decor. Their clothes reflected the vintage styles that were part of a current nostalgia craze.

The woman "at work" in front of the nearest slot machine was a classic example. She was a platinum blonde à la Jean Harlow. She was wearing a bias-cut white satin gown that swept the floor after hugging every curving inch of her body. And that actually *was* a white feather boa draped around her neck.

Madeline heard Arthur Taylor whistle softly. "Makes me feel like I've wandered into a time warp and plunged back into the twenties," he said. "Take a look at her!"

"She is . . . something," Madeline murmured.

"A big-time spender, too," Arthur Taylor noted. "Watch her toss away those dollars!"

The blonde was playing three dollars at a time, sliding the coins into their proper slots, then giving the machine's big metal lever a sharp downward tug.

Madeline heard the lady mutter an unladylike four-letter word as the machine displayed two plums and a lemon. Immediately she inserted another series of silver dollars. Then she loftily accepted a frosty, liquid-filled glass from an impeccably clad waiter who had materialized at her side.

The lady, Madeline opined, really didn't need another drink. She was already weaving and well on her way to being not only tipsy, but drunk. Fortune seemed to be smiling on her, nonetheless. Bells started to clang and then silver dollars spewed forth from the machine's base while bright lights flashed. The woman in white had hit the jackpot!

"That's unreal!" Madeline gasped.

Arthur Taylor shrugged. "Ready to try your luck?"

The casino atmosphere was getting to her. "Why not?" she decided.

"Find yourself a machine you like the looks of, and I'll get some change," her companion suggested.

Madeline started to protest, but Arthur Taylor had already started to make his way toward a cashier's cage.

For a moment she stood irresolute. She felt not only inexperienced, but somewhat underdressed in this environment. She'd literally let down her sable-brown hair tonight, releasing it from the contemporary version of a French twist she usually wore. It touched her shoulders, swirling slightly when she moved, giving her a pleasant, admittedly feminine feeling. She was wearing a simple blue silk dress that was as expensive as its excellent cut suggested. But she in no way matched up to an elaborate platinum blond coiffure, a white satin gown, and a feather boa!

Also, one slot machine looked like another to her. She gazed helplessly at the row of machines she was confronting, trying to read something into the visible assembly of plums and cherries, lemons and oranges that might, in a mysterious way, spell luck.

As she peered ahead intently, she heard a low-pitched masculine chuckle. A matching voice with a definite American accent observed humorously, "There really are no magic formulas to decipher. A slot machine is a slot machine is a slot machine, with the odds usually stacked in favor of the house. So, you take your pick and cross your fingers as you pull the lever."

Madeline turned toward the speaker. He was sitting on a high stool in front of the slot machine to her right, about to insert a silver dollar. The lights in the casino mixed blue and rose and white in a way that created an entirely new color spectrum and made the people look almost as surreal as the setting itself. Half of this man's face was bathed in a rosy glow, while the other half was cast in blue. But he was attractive, and about her own age, Madeline estimated. She was fairly adept at guessing ages. She placed him in his mid-thirties.

It was impossible to tell the color of his hair or eyes accurately in this light, but she liked the way his features were put together. She also liked his smile and the pleasant timbre of his voice.

Indicating the machine next to his, he said, "No one's been playing that one since I've been here. Why not give it a whirl when your husband gets back?"

Her husband? It took a second for Madeline to realize that her compatriot was referring to Arthur Taylor. She shook her head, smiling. "He's not my husband."

"Your father, then?"

"No. Just a friend."

After she'd spoken, she evaluated her sentence. The word "friend" had become such a multifaceted expression. She was about to explain that she and Arthur Taylor had met only today, on the flight down from the States. But explaining too much could sometimes be like protesting too much, so she held back the words.

Arthur Taylor appeared at her elbow, holding out a large cardboard cup filled with silver coins. "Casino dollars," he announced.

Madeline fumbled for her handbag. "Here . . . let me pay you for them."

He grinned. "I'm going to trust in your luck. Go ahead, let 'er rip."

Following his instructions, Madeline inserted a coin and tugged the lever. The slot machine whirred into action. But when the first symbol to appear was a bright yellow lemon, the man at her side said, "That means you've struck out first time around. Try again."

She did, and this time a bunch of cherries was the first symbol to appear. As she heard the exciting sound of coins clanging into the tray at the base of the machine, Madeline laughed with delight. Then she discovered that she'd won only two casino dollars.

Chagrined, she said to Arthur, "How much did you invest in me?"

"Twenty dollars. Stop worrying about it, will you?"

"The way I'm going, it'll be a long night before I win back your money," she informed him wryly.

"You've got plenty of time," he reminded her. "You're going to be here two weeks." He glanced at the man by her side, evidently concluded she was in good company, and said, "Well, now that you're settled in I think I'll toddle along. We'll meet tomorrow, I'm sure."

"Definitely we'll meet," Madeline said resolutely. "I intend to catch up with you and pay you back."

Arthur left her with a parting paternal pat on the shoulder, and she again addressed her attention to the slot machine. But another lemon appeared and Madeline frowned. Turning to the man at her side she asked, "Are you having any luck?"

He held out a paper cup like the one she was holding and grinned. She saw two silver dollars nestled in the bottom. "And it was half full ten minutes ago," he informed her ruefully.

"Evidently they pay off once in a while," Madeline mused. "I just saw a woman win a jackpot."

"The blonde?" the man at her side queried. "In white, tonight, I believe. Last night it was red. The night before that it was pink . . ."

"I take it you've been here a while."

He nodded. "Nearly a week. And you? You're new, aren't you?"

"I arrived this afternoon."

"Then I'm sure you've already been warned to watch out for too much exposure to the sun, and to ask for a stalk of aloe plant if you feel yourself getting burned."

Madeline smiled. "Sounds like a routine pitch," she commented.

"It is, but it's also necessary. The sun here is wicked, even though there's always a breeze blowing—the trade wind," he amended. "It has a rather deceptive effect. You lose sight of how hot it really is, of how strong the sun is. We're only a few hundred miles from the equator, after all."

As he spoke he inserted a dollar in his slot machine and tugged the lever. Three bells appeared in a row, followed by the cascading sound of coins tinkling into the metal tray.

"I'll be damned!" Madeline's fellow American exclaimed in astonishment. He turned to her. "That's the first time I've hit since I've been here," he said, then added, his voice lower, "It's also the first bit of luck I've had in longer than I like to remember."

The statement piqued her curiosity, but before Madeline could frame a reply that wouldn't sound too inquisitive, she saw the woman in white wending her way toward them. She was clutching a drink in one hand and a wooden boxlike affair in the other. There were six of the paper coin cups nested side by side in the wooden box, each brimming with casino dollars.

The blonde paused by the man at Madeline's side and tapped him lightly on the shoulder. "Hi, handsome," she greeted him, as if she'd just stepped out of a Roaring Twenties movie. "How's it going?"

"Okay," he said. "How's it with you, Theda?"

"Couldn't be better," the woman slurred, her English faintly accented. Her glance fell upon Madeline, then veered to the slot machine in front of which Madeline was standing. "You using that machine, honey?" she asked.

The woman was actually nudging her. Madeline, edging away, fibbed reluctantly, "No, I was just about to move on."

She caught the reproachful look her fellow American slanted her—a look that was equivalent to stating, out loud, that she was being a traitor to leave him in Theda's clutches.

Smiling at this, Madeline found a vacant machine at the end of another row. This one was next to a man and his wife who struck up a brief conversation with Madeline, telling her they were from Venezuela. They were taking turns feeding their dollars into the slot and then bemoaning Fate in fluent Spanish each time they lost.

For the next half hour, Madeline fed her machine. She discovered there was an interesting euphoria in plunging the coins into the slot, pulling down the lever, then waiting until the mechanical win-or-lose message was spelled out. She encountered her share of lemons, then the machine bestowed three oranges in a row and she promptly won sixteen dollars. And so it went.

Finally her paper cup was half full of casino dollars, which could be turned in for the real thing at the cashier's window. Tired at this point, feeling the effects of her long day of travel, she was about to head for the cashier's cage when an accusing voice halted her in her tracks.

"You!"

The voice was so venomous that most of the people in the immediate area automatically stopped what they were doing. With the machines temporarily silent, a strange hush ensued.

Madeline turned to see the platinum blonde weaving toward her. The woman had passed the stage of tipsiness. She was definitely drunk. Also, she was furious.

She pointed a scarlet-nailed finger accusingly at Madeline. The blonde's blood-red lipstick was smeared, lending an added macabre touch. Ribbons of colored light banded the woman's face as she advanced. At one point her hair was like pink cotton candy. The next, it looked as if nature had played a trick on her, turning her hair to snow and painting her skin blue.

"She's the one," she screeched, waving her finger violently at Madeline as she spoke. "She stole my money! It was next to the slot machine I was working when I went to the john. When I came back, it was gone. And so was she, with that nice-looking lame guy."

Nice-looking lame guy?

A short, dark-haired man wearing a tuxedo hurried toward the blonde, accompanied by one of the several uniformed guards who seemed to spend most of their time lounging near the casino entrance.

"I am the manager," the man announced in Spanish-accented English. "What is the problem, señora?"

"She's a damned thief!" the blonde accused, glaring at Madeline. Again, she shook a pointing finger. In doing so, her feather boa slid slowly off her shoulders, slithering into a heap on the casino floor.

The guard retrieved the boa and held it out to her, but the blonde pushed him away. "I don't want *that*," she scoffed. "I want my money back!"

"You left your money behind you, Theda," a quiet voice stated. "One of the attendants took it to the nearest cashier's cage. I think you'll find they're holding it for you, if you ask."

The good-looking American had come upon the scene slowly, emerging from another row of slot machines. Glancing toward him, Madeline saw that he leaned heavily on a cane as he walked. So, *he* was the "nice-looking lame guy."

Habit caused her to give him a quick professional evaluation. It was his left leg that he favored, she noted. With an unconsciously appraising eye, she observed that his knee did not bend properly. There seemed very little flexibility in the joint. Also, he walked with a cautiousness that suggested his handicap was fairly new— something he was not yet accustomed to coping with. Probably, he'd been in an accident a while back and was still recouping.

Aware that she was being not only clinical, but also overt in her appraisal, Madeline tried to look away. Instead she found herself gazing directly into the attractive American's face.

It was impossible to assess color correctly, in view of the casino's lighting effects. But she would have sworn, if from his expression alone, that he was flushing . . . and knew that she'd embarrassed him.

The blonde was staggering toward the cashier's cage, followed closely by the agitated casino manager and the uniformed guard. The other people in the vicinity were returning to their personal attempts at beating the gambling odds. Briefly, Madeline and her compatriot were in their own small oasis. Chagrined, she felt at a loss for words. What was she supposed to say? "I'm sorry, I didn't mean to stare."

She settled for the obvious, and said, "Thank you for getting me out of what could have been a rather nasty situation."

"Theda's not all bad," he answered unexpectedly. "Actually, she's a lonely soul. She's part English, part Dutch, and evidently has no place she really considers home. She has more money than she knows what to do with, acquired from *three* husbands—I believe that's the right count. She drinks too much, gambles too much, but like a lot of us she's actually chasing that elusive pot at the end of the rainbow called happiness."

He broke off and smiled, a self-mocking smile. "Whew!" he observed. "How's that for philosophy? And on only two scotches, spread over a large chunk of the evening." He held out his right hand. "By the way, my name's Chris Talmadge."

"I'm Madeline Clarke."

"Hello, Madeline Clarke."

As he spoke, Madeline felt as if Chris was not only scanning her features, but visually touching them. And he was silently letting her know that he liked what he saw.

He said, "I'd say this calls for a drink. How about paying the Caribbean Room a visit? There's a combo playing in there, but the decibels aren't half what they are in here."

There was a carefulness about his suggestion that alerted Madeline to suspect Chris Talmadge hadn't asked too many women to join him for a drink lately. She wondered why. The psychological aftermath of his accident, perhaps? At least, she was assuming that his lameness derived from an accident. If so, was that his problem? Had he been through an ordeal that left some lingering self-doubts?

She sensed that her overly analytical interest was showing when Chris said, somewhat stiffly, "I imagine you're tired. Maybe another time."

Madeline realized he'd interpreted her silence negatively, and assumed she didn't want to have a drink with him. He did have some hang-ups! She summoned her brightest smile. "On the contrary," she said. "How about now?"

They moved toward the casino entrance, Chris a step or two behind Madeline. In contrast to the casino, the lobby seemed extraordinarily bright. Madeline paused and turned toward her escort, waiting for him to catch up with her. And in this new light she was given an entirely different view of him—and a new impression.

She was tall and, because she was so slim, looked even taller. But he topped her by at least five inches. Also, he was even better looking than she'd thought back in the casino. He'd acquired the basis of a good tan during his week in Aruba, and it was becoming. His thick sandy hair was smooth, with only a hint of wave. His eyes were hazel, part brown, part green. Madeline suspected the color would change according to lighting, and to the clothes he was wearing. His nose was slightly crooked, as if it'd been broken at some point, perhaps in a high school football game. His firm angular chin clefted slightly in the center. And his mouth... There was a definitely sensual curve to his lips, both sexy and generous. This was a giving man.

He was broad shouldered and narrow in the waist. He had the physique of someone physically active, someone who kept himself fit with sports and exercises he genuinely enjoyed. That made it even more likely that whatever happened to him had happened quite recently.

Madeline's assessment was generalized, but accurate. Her profession had taught her to evaluate people quickly, to get a grip on inner problems by visually locking onto telltale outer evidence.

Once at her side, Chris Talmadge said, "Excuse me for a minute, will you? Once you left my side, Lady Luck, all that came up were lemons. I'd like to cash a traveler's check. Tomorrow's Sunday, and on Sundays they're especially slow starters around here."

Madeline nodded assent and waited while Chris went to the reception desk and negotiated his financial transaction. She tried not to focus her attention on his disability, tried to suppress the doctor in herself, but it wasn't easy. She was far too accustomed to becoming professionally immersed in other people's lives, and that was exactly what she'd sworn not to do while in Aruba.

The Caribbean Room featured an intimate ambience. On a small raised platform a musical combo was playing soft music with a Latin tempo.

Chris said something in a low voice to the head-waiter who came to greet them, and they were led to a corner table for two. The table was lit by a thick pink candle in an ornate holder, and the light was flattering. Chris Talmadge, at least, looked terrific in it. Madeline hoped she was measuring up half as well.

He asked, "Do you have a preference? Or do you want to go for the local specialty and try a piña colada?"

"I think I'll settle for a vodka and tonic tonight," she decided.

Chris placed their order, but once the waiter left their table a somewhat constrained silence fell between them. Madeline had a sudden sharp yearning for a cigarette, and was surprised at herself. She'd never been much of a smoker and, in any event, she'd given up tobacco completely just a few months after her husband's death. During that very difficult period, smoking had been her crutch.

She rationalized that she wanted a cigarette now because she needed something to do with her hands. Also, if Chris were to offer her a cigarette, light it for her, then blow out the match, it would create the necessary bit of stage business between them to fill in this small void.

He leaned back in his chair and eyed her rather speculatively. Madeline had the uncomfortable feeling that he was on the verge of asking her a lot of questions, very probably questions she wouldn't want to answer.

She also became aware of the dance floor in the middle of the cocktail lounge, and of the couples moving to the liquid tempo of a Mexican waltz. She saw Chris's gaze focus on the people dancing, and saw the bleakness drifting across his face like a passing cloud. She sensed he was fighting a threatening black mood, and empathized with him. She'd traveled that route herself.

She caught his glance and smiled, not realizing how much the smile lit her eyes, making them seem more turquoise than blue. She asked, "Where are you from, Chris?"

He looked at her blankly. Madeline watched him refocus and return her smile. He said, "Upstate New York. Lakeport. It's a small city on Lake Champlain about fifty miles short of the Canadian border. And you?"

"Bangor, Maine," she told him. "That's pushing up toward Canada, too."

"So," he observed, "our friends back home are probably wallowing around in a foot of snow, whereas we..."

Madeline laughed. "I flew out of Boston this morning," she informed him. "And I hate to puncture your balloon, but the ground was bare when I left."

"Wait till tomorrow," Chris challenged, grinning. "What'll you bet the hotel's morning bulletin will say something about a deep freeze somewhere up North?"

"A chamber of commerce act?"

"Well, people don't come to the Caribbean to throw snowballs. I presume you're here on a holiday, Madeline?"

"Yes," she said, nodding.

"Alone?"

She hesitated, but realized that if Chris Talmadge was interested he could easily find out the answer. "Yes, I'm alone." She took the plunge. "What about you?"

"I'm on vacation, I'm alone and..." It was his turn to hesitate. "And...I've been bored as hell."

Madeline leaned forward and put a finger to her lips. "Shush!" she cautioned. "Suppose there's a chamber of commerce spy at the next table? You'll be deported."

"Yesterday," Chris answered, "I wouldn't have given a damn about being deported. Having Lady Luck suddenly turn up next to my favorite slot machine tonight does, I admit, put a different complexion on the matter."

He took a sip of his scotch. Then, frowning slightly, he said, "I'm afraid I'm giving you the wrong idea. About Aruba, that is. It's not the island that's responsible for my ennui. It's me. I thought coming down here would be like getting out of jail, but it hasn't worked that way, because—" He broke off. "Enough of that," he said firmly. "Did you have a chance to get out on the beach today?"

"No, I didn't. After we checked in this afternoon I took one look at the bed in my room and passed out on it for a couple of hours. Tomorrow will be time enough for the beach."

"Your friend said you'll be here two weeks?"

"That's right."

"You'll find plenty of diversion," Chris assured her. "There are some interesting island tours to take, and there's a different party almost every late afternoon at one of the hotels along the beach. Anyone staying in any of the hotels is invited."

Madeline shook her head. "I doubt I'll go for that," she confided. "I didn't come here for the social scene. I just want to rest and unwind for a while. And go swimming. The thought of swimming in February sounds absolutely sybaritic to me."

"The water's great," Chris agreed.

He tilted his head slightly, and Madeline realized that again the music was catching his attention. She saw him unconsciously keeping time with his fingers, tapping them against the tabletop.

She, too, responded instinctively to music, and was catholic in her musical tastes. She liked classical, jazz, and rock. She liked the throbbing Latin rumba the combo was playing now, slow and sexy. It was easy to imagine herself dancing with this very attractive man sitting opposite her. He would guide her with a hand pressed firmly against her back, at that point where her slim waist blended into the soft roundness of her hips. They would look good together dancing, Madeline thought abstractedly. She could imagine the touch of his hand upon hers, perhaps the warmth of his cheek against hers....

She brought herself up short, reminding herself that this man couldn't possibly dance. But she felt sure that not long ago he had. And very well, too. His tapping fingers were keeping a perfect tempo.

He said suddenly, "That song they're playing . . . it's called *Solamente Una Vez*. My Spanish is only high school level, but translated loosely that means, 'Only once.' Or maybe you already know that?"

"No," Madeline admitted, "matter of fact, I don't." Once she'd bought a Spanish language course on cassettes because some of the patients consulting her in Boston, at that time, were Hispanic and spoke little English. But she'd never had time to master even the first lesson.

"The other night," Chris continued, "there was a South American guy in here. We were sitting next to each other at the bar. He was in the process of drowning his sorrows. They were playing that song and he insisted on translating it for me. What it says is that a person only truly loves once in a lifetime." Chris's hazel eyes seemed more brown than green at that moment, and were intensely thoughtful. "Do you believe that?" he asked.

The question took Madeline aback. It would have been easy to think he was merely making conversation, yet she sensed her answer was important to him. And in an unexpected and strangely illuminating moment, it became important to her, too.

She settled for the truth.

"No," she said. And it was crazy but, as she spoke, she suddenly felt as if an oppressive weight had been lifted from her shoulders.

CHAPTER TWO

"THANK YOU," Madeline said, diverting her attention from the spectacular view of the Caribbean beyond the sliding glass door to her small balcony. She smiled at the room service waitress who'd just brought her a tray of coffee and croissants.

"You are most welcome," the girl assured her. Her English had an intriguing, unidentifiable accent, and she was beautiful, too. Dusky-skinned, with gorgeous dark eyes and raven hair, and features of a definite Dutch cast. But then this island had long belonged to the Netherlands, Madeline remembered.

Aruba's people were fascinating. From the moment of her arrival, Madeline had noticed the interesting effects caused by a blend of background nationalities. Several of the customs officers had shown this same touch of Dutch heritage, although their skin was dark brown.

The girl left and Madeline returned to contemplating the view from her ninth floor room. The Caribbean was a visual feast of colors, bands of turquoise and tourmaline water shading to a deep lapis blue far offshore. Her private balcony held a round table and two chairs. On an impulse, Madeline slid the door open, picked up the tray that had been left for her, and carried it outside.

A warm, humid breeze assaulted her. The contrast to
the air-conditioning in the room behind her was intense. She exhaled sharply. It was only eight-thirty and
already on the hot side. And the temperature was sure
to soar as the sun climbed higher.

Delaying her breakfast for a few additional minutes,
Madeline edged to the balcony's concrete wall. Peering
over, she looked down on a large free-form swimming
pool, its adjoining patio lined with beach chairs upon
which attendants, working at a leisurely pace, were
placing full-length bright blue cushions. There were already a few sun worshipers lying out on the chairs, but
the pool was empty, its sapphire water sparkling with
golden sun motes.

Beyond the swimming pool patio, shallow steps de-
scended to the pale beige beach. The stretch of sea visible from Madeline's vantage point was also devoid of
swimmers. Too early in the morning for most people to
get up enough energy to be athletic here in the tropics,
she surmised.

Closer to the hotel, the beach was studded with a
series of open thatched-roof shelters. Blue-cushioned
lounge chairs had also been set out in a number of
them, with additional lounges placed on the sand for
people who wanted to have the full sun.

Glancing toward the sea again, Madeline's attention
was captured by the long line of freighters dominating
the horizon. Riding at anchor, they stretched as far to
her left as she could see. She counted twenty-three ships
within her range of vision, probably all oil carriers. She
knew that the Lago oil refinery—reportedly the largest
oil refinery in the world—occupied the far southeast-
ern end of the island, a dozen or more miles removed
from the immaculate sand of Palm Beach.

Madeline had meant to read up on Aruba's history, geography and culture, but there'd only been time to scan a book about the island that she'd borrowed from the Bangor library. She did remember, though, that crude oil was brought here primarily from Venezuela, and that the coastline of Venezuela was only fifteen miles away.

She averted her gaze from the ship-filled horizon, pulled a chair up to the little table, and focused her attention on her breakfast. The coffeepot was heavy metal, so the coffee was still hot—as was the pot of milk that accompanied it. She mixed a brew of *café con leche*, added sugar, and savored the delicious result.

She spread a croissant with guava butter and munched slowly. She only had a slight appetite, but was determined to eat. She'd been told by her doctor that she needed to gain weight and vastly improve both her eating habits and her general life-style.

Madeline smiled, remembering this. It gave a doctor an odd feeling to play the reverse role of patient. Nevertheless she'd virtually been forced by her colleagues to take this holiday. She'd collapsed one day, five minutes before beginning rounds at the Bangor hospital where she was a staff physician. And if that wasn't a cue....

Since her husband's death slightly more than two years ago, she'd been working much too hard. She knew that. She'd moved from the Boston medical scene to the post in Bangor, and set herself a pace no one could hope to keep up for very long. Actually, she thought wryly, she'd been due for a breakdown months before she'd finally collapsed. But her work had been the glue that held her together. Then even the glue had crumbled and, temporarily, she'd fallen apart.

Her job now, she knew, was to prove she could do to this particular Humpty Dumpty what all the king's horses and all the king's men hadn't been able to manage with the nursery rhyme figure. She had to put her pieces together again. It wasn't a job that could be accomplished during just two weeks in Aruba, but she could make a real beginning. Once back in Maine, she could—as her colleagues had pointed out with cold logic—amend her ways. While meeting the rigorous demands made on any conscientious physician, she could also learn to start living a life of her own apart from her work.

Thinking about medicine and doctors made Madeline's thoughts swerve to Chris Talmadge. Last night they'd left the Caribbean Room after having just one drink. Chris had suggested another, but she'd declined, to his apparent relief.

Fatigue had been written on his face as they'd moved slowly toward the elevators together, and Madeline imagined he would be glad to get back to his room and rest. Chris's room, she'd discovered, was on the fifth floor. He'd gotten off the elevator first, giving her a charming smile as he said good-night.

He was a very attractive man, she mused now, finishing her croissant. But also, she suspected, a very troubled man. She was admittedly curious about him . . . and not entirely in a professional way, though there was that element, too.

She wondered if she'd bump into him today, and couldn't see how she wouldn't, unless Chris tended to keep to his room. And she doubted that, in view of his nicely tanned face and hands.

Draining her coffee cup, Madeline decided it was time to explore the beach. She went back into her large bedroom, this decorated in a colorful tropical motif. The furniture was white, while the bedspreads, drapes and upholstery blended shades of lime, yellow and tangerine.

Her old bathing suits had been too big for her. The new one she'd bought for this trip was a scrap of deep pink material. She put it on, slipped a matching terry robe over her shoulders, and set her straw sun hat firmly on her head. Then she stashed a paperback novel, some tanning lotion and a package of tissues into a tote bag, and set forth.

The exit to the beach was on the hotel's lower level and opened out upon the pool area. Madeline skirted the pool, seeking the small stand from which beach chairs could be rented, as well as oversized blue beach towels bearing the hotel's crest.

The dark-skinned, handsome young attendant who came to help her took one look at Madeline's fair complexion and cautioned, "It would be best if you take a chair in one of the shelters today."

"But I want to get a tan," Madeline protested.

He laughed. "You will get a burn, not a tan, unless you are extremely careful," he warned. He led the way onto the beach, and to the last of the shelters facing the sea. "You can pull out the chair for a time, and then place it back in the shade again," he suggested, speaking with that slight accent she found so intriguing. "But no more than five minutes in the sun at a time for the first day or two. Please!"

Madeline nodded obediently, and decided to acclimatize herself by staying in the shade for a while until she got used to the humidity and the steadily blowing trade wind. She stretched out on her beach chair, picked up her paperback and started to read, but after a few minutes she gave up. Her reading was almost constantly interrupted by gusts of warm wind that came swirling around the chair, playing havoc with the pages. The trade winds never seemed to let up, but it was easy to imagine that, without their ameliorating presence, life on this island—and probably most of the Caribbean islands—would be almost untenable the major part of the year.

She put the book aside, closed her eyes, and felt her tensions beginning to ebb away. There *was* something to be said for the tranquilizing affect of a tropical climate.

Madeline chuckled silently, remembering an incident earlier this morning when she'd splashed her face with cold water, only to find that the cold water tap ran warm—quite warm.

The chambermaid had arrived just then, and Madeline had pointed out her predicament, at which the woman's pretty, dark face creased into a wide smile.

"That *is* the cold water," she explained, "or as cold as any running water we have on Aruba. All of our water pipes are above ground. The water is taken from the sea and distilled. It is very pure, and safe to drink."

Madeline grimaced involuntarily. She could not conceive of drinking water as warm as this, unless she was literally parched.

The lack of available water, and the ingenuity by which seawater was converted into something potable, was something else about Aruba she had found fascinating. There would be much more, she promised herself—new things to see, new places to explore, for the next two weeks.

As she drifted into shallow slumber, Madeline admitted to herself that it would be pleasant, very pleasant, if she had someone like Chris Talmadge with whom to share her explorations.

FROM THE PRIVACY of his balcony, Chris watched Madeline follow the pool attendant down the steps to the beach, and saw her take up temporary residence in the farthest of the thatched-roof shelters. He was surprised at the urgency of his sudden desire to join her.

He was wearing pajama bottoms—he never wore a pajama top—and most of the breakfast he'd ordered up from room service was still unconsumed. He wished last night he'd invited Madeline to share breakfast on either his balcony or her own. The view was tremendous and would take on an added dimension with her enjoying it at his side.

There were times when a person needed to share an experience. A holiday in Aruba was one of them, Chris thought wryly. This last week had only emphasized his loneliness.

He finished his coffee, went inside and struggled into a pair of snug-fitting navy blue swim trunks. His damned leg made everything more difficult to do. Getting dressed, or undressed, took twice the time and ten times the effort it had before that terrible night last summer when his entire life—literally—had nearly been blown away.

He forced himself to block out the memory of the disaster that had taken such a toll on him in every possible way. He picked up an oversized beach towel, flung it over his shoulders, found his book and sunglasses, and reached for his cane.

Slowly he limped to the door. The orthopedic specialist in the rehabilitation center where he'd been a patient had assured him the leg would improve with time. But it would never again be perfect. He had to accept that.

Eventually it might be possible to dispense with the cane. And yet Chris knew that getting rid of the cane wouldn't be enough. He wanted to dispense with the limp, wanted to go back in time beyond early last July. He wanted to reset the clock and then move forward, averting the catastrophe that had changed his life.

He winced as he thought of Theda von Storch calling him "that nice-looking lame guy." And he cringed at the memory of sitting opposite Madeline Clarke in the Caribbean Room, aching not because of the pain in his leg—though there was always some of that—but because he'd wanted to dance with her so much it had actually hurt. He'd always loved to dance, and had the instinctive feeling that Madeline Clarke would be a naturally good dancer, too.

He'd wanted so very much to hold her in his arms last night. He'd wanted to feel her warmth and softness, and smell at close range the perfume whose subtle fragrance was wafting toward him as he sat across from her, behaving like a moody fool.

Then there was that question he'd asked her about a person being able to love, genuinely, only once in a lifetime. What in hell had prompted him to pose such an idiotic query? Though she'd been polite in answering him, what must Madeline have thought of him for phrasing something like that in the first place?

Filled with self-anger, Chris savagely jabbed the elevator button and, while waiting for the elevator to ascend—the tempo of the elevators matched the tempo of life in the Caribbean—he forcibly reminded himself of what King had said to him not once, but a thousand times. King Faraday, the surgeon who had saved his life last summer, the man who also happened to be his best friend, had told him he was lucky beyond belief to be alive, and should be thankful that he could walk at all.

Chris silently repeated King's words as he headed for the swimming pool, paused there briefly, then continued to the beach. As he approached Madeline's chair, he thought at first she was asleep. He ventured a tentative "Hi" and was surprised when her eyelashes fluttered. He found himself staring into twin counterparts of the deep turquoise stretches that banded the Caribbean.

Chris swallowed hard, further surprised by his reaction to this woman. God, but she was lovely! Her pink bathing suit, while not nearly as abbreviated as most of the bikinis that bloomed along the beach, somehow managed to be much more seductive. The fabric melded to the gentle curves of her body. She was a shade too thin, he conceded, but still. . . .

He'd seen the shadows under her eyes last night, and had put them down to travel fatigue. But now he speculated that perhaps she'd been ill and had come to Aruba to convalesce as well as enjoy a holiday, which was pretty much what he was doing himself.

"Chris," Madeline said.

He was delighted that she actually seemed pleased to see him. After his moody performance last night, he wouldn't have blamed her if she decided to avoid him for the rest of her stay.

It took courage to ask, "May I join you?" Since his accident, and especially now that he was out on his own again after a long hospital confinement, Chris felt disturbingly insecure. He'd never had a problem with women before. Well, that wasn't true, he amended wryly. Once he'd married in haste, the marriage had terminated in a hell of a mess, and he'd had plenty of time to repent.

Madeline's immediate "Of course" heartened him.

Chris looked up, noticing the pool attendant hurrying toward him. "A lounge in the shade, sir?" the attendant suggested.

"No thank you, I'd like to lounge in the sun. Maybe I'll go for the shade later, but not now."

Madeline asked, "Would you move my chair into the sun for a while, please?"

She was addressing the attendant, but Chris wished he could do what she requested. He couldn't. There was no way he could handle the cane, his bad leg, and the rather heavy lounge chair simultaneously.

Madeline rose gracefully, and the attendant tugged her chair out onto the open sand. He placed Chris's chair right next to it, perhaps a tad closer than Chris would have positioned it himself. Still, it was a satisfactory compromise, and Chris tipped him well in addition to paying the small rental charge.

He lowered himself carefully onto the lounge, silently cursing his awkwardness. Madeline had already stretched out again, and Chris was thankful she wasn't looking at him. The oversized beach towel was still flung around his shoulders. He removed it and folded it at the foot of the chair, then slowly uncoiled to his full length.

He was hoping Madeline wouldn't notice the scars on his left side and on his leg. They'd already faded, and he'd been assured they would fade further with time. But the areas they covered would never tan. Viewing those white patches in the mirror this morning, Chris had cringed, finding them ugly.

Madeline noticed the scars almost immediately. But she assumed her professional face so instinctively that not the slightest trace of her reaction was conveyed to Chris. Then, using the pretext of having to squint against the glaring sun, she donned her sunglasses so she could study the scars covertly.

He'd had them for several months, she guessed, but not much longer. She wished she could come right out and ask him directly what had happened. Swiftly she reminded herself that she couldn't without appearing blatantly curious. She was on a holiday, not in a medical office or a hospital.

The wind died down briefly, and Madeline quickly got a good idea of the sun's intensity at this latitude. Even when the wind resumed again, she stirred restlessly.

The movement attracted Chris's notice, and he asked lazily, "Sun getting to you?"

"A bit, perhaps," she confessed.

"Don't overdo it, Madeline," he cautioned. "There's tomorrow and the next day and the next. Anyway, you're white as an Easter lily...."

"I know," she interposed. "And if I'm not careful, I'll be asking the attendant for a stalk of aloe!" She sat up and brushed her hair back from her shoulders. "Care to join me for a swim?" she suggested.

"You go ahead," Chris hedged. Of late, getting in and out of the water made him feel like a lumbering hippopotamus. Just as awkward, anyway.

Madeline whisked off the dark glasses and looked him right in the eye. She found she couldn't totally submerge her professionalism. "I should think," she said levelly, "that swimming would be good therapy for you."

The ensuing silence had its own sound. A herd of elephants trampling down jungle underbrush crashed through Chris's head. If he'd been able to turn purple, he was sure he would have.

He groped for a light way of putting it, but couldn't entirely conceal his embarrassment. "You sound like my doctor," he told her.

"So?"

"Okay," he conceded, managing a faint grin. "Swimming is good therapy, highly recommended. But I've been limiting my swimming to the pool. I can prop my cane somewhere and dive in, then retrieve the cane later without falling flat on my face." He added ruefully, "I never knew getting from one place to another could involve such logistics."

"If you'd consider taking my helping hand, you wouldn't need your cane," Madeline pointed out. "Then we could both go swimming in the Caribbean. The pool looks fine, but I'd like to try the sea. How about it?" She was smiling as she spoke, simply stating facts and not making an issue of them.

Chris felt a surge of gratitude toward this lovely woman sitting next to him. She was tactful, understanding—and beautiful. It would be extremely easy to fall in love with her, especially in this setting. Easy to share a tropical romance.

He fantasized a backdrop of soft tropical breezes, a golden moon suspended over indigo water, swaying palm trees, the magic echo of a steel band in the distance, and the fragrant perfume of exotic flowers, scented aphrodisiacs. . . .

Chris's thoughts nearly spun out of control. He pulled them back abruptly before they plunged over the

brink, and grinned at Madeline. "Lend me that helping hand, will you, Lady Luck?"

THE WATER was like a silk dressing gown warmed by the
sun as it caressed Madeline's skin. She floated on her
back, closing her eyes against the brilliance of the mol-
ten gold coin suspended in the deep aqua sky. There
wasn't a cloud in sight. But then it seldom rained in
Aruba, she remembered reading. One reason for their
water problem.

At her side, Chris said, "I should swim out to the
ropes and back one more time."

The swimming area was ringed by ropes. The sea beyond the ropes belonged to the boats—and there were
many. Speedboats and sailboats, catamarans and cabin
cruisers, glass-bottomed sight-seeing boats, windsurf-
ers, rowboats, and some funny little mechanical con-
traptions that looked as if they'd been made from
oversized rubber tires.

Madeline said, "If you're feeling half as lazy as I am,
you won't even consider swimming out to the ropes
again...no matter how good it might be for you."

"Thank you, ma'am," Chris told her, laughing. "I'm
relieved to hear that. You were beginning to make me
feel the way my high school Latin teacher used to. He
made sure, in advance, that I'd start off on a guilt trip
if I didn't do my homework. I think he was the first
person to instill the feeling of guilt in me."

"I had an English teacher who did the same thing,"
Madeline confessed.

Chris turned his head toward hers, and their eyes met.
He said, "So, I'm reprieved."

"You're reprieved, for today."

He liked hearing that. It meant there would be a to-morrow with her. He'd already known that, if he was to have his own way, there would be a tomorrow for them, and a tomorrow after that. But he liked hearing this in-dication that Madeline felt the same way.

They paddled lazily back to shallow water, and when Madeline helped him out as she'd helped him in, Chris decided that needing assistance wasn't all that bad. How else could he possibly have elicited so much concern from someone he'd known for approximately twelve and a half hours?

When they reached their beach chairs, Chris cast a quick glance around for the attendant. He knew both chairs should be pulled into the shade at this point. Madeline had already taken all the direct sun she should. He'd made her cover herself liberally with lo-tion earlier, but the water had washed most of it off.

The thought of lotion—or anything else—being lapped off her soft pearl skin evoked an undeniably erotic picture. Sex had played a nonexistent role in Chris's life these past seven months. Now he was pleased to discover that his inherently physical re-sponses to certain stimuli were not dead, as he'd feared they might be. Obviously they'd merely been dormant.

Madeline was drying herself off with her beach towel. Chris's eyes followed her movements, enjoying every-thing she was doing. She was unconsciously graceful in the way she bent, in the way she arched her head for-ward to rub her hair dry. He liked the way she handled her body. But in another minute she'd be ready to stretch out again, and he hated the thought of asking her to move the beach lounges because he couldn't.

At that moment the attendant appeared with a late-comer who wanted a lounge in the shade, and Chris cornered him. The young man took care of moving both beach chairs, and also nodded affirmatively when Chris whispered a request in his ear.

Chris and Madeline stretched out again and, after a few minutes, the attendant reappeared with a tray upon which there were two frosty piña coladas.

Chris spoke Madeline's name softly, and had to repeat it. Already, she was dozing. She looked up at him sleepily, and a smile curved her lips.

Proffering one of the drinks, he said, "A surprise for you. A thirst quencher."

She sat up and accepted it. "You're right, I am thirsty," she agreed. She sipped, then murmured appreciatively, "That's delicious... and probably very potent." She glanced toward the sun. "It's nowhere near over the yardarm, you realize."

"Somewhere it is," Chris corrected. He sampled his own drink, then nodded approvingly. "Somewhere in the world it's dark and people are asleep."

"So there's no five o'clock limit?" Madeline teased. "Back home we always say one should hold off drinking until after five."

"Depends on what time zone you want to be in," Chris insisted.

"You should have one of those watches that tells the time in a dozen different places all at once!"

"I do," he laughed. Then he urged, "Tell me more about back home, Madeline. Are you from Bangor?"

"No, I just work there."

"How long have you lived there."

"About a year and a half." She hesitated briefly before adding, "I moved to Maine a few months after my husband died."

Although she spoke levelly, there was a slight quaver in her voice, and Chris said quickly, "Madeline, I'm sorry. I didn't mean to pry...or reopen a wound."

"You haven't done either, Chris," she told him firmly. "I've...adjusted. At least, I think I have. My husband was a very vital man. It's still hard to realize he's gone." She continued after a moment, "He was a neurosurgeon on the staff at New England Deaconess Hospital in Boston. He worked like an idiot, and had a massive MI—a myocardial infarction, a severe heart attack—when he was forty-two. He never pulled out of it."

"That's rough," Chris said quietly. "Very rough. But then I've discovered that doctors, good doctors at least, work much too hard. Sometimes they give themselves to medicine fully, maybe more fully, than priests give themselves to the church. My best friend's a doctor, an excellent surgeon. In fact—" Chris stumbled slightly "—a few months ago, he saved my life."

He sought words that wouldn't exactly change the subject, but still would steer the conversation in a different direction. He said, "It must have been difficult being married to a doctor, a surgeon especially. Hard to cope with such a demanding schedule."

"Well, I can't say that it was difficult for me to cope with Jeffrey's schedule," Madeline replied slowly. That was true enough. There had been times when she'd found it almost impossible to cope with *Jeffrey*—but not because of the demands medicine made.

She caught Chris's inquiring gaze and knew there was no point in hedging any longer. If they were going to progress on anything other than a totally superficial level, he'd have to know about her career.

She said, "I'm a doctor, myself, Chris."

She laughed at his astonishment, then protested, "Please, don't follow the crowd! Don't tell me I don't look like a doctor...."

"Well, you don't!" Chris admitted. "I would never have guessed—" He broke off with a laugh. "That's not exactly flattering, is it?" he asked. "But I didn't mean it that way. I've known some very attractive female doctors. One orthopedic specialist who dealt with me in the rehab center was not only gorgeous, but intensely feminine. She was also old enough to be my mother. And...not at all like you, Madeline."

Madeline smiled, and it was a heart-flipping smile. Temporarily he forgot about his problems and concentrated entirely on the lovely woman at his side. It was pleasure that made him look younger, erasing the strain from his face and leaving in its place a vibrancy, a vitality.

With a husky undercurrent of sexiness in his voice Chris stated, "Doctor or no doctor...you're a very special woman."

CHAPTER THREE

CHRIS SUGGESTED LUNCH at the poolside café-bar. It was a lazy tropical Sunday and Madeline, pleasantly giddy from her late morning piña colada, gladly agreed. As they strolled around the pool patio toward the awning-shaded café, she discovered she was hungry for the first time since she could remember. Genuinely hungry. Starving!

She also discovered they made piña coladas in huge containers at the bar, filling a seemingly never-ending number of requests for them. Seconds of the frosty drink for Chris and herself were among those requests.

"We'll eat enough to offset the effects of the alcohol," Chris promised.

This proved true. The charcoal broiled ribs Chris ordered were a house specialty. "That, and chicken," he informed her. "Next time we'll have the chicken," he added, glad to make this suggestion.

Chris had previously made friends with their waiter, who greeted him jovially today. Watching them chatting together, Madeline had a sudden vision of the solitary meals Chris evidently had been eating since his arrival in Aruba. Solitary because of his choice, she was sure. Chris Talmadge was much too attractive to remain alone for very long, unless he wanted it that way.

He introduced the waiter as Jacob and Madeline recognized in the man's features those familiar traces of partly Dutch heritage. Jacob approved their menu choice and so did she, once the food had been set before them.

They ate the ribs with their fingers, dipping each piece into a delicious spicy sauce. French-fried potatoes came with the order, crispy on the outside, fluffy on the inside. These, too, went marvelously with the sauce.

"I've never tasted anything so good," Madeline said honestly, unabashedly licking her fingers.

Her face was tinged with color from the sun and her dark brown hair tumbled around her shoulders in charming disarray. She'd put on her terry robe, but hadn't pulled it around her or tied the front. Open, it revealed the deep vee cut of her bathing suit. To Chris, facing her across the wooden table, the gentle swell of her creamy breasts was clearly visible. He felt a slow, wonderful surge of desire for her.

Behind them, a chef working at the charcoal grills began singing an island song, his voice deep and throaty. Some of the other chefs joined in. There was a lilting calypso rhythm to the song. Unconsciously, Chris began tapping his fingers to the tempo.

The song ended, and the men shouted back and forth to each other in a language totally indecipherable to Madeline.

"Papiamento," Chris explained when she mentioned this. "It's the native language the Arubans speak among themselves. But they're all quatrolingual. In school, Aruban kids learn English, Spanish and Dutch simultaneously, and then speak Papiamento at home. I find it sad, after being here, to think of some of my friends in the States who are first generation Americans but won't teach their kids their mother tongue because they're afraid it would confuse them." Chris paused. "Another piña colada?" he suggested.

"I'd love one, but I wouldn't be able to walk out of here," Madeline confessed.

"Then how about some iced coffee?"

"Terrific."

They lingered at the café, and after a while several musicians set up a series of steel drums in a shaded area near the pool. The men worked in the same unhurried way everyone seemed to do everything in Aruba, and when they started playing it was in a slow, lazy tempo. Gradually, though, the tempo increased, until the steel band escalated in a frenzy of sound. This was wonderfully primitive music with a throbbing tropical beat. Incredibly sensual, it sent the blood flowing in hot rivers through Madeline's veins.

Listening, his senses fully engulfed, Chris glanced toward Madeline. She had propped her elbows on the table and was leaning forward, her chin resting against her clasped hands. Her eyes were half closed and she was totally relaxed, obviously unaware that she was swaying slightly, moving in rhythm with the pulsating music. Chris felt a knot in his throat, felt his muscles tighten, felt the deep swell of arousal. And knew how much he wanted her.

This woman had only been in his life for part of an evening, part of a morning, and part of an afternoon. But his sudden need for her was enormous, his desire for her overwhelming.

He spoke, unconsciously coining another nickname for her. "Maddie."

She opened her eyes wide, and he saw he'd startled her. "What made you call me that?" she asked curiously.

"I don't know," he confessed. "Nothing . . . coherent. Just an impulse." *Just one of many impulses regarding you that are threatening to take over,* he added silently.

Madeline didn't pursue the point. She said softly, nodding toward the musicians, "They're wonderful. It's the first time I've ever heard a steel band play live. It really . . ."

"It really what?" Chris encouraged.

"It gives you quite a feeling."

The music climaxed abruptly, then ended. But an afterbeat seemed to linger in the moist tropical air. Madeline said, her words in counterpoint to the echo in her head, "You know . . . I think I'm going to go up and take a siesta."

Chris held his breath, wishing she'd say more. He would have given anything he owned at that moment to have been able to garner the nerve to suggest, "May I come with you?" But he couldn't do that. Logic told him he hadn't known her long enough. He could only expect resentment from her in the wake of such an unrestrained overture.

It was hell, sometimes, to yield to logic!

He reached for his wallet, in which he'd stashed some cash and his credit cards, only to fumble and drop it on the ground. Several papers escaped in transit, and Chris swore under his breath. One of the more difficult things in his life, these days, was attempting to stoop down and pick anything up.

Madeline acted even before he'd finished swearing. With one graceful gesture, she gathered up the wallet and the spilled contents, and held both out to him. Only at the last instant did she glance at the material in her hands. At the top there was a color photo, face up.

Curiosity prompted her to look at the photo more carefully. She at once recognized Chris in the center. He was supporting himself on crutches, but garbed quite formally, and there was a beautiful black-haired girl wearing a vivid green satin dress standing at his side.

It was childish, ridiculous, to feel even the slightest spasm of anything that might be diagnosed as jealousy. But Madeline did. Especially when, looking closer, she saw how the girl was looking at Chris, the adoration in her eyes as plain as a camera could make it.

Madeline drew in her breath ever so slightly, then said with professional calm, "She's lovely, Chris."

He was still chagrined because of his awkwardness, but now he reached for the things she was holding out to him and his eyes fell upon the photo.

"That's Lorna," he said, as though that in itself should explain anything there might be to explain.

Madeline felt a slight surge of irritation. "Lorna?" she queried politely.

"She was my nurse all the time I was in the hospital in Lakeport," Chris reported. "That picture was taken at the wedding."

"Wedding?" Although she was painfully aware that she was being ridiculous about this, Madeline's pulse skipped at least one beat. "Your wedding?" she added when he didn't respond to her query right away.

Chris was sorting out papers, cash and credit cards. But he stopped short at her question. "*My* wedding?" he echoed. "Good God, no. That picture was taken at King and Claire's wedding, last December. King Faraday, the surgeon I spoke to you about? I was best man. Anyway, this picture was taken at the reception."

Chris was scanning the wallet's contents as he spoke and produced another color photo. "The newlyweds," he explained, holding it out to Madeline.

Madeline found herself looking down at a picture of an incredibly handsome, very blond man, and a beautiful woman standing next to him.

"They make a stunning couple," she managed, still thinking of the girl named Lorna.

"Yes, they do," Chris nodded. "And they belong together, if two people ever did." He smiled slightly. "Being at their wedding was almost enough to make me believe in marriage again."

Again? Questions raced through Madeline's mind, but there was no chance to pose them. Chris was leaving a tip for Jacob. Then he reached for his cane and awkwardly got to his feet.

He said, "I think I'll stretch out by the pool and get a little more sun. Maybe, after a while, I'll do some swimming. More therapy," he added wryly.

Madeline stared up at him, then asked suddenly, "How did it happen, Chris?"

He'd known the question would come sooner or later, but hadn't expected it at this moment, in this paradise setting. And he didn't want to answer, because talking about what had happened would bring back the searing memory of a night horrible beyond belief. Yet it would be stupid, as well as ill-mannered, to turn her query aside.

He put it as simply as he could. He said, "I own—or I owned, actually—a plastics factory on the outskirts of Lakeport. Early last July, there was an explosion. Several people were killed, several more were injured. Believe it or not, I was one of the lucky ones. Thanks, in part, to the skill of my doctor friend I told you about."

Chris drew in a long breath, fighting away visions of flames and screams and the horrible cacophony of an entire building falling into pieces around him.

Madeline said gently, "I'm sorry. I shouldn't have pried."

Chris shook his head. "You weren't prying," he said. "I noticed you…looking at me last night in the casino. And again today, a few times when you didn't think I was watching. I'll admit at first I put it down to curiosity. That's something I've had to learn to deal with. But when you told me you were a doctor, I realized that with you it's a matter of…clinical interest, shall we call it?"

Madeline frowned. "I'd say it's more than that," she replied, and added enigmatically, "In fact, it could become considerably more than that."

Her voice was edged with tension, but Chris couldn't respond to it. He was trying to assimilate what she'd just said, trying to interpret exactly what she meant. And he stood, staring after her helplessly, until Madeline had walked the full length of the path to the hotel and disappeared inside.

"I HOPE I didn't wake you up."

"No," Madeline assured Chris. She was sitting on the side of her bed, holding the phone receiver, wearing only a thin dressing gown. She'd slept for over two hours, and upon awakening had decided to take a cool shower. Except there was no such thing as taking a cool shower on Aruba. She'd forgotten that the cold water tap ran warm, and the hot water tap ran very hot.

She waited for Chris to continue, but there was a fairly long pause. She was about to insert a comment off the top of her head, something that might invite a dialogue between them, when he said hesitantly, "Look, I don't want to be a pest."

Madeline laughed out loud. The last thing in the world she could imagine Chris Talmadge becoming was a pest. Then she sobered. The terrible explosion in which he'd been so severely hurt had done a lot more than injure him physically. She'd already diagnosed that he was carrying around not only the cane he needed in order to walk, but an inferiority complex, as well.

She wished she could cut through the sugar frosting of politeness and tell him bluntly what he should do with his complex. She wished she could tell him he was the most attractive man she'd met in years. He was not only handsome, he was considerate, innovative, resourceful, and had a delightful sense of humor. And though they'd only touched the surface of their mutual likes and dislikes during their brief acquaintance, Madeline was sure they would find they had many things in common.

There was no need for him to carry an added burden of inferiority because he had a lame leg. It wasn't worthy of him. She'd only known Chris a very short time, but was keenly aware of his latent strength. There was a quiet assurance about this man that—fortunately—usually triumphed over his moments of moodiness or hesitation. Damn it, someone really should set him straight!

She wondered why the brunette in the wedding photo—Lorna, the girl who'd been his nurse at the Lakeport hospital—hadn't done so before now. Certainly, if one could read anything from an expression in a picture, Lorna was in love with him.

Chris's voice echoed through the phone. "Madeline? Are you still there?"

"Yes, I'm still here," she said rather shortly, deciding after they'd known each other for another day she'd probably set him straight herself.

She wished he were here with her right now. Then maybe she could make herself discuss this problem with him without wasting any more time. Thinking this, she inadvertently glanced down at her sheer dressing gown and wondered impishly what Chris's reaction might have been if he'd come to her door instead of phoning—and she'd opened the door wearing this!

She brushed the thought aside and asked lightly, "Chris? Are *you* still there?"

He laughed. "We sound like we're playing word games. Anyway," he repeated, "I don't want to be a pest." This time when he said it confidence triumphed. He didn't sound at all like he really thought he could be a pest. "But there's an interesting floating restaurant down by the harbor in Oranjestad . . ."

Yesterday—could it possibly be only yesterday?—the minibus from the airport had driven through a section of Oranjestad, Aruba's capital city, Madeline recalled.

"It's called the Java," Chris continued, "and they feature Indonesian food. Especially the *Rijsttafel*. Have you ever had one?"

"No. What is it?"

"It translates as 'rice table,'" Chris informed her. "It's a real feast. Rice is the basis, but a couple of dozen side dishes are served with it. Some of them are mild, some of them scorching hot. They blend all sorts of herbs and spices, and feature meats and shellfish and vegetables and fruit, all in their own special sauces."

"You're making me hungry," Madeline complained.

"I was hoping I would."

"Why an Indonesian restaurant in Aruba?" she inquired. "Or am I asking a stupid question?"

"You could never ask a stupid question, Lady Luck," Chris teased. "The Dutch were big in Indonesia in an earlier age," he reminded her. "They owned Java once, so *Rijsttafel* became an exotic menu item back in the Netherlands. When I was in the Netherlands a few years ago, I went to a couple of excellent restaurants in Amsterdam that featured it. I think you'd enjoy it."

Madeline was tempted to tell him he didn't need to do such a selling job. She'd already made up her mind.

"I think I'd enjoy it, too," she agreed.

"That," Chris said after a moment, "was a very easy capitulation, Madeline. Shall I make a reservation for, oh . . . say, seven? We can take a taxi."

"Seven would be fine," Madeline said, but she was glancing at the clock as she spoke. It was over two hours until seven, and she wished she didn't have to wait that long to see Chris again.

Those hours did not pass quickly. Madeline had brought a minimum amount of clothing with her, but she did have a choice of three different outfits she could wear to dinner. Fortunately the air-conditioning in the hotel was highly efficient, or her dresses would have been hopelessly wilted by the time she tried each of them on for the third time.

She settled for a pale pink cotton dress that had a form-fitting bodice with a sweetheart neckline and a softly gathered skirt. Viewing herself in the mirror, Madeline thought whimsically that she looked like a valentine. But . . . it suited her mood.

Chris was waiting for her in the lobby when she went downstairs. He was wearing a cream-colored tropical suit and a yellow shirt, open at the throat. He looked handsome, really terrific...and virile, Madeline thought, adding the adjective and getting a pulse-accelerating reaction from it.

The concierge had called a taxi for them, and it was waiting in front of the hotel. As they settled inside, Madeline said, "I like the Aruba license plates."

"Hmmm?" Chris queried, distracted from his total absorption with Madeline. She'd told him she was almost thirty-four—just a year younger than he was. They'd discovered that they both had March birthdays, his the day before St. Patrick's Day, hers the day after. But she looked at least ten years younger than she was.

He murmured, "I think Aruba agrees with you." Then he added, "What did you say about license plates?"

"Well," Madeline teased, having noted his absorption, and having guessed that she was at least partially responsible for it. "They're blue, with gold letters."

"What's so unusual about that?"

"It's the slogan I like," she explained. "'The Happy Island.'"

Chris reached for her hand and entwined her fingers with his. "Right now," he said, "I think this must be the happiest island in the world."

The boulevard along which they were traveling was brightly lighted. Pink oleanders and red hibiscus bloomed by the roadside, and there were many other tropical trees and bushes not so easily identifiable.

"I think most of those trees and shrubs were planted and are carefully nurtured," Chris commented. "I'd imagine so, anyway. From what I've read about Aruba, not too much grows naturally here—aside from cacti and similar plants that require little or no water. And, of course, the divi-divi trees.''

''Divi-divi trees?''

''Intriguing name, isn't it? Maybe you've noticed them. They're straggly looking, with short trunks that bend over so the crown of the tree looks horizontal. They look as if they're eternally windblown, which I guess most of the time they are. The divi-divi is the national tree of the neighboring island of Curacao, but plenty of them grow here, too.''

''Where did you learn all this?'' Madeline asked, fascinated.

Chris grinned. ''I picked up a booklet about the trees and flowers of the Caribbean in the hotel gift shop,'' he admitted.

''And here I was thinking you must have the world's most retentive memory!''

''Not guilty as charged,'' Chris assured her. ''About the divi-divi, though. It's not much to look at, but it's a kind of compass.''

''What do you mean?''

''The trade winds on the island blow in one direction, toward the leeward side. So the divi-divi's fernlike leaves always blow the same way. If you're lost and follow where the divi-divi leaves are pointing, you'll find your path again.''

''I like that,'' Madeline said. ''It's a charming legend.''

''It's not just a legend,'' Chris corrected. ''It happens to be true.''

It was a fifteen minute ride from the hotel to the harbor-side restaurant and Madeline was immediately intrigued. The Java had been built on a permanently anchored barge, and looked like a Chinese pagoda. It

was reached by a wooden bridge illuminated by colorful paper-shaded lanterns.

The atmosphere was tropical and romantic, and the
Rijsttafel was everything Chris had promised. Madeline sampled each of the more than two dozen side
dishes, sputtering and hastily reaching for her cool
Dutch beer when she encountered one of the spicier
foods, but giving all of them her vote of approval.

She and Chris talked about a variety of things as they
enjoyed their unusual dinner. Chris told her about
growing up in Lakeport, New York, and getting interested in music at an early age because there was a school
of music in the big old house right next door to him.

"I took piano lessons for years from Miss Delia Parmeter," he confessed. "I still play for the fun of it. I
never had any aspirations about becoming professional, although Miss Delia used to try to nudge me in
that direction. But I wasn't willing to put in the hours
of practice it requires to be an excellent musician. After I'd been practicing for a while, the lure of the out-
doors would get to me and I'd escape."

"To do what?" Madeline questioned.

"Oh, all sorts of things," Chris said vaguely.
"Lakeport's very close to the Adirondack Mountains.
I've done my share of climbing and in the winter my
friend King and I used to go skiing every chance we got.
More recently, I started windsurfing. Gliding out on the
water under your own power is a terrific feeling. Have
you ever tried it?"

Madeline shook her head. "I've never been too much
for water sports, except swimming," she said. "That's
because there's a swimming pool available almost
everywhere, but lakes and oceans, generally speaking,
have been somewhat lacking in my life to date."

The waiter came to clear their plates away, then brought them slices of fresh tangy fruit for dessert.

"Amazing, isn't it," Chris said, sprinkling lime juice on a slice of papaya, "how absolutely everything in the way of food has to be imported into Aruba? It must be strange to live in a place where it's virtually impossible to grow anything—at least anything that can be eaten. I've been wanting to take the bus tour around the island to get an overall picture. Palm Beach certainly isn't typical!"

"No, I don't imagine it is," Madeline agreed dryly.

"Would you like to try the tour?" Chris asked, still holding back, she saw, when it came to issuing an invitation.

"Yes, I'd love to," she assured him promptly. "I'd say let's save it for a rainy day so we can go on enjoying the beach, but I guess there literally aren't any rainy days on Aruba."

"Very few," he nodded. "And none at this time of year. I think someone mentioned that what rainfall there is generally occurs in autumn."

He motioned to the waiter to bring the check, then said, "Want to try your luck in the casino again tonight?"

"I don't know," Madeline hedged.

"Why so hesitant...when you're Lady Luck herself?" Chris teased.

"My finale last night wasn't exactly glorious," Madeline reminded him, remembering the platinum blonde.

He laughed. "I ran into Theda after I left you this afternoon," he said. "I sensed she was feeling somewhat ashamed of herself. People like Theda don't usually come out and admit things like that. Anyway, I'd go so far as to guarantee that she won't put on a repeat performance, where you're concerned. Chances are she'll try to make friends with you.''

"I'm not sure I could deal with that," Madeline admitted.

"As I told you, she's not all bad. Lonely, more than anything else. Loneliness can do strange things to people.''

"You sound like an expert on the subject... which I find hard to believe," Madeline said. "I can't imagine your ever having been lonely for very long, Chris."

"Thanks for the implied compliment," he said. "But... I've put in my share of lonely days and lonely nights, believe me." He shrugged, as if to cast off a lingering shadow. "Let's not get into that, okay?"

Madeline had no wish to pry. Chris wasn't a person who'd take kindly to prying. Yet in many ways, he mystified her. She recalled the comment he'd made this afternoon about the wedding last December between his two best friends in Lakeport. He'd said that it almost made him believe in marriage again.

Again. She wished she'd had the nerve to pursue that telltale word. Still, why should she be surprised, even a little taken aback, to think that Chris Talmadge might once have been married? It seemed obvious that he no longer was. Thinking about it logically, it seemed doubtful that he had any serious ties—even to the girl in the picture. If so, he wouldn't be here in Aruba convalescing by himself. Not, that is, if he were attached to any woman in her right mind!

If he were mine... The words popped into Madeline's head and she quickly forced them away. Probably, Chris had been married. And, evidently, had been disenchanted by it. Madeline grimly reminded herself that he was not alone.

He smiled across the table at her. She was struck anew by his attractiveness, and by something more—an enormously appealing quality she couldn't put into words.

It had been so long since she'd *wanted* a man. Now the suppressed desire began to teach her that—like a plant surviving winter—something could be dormant without altogether dying. But her feelings with Chris, when he took them a step further, were not akin to plants struggling for a new grip on life. Nor were they old coals being stirred in search of lingering embers. Rather, these were embers already glowing, new embers ready to burst into flames—pure, bright and hot.

Madeline was so surprised at her self-analysis that her eyes widened as she looked at Chris. He felt as if he were gazing into deep turquoise pools in which he'd be happy to drown—if that would mean prolonging his time with this beautiful, exciting woman.

He felt surprisingly unself-conscious as he reached for his cane and stood up. And there was a catch in his voice as he said, "Come on. Let's get a cab and go invade the casino. I have a feeling that with you around, this is going to be my lucky night!"

A night, he thought privately, that he wished could go on forever. A night that he wished would become more and more intimate as the minutes progressed.

But it was too soon for that, especially with a woman like Madeline. Her reserve was a quality that he'd noted from the beginning—and respected.

He took her arm as they walked back over the little bridge, and held her hand as they waited for their cab. The night was dark and Chris couldn't see the expression in Madeline's eyes. Or he might have realized how close she was to tossing both reserve and caution to the ever-blowing trade winds.

CHAPTER FOUR

MADELINE DISCOVERED there was a difference to visiting the casino with Chris. Her awareness of the heady atmosphere was heightened, her sense of excitement enhanced. Life had been blurred around the edges these past couple of years. Now she was beginning to see again, and she liked the sensation that gave her. With a newly corrected inner vision, everything became sharp and stimulating. Colors and noises and smells were intensified—and underlined by the newfound joy of simply being alive.

The change in her was due to this man at her side, and she appreciated how he was making her feel. She appreciated *him*. Essentially they were still strangers, but the affinity between them was undeniable, something more potent, more promising, than a mutually simmering physical attraction. Something Madeline wished there'd be time to explore during these two weeks in Aruba.

"I'll get some casino dollars," Chris said.

"Come on," Madeline protested. "The least I can do is pay for my own gambling!"

He shook his head. "It'll be luckier this way."

She watched him limp toward a cashier's cage, surprised at the tenderness she felt toward him. They'd covered a lot of ground today. In a more ordinary environment, it would have taken much longer to reach the point they'd arrived at with each other. There was still so much to learn about him—and again she was reminded of the limited time during which they'd be together. At moments, though, Madeline felt herself seeing deep inside this handsome, proud, strong yet vulnerable man. And she'd also given him a few in-depth glimpses of herself.

She watched him return toward her carefully holding two coin-filled paper cups, one nestled inside the other. It wasn't easy for him to balance the cups in one hand while handling his cane with the other. The woman in her cried out to rush to his aid, but the physician's voice restrained her. Chris would have to learn to cope—with many things.

Chris handed her one of the cups and, peering at its contents, Madeline chided, "You've invested a fortune!"

"You'd be surprised how fast it can go."

"No, I got a good idea of *that* last night! Well, if I'm lucky, I'll split my winnings with you."

"On the contrary, Maddie. Winners keepers, losers weepers. Come on."

They started toward the rows of slot machines, then Chris paused and asked, "Want to try roulette or blackjack instead?"

Madeline shook her head and laughed. "I wouldn't know how to begin!"

He grinned. "I'm sure you'd find a willing teacher."

"Maybe another time. I'll have to build up to that kind of gambling." Madeline jiggled her silver dollars. "Look," she invited, "you go ahead and try the serious stuff, if you want to."

"I've been that route," Chris told her. "For now I think I'll stick to the slots."

They chose side-by-side machines. Madeline watched Chris insert a dollar in the slot and discovered she was holding her breath. All along he'd been insisting that she was "Lady Luck" to him. She wanted—absurdly so—to live up to the affectionate nickname he'd coined and was instantly disappointed when she saw lemons pop up on his first try.

He caught her expression and protested whimsically, "Hey! Don't lose faith in yourself. I haven't . . . yet!"

Madeline's smile was tremulous. "I want you to win, Chris," she confessed, knowing her seriousness was all out of proportion to taking chances on a slot machine.

His eyes caressed her. "Any man would be a winner with you at his side," he said softly.

Their eyes met, and held. Desire twisted in Madeline so sharply that she caught her breath. As her awareness of everything around her kept intensifying, so did her knowledge of the potent chemistry brewing between Chris Talmadge and herself. She'd just been thinking about how much she wanted to know this man better. Now she warned herself that only a fool would fail to realize that exploring a potential relationship with Chris would be many times more risky than gambling away a few dollars. Incredibly, Madeline discovered that this chance was one she was prepared to take!

While Chris focused his attention on the slot machine again, Madeline visually caressed his thick sandy hair, then mentally etched the outline of his profile. There was a freedom to letting herself watch him like this, and to letting herself *feel*. There was a wonderful ache to her yearnings for him. Wonderful because this twisting, this wanting, was a part of life she'd been missing for much too long.

In the beginning there'd been something like this with Jeffrey. But only in the beginning.

She heard bells clang, then heard Chris whoop, "My God, I've hit the jackpot!" Lights flashed, silver coins rained into the base of the machine and, in another instant, an attendant hurried over to help Chris cope with his good fortune.

Chris turned to her, threw his arms around her and hugged her close. Then he caressed her cheek and kissed her impulsively.

Madeline, feeling the softness of his mouth and tasting its sweetness, wanted more. She knew she was reacting to him too fast, but she had no desire to put on any brakes. She smiled with him and laughed, and loved it when he stated fervently, "You're the luckiest thing that ever happened to me!"

When Chris's winnings had been piled into additional paper cups, the attendant brought stools for both him and Madeline. She suspected the pleasant, courteous man had noticed Chris's disability, and was being tactful.

A waiter appeared with champagne, compliments of the house, and Chris and Madeline toasted each other, clicking glasses. But Madeline didn't need the bubbly, pale gold liquid to make her giddy. Watching Chris was euphoric in itself. For the moment, the fatigue and pain had vanished from his face. He looked younger, carefree—and incredibly handsome. He toasted her again, his wide grin disarmingly boyish. And as she responded to the toast, Madeline knew how very easy it would be to fall in love with him.

Chris teased, "Aren't you going to splurge and gamble a little yourself? We're way ahead now, you know."

Madeline glanced at her full paper cup. She'd yet to play the first coin.

"Would it be terrible if I dumped all those coins in my handbag, and saved them for tomorrow night?"

"No, I don't think it would be terrible at all," Chris assured her. "To tell you the truth, I don't want to make any more plays either. Anything else would be hopelessly anticlimactic, so I think I'll cash in."

Chris added urgently, as if she might suddenly vanish, "Wait for me, will you?"

"Of course," Madeline nodded. "I'll be spying at one of the roulette tables."

She stood near the croupier at the nearest roulette table and watched people place their bets, follow the spinning wheel, then react to the outcome. Expressions, gestures and exclamations ranged from the sublime to the desperate, depending on the course luck had taken.

Madeline had never been much of a believer in luck. It always seemed too intangible to put much stock in. But tonight, watching Chris, she'd *willed* him to win—and it worked.

"Come on, Clarke," she chided herself, chuckling.

Joining her, Chris asked, "Is it a private joke?"

They turned away from the roulette table and moved slowly toward the casino entrance. "Not really," she allowed. "I was beginning to think maybe I should buy myself a crystal ball, that's all."

"Why? Do you have a sudden urge to peer into the future?"

Madeline laughed easily. "As a matter of fact, I've always shied away from looking too far ahead. I've had all I could do to handle today," she admitted. "But now," she continued, enjoying her lighthearted fantasy, "I'm beginning to wonder if maybe I have some magical power I didn't know about. If you win another jackpot tomorrow night . . ."

"Being with you is a jackpot in itself," Chris said softly. "Haven't I told you that already?"

His statement rocked Madeline's emotions, and her silence spoke for itself.

When they reached the lobby Chris stopped. Moving his cane and shifting his position slightly, he said, "I meant that, Madeline. I very much appreciate your spending your time with me. This has been such a terrific day."

His smile was lopsided, and she wanted to straighten it with a kiss. He said, "Could we prolong this evening just a little bit? With a nightcap, perhaps? We don't have to go to the Caribbean Room. There's a smaller cocktail lounge right over there."

"I think I'd like that better," Madeline told him.

"So would I."

She wanted very much to be alone with Chris at an intimate corner table for two, so it chagrined her to immediately spot Arthur Taylor as they entered the lounge. Then she made the further discovery that his companion was the platinum blonde who had caused such an unpleasant incident in the casino last night.

"Damn," Chris muttered, "your friend Arthur has seen us. He's beckoning like mad. They *would* have a table for four, blast it."

It was unfortunate, but there was no way to avoid Arthur's effusive gestures. Nor was there any polite excuse to refuse his invitation when he insisted they join him.

As Arthur held out Madeline's chair he said smoothly, "You both know Theda von Storch, don't you?"

Chris, matching the older man's smoothness, nodded. "Of course. How are you, Theda?"

Theda murmured something inaudible, and Arthur added jovially, "Theda and I happened to be sunning side by side at the pool this afternoon and we discovered, in chatting, that we have mutual friends in Philadelphia."

"The Camerons," his companion added rather absently.

Madeline, sitting down, was disconcerted to find Theda's very pale gray eyes staring at her. She remembered last night's scene only too vividly, and hoped they weren't going to have a repeat performance.

Drinks were ordered, delivered, and sipped. But the atmosphere was constrained. The two men did almost all the talking. Then suddenly Theda got up, reached for her jet-spangled evening purse and said bluntly, "I need to go to the ladies' room. Will you come with me, Madeline?"

Madeline caught the plea in the question, felt Chris's eyes on her, and rose reluctantly.

Theda was wearing black tonight—a tight fitting silk dress, jet jewelry, and high-heeled black satin sandals. Her platinum hair was piled in a mass of curls on top of her head, and she was carefully made up. She presented an exotic picture, and turned heads as she wove between the tables of the cocktail lounge. Even her walk was provocative, but Madeline, observing her professionally despite herself, noted the strain on Theda's face, caught the twitching cheek muscle, and picked out other small yet telltale evidences of trouble.

She's holding herself on a leash, scared to death she's about to go to pieces, came the diagnosis.

In the ladies' room, Theda repaired makeup that didn't need repairing, patted hair that didn't need patting, and stalled until Madeline realized she was waiting for two women, assessing themselves in the full-length mirror, to leave.

Finally they did, and immediately Theda turned to Madeline. "I don't know how to say this," she blurted, "because I'm not very good at saying I'm sorry. But last night I wasn't myself, or I would have known you wouldn't have taken my money."

When something—or someone—embarrassed her, Madeline inevitably reacted by appearing to be cooler than she was. Theda had crossed that line, and Madeline said stiffly, "It's all right, really it is."

"You know that's not so," Theda cut in. "Right now, you're looking at me like I'm dirt."

"Please," Madeline protested. "That's not true." The last thing she wanted was another scene with this woman.

Theda shook her head helplessly, and her words came with difficulty. "I really *am* sorry about last night," she said. "I was drunk...and I made a fool of myself. Does that satisfy you?"

Madeline took a long look at the woman standing in front of her and felt a twinge of pity. She estimated that Theda must be in her mid-forties, despite her obvious efforts to look younger. She was fading, though. The overt sexiness she projected wouldn't last forever, and too much drinking was taking its toll. But there was more than that.

It struck at Madeline suddenly that Chris was right. Theda von Storch was lonely, and frightened. She said, more gently, "There's no need for you to feel you have to satisfy me, Theda. Your apology is enough. After all, we all make mistakes."

She heard her own words and flinched. She'd made such a Pollyannaish statement. She despised self-righteousness in others, and was chagrined to discover it in herself. Impulsively she reached out and touched the other woman's shoulder.

"Look," she said, "it's over and done with. You remember that old saying about it being a waste of time to cry over spilled milk?"

Theda laughed shakily. "Only too well."

"Then why don't we start from here?"

Theda's eyes brimmed with tears. "Thank you," she said simply. She glanced hastily at the mirror, and moaned, "Damn it, I'm going to ruin my mascara!"

A few minutes later, Madeline and Theda approached the table where Chris and Arthur were waiting. Madeline saw Chris watching her rather apprehensively. As soon as she sat down next to him, he asked in a low voice, "Everything okay?"

"Fine," she assured him.

Arthur engaged Theda in conversation, leaving Chris and Madeline in their own small oasis. She again became aware of the incipient closeness between them, and his concern seemed natural when he commented, "You girls were gone a long time."

"Theda was waiting till we could be alone, so she could tell me something."

"Did she?"

"Yes." She smiled into his anxious eyes. "It's all right," she said. "Honestly, it is."

"I wondered," he murmured, his voice so low that only she could hear him, "if you'd be that forgiving."

She was startled. "Do I seem so...unrelenting?"

He smiled. "I'd say you seem like a person with a strong sense of justice. So whether or not you forgave would depend on your assessment of innocence or guilt." He added teasingly, "Now, I'd be happy to be found guilty of some things, in your eyes—"

Arthur cut in on their dialogue. "I ordered a second round," he announced. "Hope that's all right with you."

Madeline didn't want another drink, as she'd only finished half of the one in front of her. But her ice had melted, making her drink weak and watery. So she accepted a replacement and when Arthur raised his glass she responded, "Cheers."

She felt pleased because Arthur was enjoying himself so much. Arthur was a kind man, a good man, a deeply family oriented person. From what he'd told her on the plane coming down, he still missed his wife very much. It was nice to see him relaxing and having a good time.

Even as she was thinking this, Madeline sensed Chris's restlessness. She saw him wince as he moved slightly and suspected that his leg was bothering him, which was no wonder. Chris had put in a long activity-filled day.

As soon as she could, she managed a yawn. "I think I'm going to have to leave you lovely people, and call it a night," she murmured.

"I second that," Chris promptly concurred. "It must be this tropical climate, but I'm done in."

Arthur laughed. "Theda and I were just thinking about going over to the Caribbean Room and doing a little dancing."

Madeline groaned. "Be my guest! I'd collapse if I took two steps on a dance floor." As she and Chris left the table, she turned back to say, "Have fun, Theda. I'm sure we'll see you tomorrow."

Chris had gone ahead, so this final comment put her a step or two behind him. She caught up and, glancing at his face, saw his mouth set in a tight line.

"Something wrong?" she asked quickly.

"Not exactly. I can't help but have the feeling that maybe I'm holding you back."

"What are you talking about?"

"You might like to do a little dancing yourself. Obviously, I can't volunteer to be your partner."

Madeline impulsively grasped his arm and protested, "How can you suggest that, Chris? You must have seen that I've been falling asleep for the past half hour."

"Boredom, maybe?"

She shook her head. "I'm just tired, that's all."

As they reached the elevators and waited for a car to descend, Chris seemed determined to stare ahead through empty space. Madeline was sure that his leg was giving him quite a bit of pain, and it was difficult for her not to say anything. She wanted to help him as a physician. But she also recognized a different kind of urge. She wanted to fuss over him. And she could appreciate what his reaction to *that* would be. Just now, his pride was enveloping him in a suit of armor.

The elevator arrived and, as it whirred upward, they were alone. Madeline expected the car to stop at the fifth floor and for Chris to get out there. But it continued to the ninth, and she realized he must have pushed only the one button.

When he got out of the elevator with her, her heart began to pound. Her pulse rate accelerated until she felt as if it was thumping through her body like a miniature tom-tom.

They came to her door and she stood in front of it, irresolute. Something deep inside her told her this wasn't the moment to ask him to come in. They were both tired and Chris was on edge. Though they were old enough and free enough for whatever might happen on the other side of her closed door, instinct warned Madeline that the time wasn't right. It was too soon. To rush into the unknown tonight would risk spoiling something very valuable.

Chris laughed, but Madeline detected a hint of bitterness as he said, "I'm not about to pose any problems for you, Madeline."

"Chris, please."

He ignored the protest. "I only wanted to say goodnight to you in peace, not in the hotel lobby."

Earlier this evening, when he'd won the jackpot, he'd looked so young and carefree. Now Madeline saw gray shadows of fatigue under his eyes and a weariness compounded of pain and tiredness. The tight line keeping his mouth in check had a different meaning. He'd come a long way, she was sure. But he was still far from accepting his handicap, and his frustrations tended to haunt him too easily.

She cautioned gently, "Don't imagine things."

He looked down at her, not quite meeting her eyes. "What's that supposed to mean?"

"Tomorrow's another day, Chris."

He smiled crookedly. "And what's *that* supposed to mean?"

"I think we'll both be in better shape to talk about . . . things, after we get some rest."

He surveyed her, his smile widening. "I think maybe you should have been a diplomat, Madeline, instead of a doctor. You're right, of course."

He reached out to her, and she moved into his arms. He pressed his cheek against her fragrant hair as he clutched her, his emotions whirling in a blend of sadness and sweetness and wanting. He wanted her physically, and was sharply aware of *that* need. But he also wanted to lose himself in her warmth, her softness, her closeness.

Chris was only beginning to gauge how much emotion he'd been keeping pent up inside. He'd been holding too tight a rein on his feelings since the accident—since before the accident, really. He'd always had an ability to camouflage the things that affected him the deepest, keeping them even from himself. He knew now that he'd never fully come to grips with the trauma of his marriage to Sarah, their mutual failure, and their divorce.

Madeline had neither pried nor preached—though several times he'd wondered if she wasn't going to start lecturing him. He reminded himself that she was an astute doctor, as well as a beautiful woman.

As they'd waited for the elevator, he'd been keenly aware of her concern for him. He appreciated it, but he also wanted to back away. He'd already had enough experience with pity, now that he was handicapped and could understand why handicapped people often resented it so fiercely. The last thing he wanted was to have people feeling sorry for him. Especially a person like Madeline, whom he could so easily come to care about.

He knew he was running scared because he feared that she felt sorry for him. That, probably, was why she was being so kind.

Kind? As he nestled his chin into the softness of Madeline's beautiful sable-brown hair, Chris prayed that her embrace wasn't based on kindness. Although he was almost afraid to find out, he decided to search her eyes for the answer.

He released her slowly and pulled back, then cupped her chin in one hand and tilted her head so that he could look directly into her incredible turquoise eyes. And the passion he saw reflected there staggered him.

Chris forgot about caution. He drew Madeline into his arms again and their mutual yearning surfaced, swamping them both. Their mouths melded together in a passion-filled kiss, a kiss inviting exploration. Chris, thoroughly aroused, knew how easy it would be to spin out of control.

Madeline clasped his head with both hands as their lips met again, kissing Chris with an instigation all her own. He felt her fingers fluttering across the back of his neck, her touch indescribably erotic. Stunned by his reactions, he began to appreciate how much this woman had to give.

His hands moved instinctively, sculpting the curves of her body. Through the thin fabric of her dress, her hardened nipples telegraphed her desire. But for tonight her desire—and his as well—were going to have to be put on hold.

They heard the elevator door clang open and quickly let go of each other. And by the time a portly man, and his equally portly wife, were walking past them along the corridor, Madeline was fitting her key into the lock and Chris was bidding her a proper good-night.

He started toward the elevator, then heard her murmur wickedly, "Saved by the gong, eh?"

He turned back. "Next time," he threatened huskily, "you won't be so lucky!"

"Really?" Madeline tempted. And surprised herself by adding, "I can't wait."

CHAPTER FIVE

THE PHONE on Madeline's bedside table rang at eight-thirty the next morning. She'd been dreaming but she came awake quickly, immediately forgetting the dream's content as she reached for the receiver. She was certain it was Chris on the phone.

It wasn't. It was Arthur Taylor.

"Hope I didn't wake you up," Arthur began.

"No. I was dozing a bit, that's all."

"There's a sight-seeing bus leaving at ten this morning," Arthur said. "It tours around the island and stops for lunch at a place over on the north shore. I just ran into Chris Talmadge in the coffee shop, and he's game if you are."

"It sounds interesting." The response came mechanically and Madeline hoped Arthur wouldn't catch the lack of enthusiasm in her voice. She was sure the tour would be fun and informative, and—as she'd already told Chris—she wanted to take it. But she'd looked forward to spending some private time with him today, either out on the beach or wherever they could find a quiet place in which they could be alone and talk.

On the other hand, maybe talking too much at this stage in their relationship wasn't such a great idea. "Talking" on that level meant not only asking questions but answering questions. And that could be painful. Chris was probably no more eager to soul search than she was. The setting was not conducive to it. They were, after all, on vacation in a tropical paradise.

"I've been wanting to see something of the island," she told Arthur, trying to compensate for her earlier response. "Shall I meet you in the lobby at ten?"

"Better make it a quarter to," he advised. "Meet us by the newsstand. And be sure to wear comfortable shoes."

Madeline showered and dressed, then decided to go down to the coffee shop for a light breakfast. There wasn't time to order anything from room service with the expectation that it might arrive before she was ready to depart. The room service in the hotel operated pleasantly, but with no knowledge of the meaning of haste.

The coffee shop was on the lower level. Madeline glanced around the lobby before descending to it, thinking perhaps she'd spot Chris. If she did, she was sure he'd agree to have a cup of coffee with her. But he wasn't in evidence.

Once she'd finished breakfast, she wandered through the hotel's gift shop, scouting out potential purchases—gifts to be bought later, to take home to her friends. She didn't want to lug anything along on the bus with her.

There was also a chic dress shop in the hotel's small shopping arcade, and a jewelry shop that offered excellent buys if a person was in the market for diamonds, rubies or emeralds. Madeline wasn't. Finally, there was a tiny variety store that stocked postcards, suntan oil and other essentials. Madeline scanned the postcards and selected a few, then found she had to wait in line to pay. By the time she'd accomplished this, it was nearly a quarter to ten.

Chris and Arthur were already waiting at the news-stand. When she saw Chris, Madeline experienced an internal flip-flop no physician could possibly have put a name to. He was wearing cream-colored slacks and a deep green sports shirt—and he looked fantastic.

His eyes caressed her, making her feel as if she'd taken a sudden plunge back into adolescence. As she greeted the two men, she felt flustered. It was a funny, heady sensation.

Madeline was sure Arthur had noticed the vibes humming between Chris and herself—his smile was approving, if not downright benevolent. Then he glanced at his watch and frowned. "Wouldn't you know Theda would be late?" he commented tolerantly. "Maybe I'd better phone her."

At that moment Theda sailed out of an elevator. She was a vision in pink from her cloth sandals to the broad-brimmed straw hat that dipped at an alluring angle over one eyebrow.

Together they strolled toward the hotel's main entrance, where a number of people were awaiting the arrival of the tour bus. Madeline didn't realize how cool the air-conditioned hotel was until the bus arrived and they went outside. Then the full effect of the hot, humid, tropical atmosphere hit her.

Theda said, "Whew! This is enough to make your makeup melt!"

She climbed aboard the bus and Madeline followed her, snagging a window seat just behind the one Theda had appropriated. Arthur slid into place next to Theda, but it took Chris longer to make his way up the aisle. By the time he sat down next to her, Madeline realized that this small reminder of his handicap had dampened his mood.

She warned herself not to pay undue attention to this. She mustn't let Chris know how attuned she was to his hang-ups. It would do him more harm than good. He didn't need to be mothered—smothered, Madeline corrected herself. He deserved more credit than that.

The bus pulled out onto the palm-lined boulevard that led to the airport, a familiar route to the tourists on board. After only a few miles, though, the driver made a sharp left turn onto a secondary road and began to comment first in English and then in Spanish on the sights they were seeing.

Away from the immediate coastline, the island of Aruba proved to be very barren, its flat terrain punctuated occasionally by prominent conical hills.

"That is Mount Hooiberg," the driver announced, pointing to a cone-shaped hill that stood all by itself in the middle of a wide plain. "It is a real landmark, as you can see. There is a good path to the top. You can easily climb it in an afternoon and get a very good view."

"Fat chance," Chris muttered sullenly.

Madeline was looking out the window, her attention captured by a tan and white animal she'd seen loping along. It looked like a goat, but she wasn't sure.

"What?" she asked, turning to face Chris.

"Climbing to the top of Mount Whatever-it-is," Chris grumbled. "Or doing anything else that requires even a modicum of physical dexterity. I should have stayed on my balcony and contented myself with gazing out over the Caribbean."

It wasn't like Chris to indulge in self-pity, certainly not so overtly. Madeline slanted a glance at him and decided on a direct approach. "How am I supposed to answer that?" she challenged.

Chris managed to smile. "By telling me you didn't know I was such a whining brat," he answered, then added softly, "I'm sorry, Maddie."

Only her father had ever called her Maddie. And as memories of him flooded in, she decided it was the right moment to let Chris know that everyone met up with tragedy more than once in a lifetime.

She said quietly, "That was my father's name for me."

"Oh?"

"I grew up in Scranton, Pennsylvania," Madeline began carefully. "That's coal mining country. My father was part owner of a mine, but he wasn't the office type. He loved the mine's physical operations, which was . . . unfortunate. He was killed in a mining accident when I was ten."

Chris looked stunned, and whispered contritely, "I'm sorry."

"Because you've reminded me of my father? You don't need to be. I loved him, Chris. We were very close. He and I had a special rapport. So, although it still hurts to think of him even after all this time, he'll always be very special in my memory."

Chris nodded thoughtfully. After a moment he asked, "Do you have any brothers or sisters?"

"I have two brothers."

"You're lucky. I'm an only child. Are you close to your brothers?"

"Not especially. They're both older than I am, and have long since married and settled down. One lives in Scranton, the other moved out to Seattle."

"And what about your mother?"

"My mother remarried a couple of years after my father's death. Her husband is retired now. They live out in Southern California."

"When did you decide to become a doctor?"

Madeline smiled slightly. She'd decided this wasn't the time and Aruba wasn't the place to get into asking or answering too many questions, or doing too much soul-searching!

She said, "I've asked myself that many times and I've never been able to come up with one specific answer. I think my decision was somehow connected with my father's death. True, the doctors weren't able to save him. But they did save several other miners. Even though I was very young, and my personal sorrow was so acute, they made an impression on me. I think maybe I subconsciously decided, right then, that one day I wanted to be able to do something of equal importance for other people. One thing led to another..."

Memories were again crowding in and to avert them Madeline looked out the window and saw another animal, this one black. "Are those goats?" she asked incredulously. "They're running loose like dogs!"

Chris chuckled. "I guess they are pretty much like dogs in the Aruban scheme of things. I was talking to Jacob—you know, the waiter back at the pool bar?"

Madeline nodded, her eyes on the "wild" goat.

"Anyway," he went on, "goats are important in Aruba. They provide milk and they take care of most of the garbage. So they're allowed to run free, even though most of them have owners."

"They come in all colors," Madeline mused. "I saw a tan one a while back, and now this black one, and look, there's a white one," she finished, pointing.

"Have you noticed the broken green glass?" Chris observed. "If you were to ask me to give a quick impression of the Aruban countryside—or what we've seen of it so far—I'd emphasize the goats and the broken glass. I don't think I've ever seen so much broken glass."

"They need a better litter law," Madeline decided. "It's too bad. It does make sort of a blot on the landscape."

"It also proves the citizens like their Dutch beer!"

They came to a town, and the bus driver pointed out a number of the small *cunoco* houses that were typical Aruban residences. Made of stucco, they were predominantly white or tan with red tiled roofs. Occasionally a pistachio green or strawberry pink house added a splash of color to the scene.

Stucco walls surrounded many of the properties, often ornamented with fancy cinder blocks. Tropical plants and palms flourished everywhere, while endless cactus fingers pointed skyward. But the overall portrait was of a very arid land.

Madeline said, "It almost looks like a landscape devastated by a nuclear explosion, perish the thought. It's so dry, though."

Arthur evidently heard her because he leaned over the back of his seat and said, "It was a lot worse before the Dutch government built the big new desalinization plant out in the center of the island and gave it to Aruba as a gift from the Netherlands. Till then, people had to catch what they could during the rainy season that extends from October through December. So, things have improved."

The north shore of the island presented a startling contrast to the Palm Beach coast where the big hotels flourished. There were huge rock outcroppings and old lava fields left from long ago eruptions when Aruba's conical hills had been active volcanoes.

They passed the ruins of what looked like a stone castle. The driver explained that the British had once tried gold mining on Aruba, and this had been the site of a major mine.

"But it did not work out well." He shrugged.

They stopped for lunch at a restaurant overlooking the Caribbean and a natural stone bridge. As he pulled into the parking lot, the driver cheerfully reported that sharks frequented these offshore waters. "Sometimes you can glimpse a whole school of them feeding hungrily," he announced with a laugh.

Madeline shuddered and whispered to Chris, "I think I can do without that."

Before eating, most of the tour members opted to walk across the bridge and take pictures. The reddish rock formation arched over a narrow salt water inlet and was the largest in the Caribbean, according to their guide.

Chris's mouth tightened again, and his voice was rough as he said, "Go ahead with the others, Madeline. There's no need for you to always hold back because of me."

"I'm not holding back because of you," she countered lightly. "For one thing, I didn't bring a camera. For another...well, frankly, I'd rather stay with you! Why don't we go see if there's a lounge in the restaurant. I could do with a piña colada."

Chris had his sunglasses on, so his face was an inscrutable mask. Still, Madeline suspected he was glaring at her.

"You don't have to be so damned *nice* to me, Madeline," he complained.

"And you don't have to decorate your sleeves with complexes," she retorted and started ahead.

She felt frustrated with him, yet tugged by an emotion that bordered on pity. So many simple things were difficult for Chris just now. If he could only realize that, given time, his abilities would improve.

Now I am *patronizing him,* Madeline warned herself silently.

"Hey! Wait up, will you?" he called.

She slackened her pace only slightly, an inner devil commanding, "Make him try!"

He caught up with her just inside the restaurant and asked abruptly, "Is there a cocktail lounge?"

"I don't know. Let's look around."

There was indeed a small bar with several tables along one wall. "I don't mean to be rude to Arthur and Theda, but I want you to myself," Chris said as he deliberately chose a table for two.

Madeline met his eyes and murmured, "I wasn't sure you were feeling that way."

Chris groaned. "Please, Dr. Clarke, spare me, will you?" Grinning mischievously he teased, "Are you sure you aren't a psychiatrist?"

"Very sure, thank you."

"Well, you could fool me." He brushed his shirt sleeve and asked innocently, "How difficult is it to wash out a complex?"

"That depends on how permanent the dye is."

"I don't think these are permanent dyes," Chris decided. He was toying with a match folder he'd found on the table as he added, "That's to say...the colors might not be washable, but I think they'll fade with time."

He gazed across at her and his eyes seemed especially green. To Madeline, he looked incredibly handsome. More importantly, he was showing her a courage she not only welcomed, but applauded.

She said softly, "I'm sure they'll fade with time, Chris. And...I understand the way you tend to react."

"But you don't condone it?"

"It's not a question of condoning anything. I've never been in your position, so I haven't the right to pass judgment. But I do think you owe it to yourself not to make false assumptions."

"About what?"

"You're very good company," she told him steadily. "Many people—many women—would much rather be with you than out climbing mountains, or exploring rock formations, or dancing. Take my word for it."

Chris couldn't answer her immediately, he was so taken aback by Madeline's compliment. When he did speak there was a telltale huskiness to his voice. "I think I should say thank you," he managed.

Other members of the tour group entered the restaurant, and in the din that followed serious discussion about anything became impossible. For the better, Madeline decided.

Later in the afternoon they stopped at a small church famous in Aruban history. Their entourage dutifully trooped out to see the interior of the little building, but Madeline stayed in her seat. When Chris darted questioning glances at her she explained, "It's too hot. I'd rather stay put."

Still later, they visited a rock garden studded with huge boulders. A stony path with rope guidelines led to the top of the tallest boulder. Again, a spectacular view

For a while Madeline anxiously wondered if Theda
might get tipsy again. But Theda, dressed entirely in
yellow, remained so proper that it would have been
funny under other circumstances. As it was, there was
something almost pathetic about her—Theda so desperately wanted to be liked. Madeline could see that
now, and felt a surge of fondness and pity for the
woman.

Dinner over, they moved to the small casino inside the
hotel where the personnel were devoting the evening
entirely to teaching blackjack. Arthur chuckled as he,
Theda, Madeline and Chris took seats beside one another at a blackjack table. In a low voice he confessed,
"I've played this game before."

"I'll just bet you have," Madeline murmured. "And
you, too, Chris."

"Once or twice," Chris grinned.

"And you *too*, Theda?"

"Well...a couple of times in Monte Carlo," Theda
admitted.

"So I'm the only novice!"

"You'll probably have all the luck," Chris decided.
"On the other hand, I expect you'll bring me luck—as
you always do."

Always wasn't quite accurate. And Madeline wished
Chris hadn't brought up the subject of her being his
"Lady Luck." It made her uncomfortable to think she
might let him down.

Their instructor was a lady croupier who could have
stepped directly out of a movie. Her skin was ebony,
and her black satin hair was twisted into a stunningly
elaborate chignon. She wore a slinky black silk dress
with a deep décolletage. Gold chains encircled her neck
and gold bracelets flashed on her arms. Long gold ear-

was offered. And again Madeline let the others go
without her.

Before Chris could protest, she said frankly, "If you
had the two best legs in the world, I'd rather not do that
this afternoon. Another time, perhaps."

He subsided with a wry smile. "All right, all right,"
he said mildly. "You've convinced me."

On the return trip to Palm Beach, though, when they
stopped along the main street of Oranjestad so that
people could do some shopping, Chris struggled to his
feet and ordered, "Come on!"

"Must you?" Madeline moaned.

"Yes, I must," he stated firmly. "I want to buy you
a souvenir."

Oranjestad was basking in the late afternoon sun, the
golden light emphasizing the dustiness and aridity of the
little town. Small shops offered cameras, liquor, jewelry, perfume and other imports from places all around
the globe.

"I wish there were more things made right here in
Aruba," Madeline commented.

"So do I," Chris agreed. "Not much is actually made
on the island, though. The climactic conditions force
the importation of just about everything that's used
here." They passed the window of a shop featuring
beautiful Scandinavian crystal, which prompted him to
ask, "Do you collect anything special?"

Madeline smiled. "I've always wanted to collect unicorns," she confessed, "but I've yet to start."

"Why unicorns?" he queried.

"Oh, because they're mythical, I suppose."

"Okay," Chris decided. "Let's see what we can
find."

The storekeeper was a big, florid-faced Dutchman who nodded as if there was nothing at all unusual about Madeline's request. The affable merchant produced an exquisite crystal animal with a sparkling spiral horn in the middle of its forehead. The unicorn was perhaps two inches long, perfectly made, and refracted rainbow light when held up to the sun.

"Like it, Maddie?" Chris queried casually, sneaking a long glance at her.

Madeline knew her expression was giving her away, and she tried to camouflage her delight. She knew how expensive crystal animals could be, and was sure that this miniature gem would be right at the top of the price list.

"It's nice," she said, "but . . ."

Chris shook his head knowingly and favored her with a smile so tender it almost melted her. Negotiations followed with the shopkeeper, and a moment later Madeline walked out into the dusty street clutching a small white box in which her unicorn, carefully wrapped in layers of tissue, was nestled.

Aboard the bus again, she said shakily, "I think you know . . . you shouldn't have."

"And why not?"

"Chris, I really love it. But it was ridiculously expensive and . . ."

"And I wanted you to have it," he finished, leaning and kissing her lightly on the lips. "You only have to promise me that you will always keep it, and that whenever you look at it you'll think of me."

The unicorn was immediately given a place of honor on the dresser in Madeline's room. And she was gazing at it—and thinking of Chris—when he called the next afternoon.

They'd spent the morning together sunnin beach and swimming. Then they'd had lunc poolside bar, with Jacob in attendance. Af Madeline had opted for a nap in her room wh lingered by the pool, determined to swim a few fore he called it a day.

When the phone rang, it had barely been since they'd parted. She'd not expected to he him so soon.

"I just got back inside," he said quickly, happened to see a notice on the bulletin boar lobby. They're having a steak dinner at the Bl this evening, followed by blackjack lessons. It's the beach from us, and for the price of admissi give you fifty 'gambling dollars' to wager. Wo interest you?"

"Sounds like fun."

"Then suppose I call for a taxi to pick us up seven. Meantime, I can buy our tickets right stairs at the registration desk." Chris hesitate added, "Arthur appeared as I was reading the Would you mind very much if he and Theda along?"

"No, not at all."

That was the truth, although not the whole Madeline doubted there'd be a time when she wo prefer being alone with Chris. Still, she was su evening would prove to be enjoyable for everyon

The Blue Delft was very different from the A Palace. It was a cottage-type resort, strung alo beach closer to Oranjestad. Dinner was served in a screened room built right at the edge of the sand. were broiled over glowing coals, and the constan ply of wine was "on the house."

rings dangled from her ears, and diamonds sparkled on her fingers. She was swift and efficient, her exquisite face totally expressionless as she dealt the cards and talked in a low monotone.

On the very first hand, Chris turned over his cards and succinctly stated "Blackjack." Under his breath, he whispered triumphantly to Madeline, "You see?"

"Yes, I see," she said, smiling, wishing she could forever continue to be Chris's lucky charm.

It was late when they got back to the Aruban Palace. Even so, the cocktail lounge was still open for business.

Arthur asked, "Anyone for a nightcap?"

"Not me, thanks," Madeline declined. "I'm ready to call it a night."

Chris echoed her sentiments, but Theda said primly, "I wouldn't mind one last scotch."

"That's the girl," Arthur approved, taking Theda by the arm. "Sleep well, you two," he told Chris and Madeline. "We'll catch up with you tomorrow."

An empty elevator was waiting for them. Chris pushed nine, and then hesitated. As the car started to move slowly upward, he said softly, "I . . . think you know what I want to ask, Madeline."

She knew. All evening Chris's proximity had been doing strange and wonderful things to her. She'd been aware of him every second, absorbed with the marvelously enticing, sensual impact he made on her.

Now she whispered, "You don't have to ask, Chris."

"Madeline . . ."

She shook her head slightly. "Don't say anything," she cautioned. "There's no need to . . ."

"But . . ."

She touched his lips tenderly. "Shush, darling," she hushed him, and added almost shyly, "Don't you know how much I want you?"

There were still questions in Chris's eyes as they entered her room. Madeline switched on a lamp and in its soft glow she smiled at him. "Come out on the balcony with me," she invited as she opened the sliding glass door.

Chris followed her slowly. Pretending not to notice the careful distance he was maintaining she murmured, "Isn't the beach beautiful? It has more of a curve than you'd think. And the distant lights of the other hotels and Oranjestad sparkle so." She laughed, trying to conceal her nervousness. "Is that really the same moon we see in the sky back home?" she asked him.

For a moment Madeline thought Chris wasn't going to answer her. It was a long while before he said anything. Then he ventured in a low voice, "I don't know how to say this."

"Say what, Chris?"

"I feel at sort of a weird disadvantage," he confessed.

"There's no reason why you should feel at any disadvantage."

"It's been a long time, Maddie," he reflected huskily, the words wrung out of him. "Since the accident, needless to say. But . . . way before that. After my divorce, after I went back to Lakeport, there . . . wasn't anyone."

Madeline smiled into the night. "It's been a long time for me, too, Chris," she revealed. "But I don't think that really matters, do you?"

His face was in the shadows, so she couldn't read his expression clearly. Still she sensed his tenseness and reached out to him first. She cupped his face between her hands and stood on tiptoe to kiss him. And when their lips brushed, Chris tossed the last of his caution to the trade winds.

Time lost all meaning. He felt as though he'd wanted her forever—ever since that first night when they'd sat together in the Caribbean Room and he'd wished so intensely that he could dance with her. He'd yearned to hold her close, to match her movements to his.

Well, he couldn't *dance* with her. But as he drew her against him, Chris knew he could do everything else she wanted. Everything else they both wanted.

Caught in the moonlight's magical web, their embrace became more and more fervent. Chris found and gently tugged at the fastener on Madeline's dress. The soft material fell away from her shoulders and slid tantalizingly to the floor.

She stood before him wearing a pale satin teddy that skimmed her slim, lovely body. She was beautiful. Chris swallowed hard as his eyes caressed her, a deep longing for her assaulting him. Then he felt her fingers grasping his polo shirt. Acting purely on instinct, he helped her pull it over his head.

Next those probing fingers tentatively moved to the wide bronze buckle that secured his belt. Madeline slowly unclasped the buckle...then she stopped. It was Chris's turn to softly laugh. "I guess you can see what you've done to me," he whispered.

She nodded, searching his face before she slowly continued her task, tugging at his zipper, her fingers burning him even through the cloth of his slacks. It was a delicious fire, but there came a moment when he had to step out of his pants and he cursed his clumsiness.

Madeline said softly, "Pretend we're on the beach, coming out of the water. Put your hand on my shoulder..."

He did so, and chuckled playfully. "I'd say we're just getting into the water," he amended. "And very soon I'm going to be in over my head."

In another minute, they were like mobile Grecian statues, brushed with the moon's silver-white brightness. Their hands explored flesh that looked like marble in the moonlight, but was warm and vibrantly alive. Passion flowed between them as they kissed, stroked and caressed, each shared gesture carrying them higher and higher still on their path to the stars. And, when finally they sought Madeline's bed, it was to come together in a culmination so swift and overwhelming it left them both gasping.

Once she was able to speak, Madeline whispered incredulously, "I can't believe it. How could anything so... beautiful, happen so quickly?"

Chris murmured, "Sometimes miracles happen that way, Maddie." Gazing deeply into her eyes, he reached for her and added, "But this time there's no need to hurry."

CHAPTER SIX

MADELINE DIDN'T WANT to be conscious of the passage of days, but she couldn't help counting them as she began her second week in Aruba. And each hour became more valuable than the one just past.

She spent most of her time with Chris. During long lazy mornings on the beach together—with Madeline often keeping to the shade at his insistence—they slowly got to know each other better. Sipping piña coladas in this tropical paradise, it was easy to exchange confidences that might have remained unspoken in a more mundane setting.

Chris would be staying on the island for another week after Madeline left. He groaned at the thought. "I can't imagine what I'm going to do with myself once you're gone."

"You can sleep days and win a lot of money in the casino at night," Madeline suggested mischievously.

"Without Lady Luck at my side? You're out of your mind!"

They were joking but their raillery was strictly on the surface. Underneath they were both dreading their upcoming separation.

One afternoon, as they lingered at the poolside café-bar sipping the frosty drinks Jacob had tempted them with for "dessert," Chris confessed that he was not looking forward to going back to Lakeport.

"It's not the place," he said. "It's what I expect to find there."

"What, exactly?" Madeline asked. As she posed the question, she remembered the beautiful brunette pictured with Chris at the wedding of his friends, King and Claire Faraday. Was she—Lorna, that was her name—going to be among Chris's "findings" once he returned home?

"Before I left," he said ruefully, "I persuaded King to drive me out to the factory. I hadn't seen it since the explosion and King didn't want me to go. He said it was a hell of a way to start a vacation. But...I had to know what I was facing."

"It was *that* bad?" Madeline queried, her deep turquoise eyes mirrors of sympathy.

"There was nothing left," Chris answered dully. "I suppose I expected to find charred ruins and a lot of rubble. But everything had been cleared away while I was in the hospital. You might say I'm down to a basic concrete cellar."

"Are you going to rebuild, Chris?"

He considered this and his brow furrowed. "Frankly, I don't know what to do. Sometimes I wish I was ten years younger."

Madeline laughed. "And you're not quite thirty-five?"

"Not exactly ancient, I admit. But it's still late in the day to start a new career. Or, more correctly, to go back to an old one."

"An old one?"

Chris nodded. "When I was in college I became interested in the use of plastics in medicine—especially their future potential."

"You wanted a medical career?" She was surprised by that.

"I didn't want to be a doctor, if that's what you mean. What I wanted was to go for a doctorate in science and then pursue a career in medical research. My first interest in plastics was in connection with their use in prosthetics—in artificial arms and legs. Then, well, I became more and more interested in the things that can be done with plastics in connection with heart surgery, to the point of developing a really effective artificial heart. There's a long way to go before anyone'll get to the horizon, where that sort of thing is concerned. There's constant room for innovations and improved design."

Madeline liked his enthusiasm. "Whatever made you give up on a field like that?" she asked curiously.

He met her eyes directly and said, "I fell in love with the wrong woman. Sarah was not about to sit around and wait for me while I experimented in my ivory tower. Because of her I took a job after college with a plastics manufacturing firm in the city. New York, that is. Sarah liked the bright lights. She liked a lot of things we would have been better off without."

Madeline reached out quickly and clasped her hand over his. "I didn't mean to pry, Chris," she apologized.

"You weren't prying, Maddie. Hell, I want you to know all about me. So, to be honest, my gimpy leg wasn't the only reason I was gun-shy when I first met you." He spoke as if that meeting had taken place a long time ago.

Chris took a deep breath then stated bluntly, "You see, one man wasn't enough for Sarah. She was great in the beginning . . . but let's say it wasn't a very long honeymoon. After a while she didn't even try to hide her infidelities, and that . . . hurt.''

"It must have hurt terribly."

Chris shrugged. "I've always been an idealist," he confessed, "so I tried to put the pieces of our marriage back together. But it became far too complicated a puzzle for me to deal with. Finally, both Sarah and I made the decision that divorce was the only logical answer."

"You don't have to tell me this, Chris."

He favored her with a crooked smile, but continued, "Here's the clincher, Maddie. I'd scarcely gotten my final decree when my grandfather died and left me some money. I hate to say it, but maybe Sarah wouldn't have been so quick to agree to ending our marriage if that had happened sooner. The money gave me a fair bit of independence—enough to go back to Lakeport and build my own company on some land I'd also inherited. And . . . that's about it. The saga of a sour marriage and an equally ill-fated business venture," he concluded.

It was difficult to reply, but after pondering what he'd told her Madeline finally asked, "Your factory was insured, wasn't it?"

"Yes, but the settlement's still pending. There's a question of possible arson that hadn't been entirely settled when I left to come down here."

"Was it arson, Chris?"

"I very much doubt it. The original theory was that the explosion was caused by a fire that resulted from an outbuilding being hit by lightning. I buy that, but the insurance investigators have to justify their pay, I guess. It makes things drag on for so long, though."

"Instead of rebuilding, why not go back to school and work on your doctorate?"

"I'm not a schoolboy, Madeline," Chris ruefully conceded. "I'd feel totally out of place in a classroom full of kids."

"Most people working for doctorates can hardly be called kids!"

"I know, I know. To tell you the truth, I wasn't that far from getting my degree. I'd started on my thesis—"

"Then go back and finish it, for heaven's sake!"

"That's easier said than done," Chris told her. "Before the accident I *had* thought about doing exactly that. I was also about to start work on a plastic valve for use in coronary surgery...."

"Chris, if you have something like that to offer, you can't just toss it away," Madeline insisted.

"I guess I lost my motivation," Chris replied absently. He finished his piña colada, then asked suddenly, "How's your unicorn?"

"What?"

"The unicorn we bought in Oranjestad, Maddie. Remember?"

She looked at him and began to smile. "My unicorn's fine," she said. "He's upstairs on my dresser. Maybe a little lonely...."

"Perhaps we should pay him a visit," Chris ventured.

CHRIS AND MADELINE made love in her room that afternoon. Attuned to the lazy tropical atmosphere, they went slowly, savoring each gesture, exploring each nuance of feeling to the fullest. Finally their passion crested and they yielded to its glory. Then, as late afternoon shadows muted the sunlight filtering through the curtains, they lay side by side for a long while, holding hands like innocent children as they talked about all sorts of things.

Nothing they discussed was deeply personal. There'd been enough self-revelation—on Chris's part at least—for one day. Madeline, thinking that she knew him better than ever, realized her time would come. He deserved to hear a few confidences from her.

Her time came earlier than she expected. They went swimming the next morning and had stretched out on lounge chairs when Chris suddenly commented, "You've never said much about your husband, Maddie."

She repressed a smile. "What would you like to know, Chris?" She realized that a direct approach was the best way to go with him. "About Jeffrey, that is."

"Well..." Chris seemed to struggle, then finally said, "It's easier to talk about Sarah, I suppose because she isn't . . . dead."

"I guess that's so, to a point," Madeline acceded. "But death doesn't necessarily sanctify a person." Speaking carefully, she continued, "Basically I had a good marriage. I don't think there's any such thing as a *perfect* marriage, because people are imperfect in themselves."

"True."

"Oh, I loved Jeffrey," she added hastily. "Don't misunderstand me. And he loved me. In many ways, he was a wonderful husband. He was generous and passionate—challenging on every level. Which, in a nutshell, was our problem."

"How so?" Chris asked skeptically.

"Simply put . . . Jeffrey was a perfectionist. He demanded perfection from himself, especially in his work, and he expected it from others. He wanted a consistently excellent performance from me—as a woman, as a wife, and also as a physician. It was a hard role to play because I'm not a perfect woman. So at times I let him down, and quite badly, in his opinion.

"Nevertheless, we had a good personal life together. And, professionally, he was always there when I needed him, always ready to give me the benefit of his vast store of medical knowledge." She paused reflectively, then added, "So much of my life was wrapped up in Jeffrey that when he died I was like a boat without a rudder. I'd never learned how to steer my own course. I married him the week after I graduated from med school, and if anyone was ever naive, it was me."

"Was he a lot older than you?" Chris queried hesitantly, wanting to know what kind of a man Madeline had been married to, yet apprehensive about finding out too much. It dawned on him that though Jeffrey Clarke was dead, he was still a force to be reckoned with.

"Ten years older," Madeline said. "He was the first person I ever saw operate. I was on a surgical rotation my third year in med school, and he was the attending surgeon. I was impressed, let me tell you."

"He must have been excellent."

"Yes, he was. And, in a way, that was another of our problems. I often felt that Jeffrey was more like a father to me, rather than a husband or lover."

She wanted to tell Chris that she'd never reached the sensual pinnacles with Jeffrey that she'd already reached with him. But that wasn't an easy thing to admit. Although he'd come into her life so recently, Chris had already left an indelible mark.

Chris didn't try to pick up the threads of her statement. He waited judiciously, then asked instead, "Do you plan to stay in Maine, Maddie?"

"I don't know. Tom Lucas, a good friend and colleague of mine in Bangor, has been telling me lately that I should try something else for a while, but I'm not sure I want to do that."

"What does he suggest?"

"He tossed out the idea that I might apply for a grant and do some research in my field. Specifically in gastroenterology. Something that would open up a few windows in my life."

Her eyes sparkled as she softly added, "But lately, windows have been opening up on their own."

THE NIGHT BEFORE Madeline was to leave Aruba, Arthur Taylor insisted upon hosting a small dinner for her. It was difficult to say no because the life that revolved around the Aruban Palace was insular. There weren't too many viable excuses to offer, Madeline realized dismally.

When Chris heard she'd accepted Arthur's invitation, though, he was very annoyed.

"I'd have thought you might consider it important for us to be together your last night here," he stated testily.

"I have every intention of spending my last night here with you," Madeline assured him impishly.

"That's not what I mean, and you know it! Damn it, I don't want to share you, not this evening."

"Darling, it'll only be for a couple of hours. Then we can fade into the moonlight."

"Fat chance," Chris grumbled.

The situation worsened when it developed that Arthur had booked a table in the hotel's main dining room, where the decor was formal, the cuisine was French, and an excellent orchestra played for dancing.

Arthur had invited Theda plus two other couples whom they'd met the night they went to the Blue Delft for blackjack lessons. It was a convivial group—or would have been, except for Chris, who wasn't at his best.

The other men all asked Madeline to dance from time to time, and it would have been more pointed to refuse than it was to accept. She might have enjoyed herself, except that with every step she took on the highly polished dance floor she became increasingly aware of Chris, sitting in stony silence, his thoughts turned inward.

Madeline felt that he was behaving very badly, but she couldn't entirely blame him. Tension had stretched between them these past couple of days, as the time for her departure neared. Last night they'd made love almost frantically, as if determined to live a lifetime within the space of an hour or two.

Now, as Arthur led her back to their table after a waltz, she felt a headache begin to press at her temples.

Theda was sitting with Chris and it looked as if they'd been having a very one-sided conversation. Arthur claimed Theda for the next dance. And when a waiter hovered nearby, Madeline asked him for a vodka and tonic. Chris glanced up at this and gave his order for another scotch.

He looked so miserable that it was difficult to be angry with him. But he'd done nothing to make the best of the situation tonight and that had annoyed her.

Madeline knew she couldn't let it pass. She had to say something to him. Her head was beginning to pound and she felt tired and irritable. "I wish you'd be a little more pleasant," she chided. She hadn't intended to snap, but that's the way her words came out.

"Pleasant?" he echoed. He raked her with an accusing glance. "How the hell can you expect me to be *pleasant*?"

"It's my last night, after all."

"Don't you think I know that?"

"Yes, of course you know it. But you might think of *me* just a little bit instead of wallowing in self-pity."

"Wallowing, eh?"

"Well, haven't you been?" she challenged.

She saw his mouth twist. "It hasn't been the easiest of evenings for me," he allowed.

"Because I've been dancing with a couple of men old enough to be my father? Come on, Chris."

He scowled. "I'm not jealous, if that's what you're implying," he told her stiffly. "Anyway, I'd feel the same if they were as old as your grandfather. They *can* dance with you, Maddie, and I can't. That's the issue."

Madeline sighed impatiently. "Dancing isn't important."

"Isn't it? It's important enough to me that right now I'd give ten years of my life to take you out on that dance floor."

"That's the most ridiculous thing I've ever heard!"

"Is it?"

Chris was glaring at her and Madeline glared back. Then suddenly she saw him draw a deep breath.

"My God!" he observed, actually smiling. "We're having our first fight. That sort of rounds things out for us, wouldn't you say?"

"What do you mean?"

"Well, speaking for myself, you've seen my best side, and now you're seeing my worst. So you know what a lousy disposition I really have."

"Do you?"

"Yes," he said. "No...I don't know." His eyes seemed to mist, then he whispered, "All I know is...I love you."

Madeline lost her voice and warm tears filled her eyes. Appalled, Chris reached out a hand and gently touched her arm. "I didn't mean to upset you," he implored. "I know I'm rushing things, but..."

Her smile was shaky. "Don't protest so much, okay?"

She knew he was waiting for her to say more than that. And she wished she could. But so many thoughts were crowding in—thoughts of tomorrow, thoughts of the past, thoughts of reality back home—that Madeline still couldn't speak.

The others returned to the table and she heard someone ask Arthur how he liked retirement. Arthur confessed that he wasn't thrilled with it.

"I'm not cut out to be idle," he admitted. "So when I get back to the States, I'm joining an organization of retired executives, a firm that helps people in need of specific business expertise."

Then everyone began talking about their post-vacation plans, and Theda laughingly declared it was about time to start searching for her fourth husband!

Madeline evaded discussing anything to do with her future, and so did Chris. But Chris did begin making a concerted effort to be pleasant, although only she sensed how difficult it was for him to turn on the charm.

Later, when they were alone in her room, she hugged him and said, "Thank you."

"What for?"

"For trying. I appreciated it. I think the others did, too, although I doubt they put their fingers on exactly what was wrong."

"My gloominess made that much difference?"

"To me it did."

Chris moved to the sliding glass door that opened onto the little balcony and stared out at a black sea. Madeline went to him and wrapped her arms around his neck. "The way you feel," she said softly, "makes a lot of difference to me."

"The way you feel makes *all* the difference to me," Chris answered. He seemed about to say something more, but instead he sighed. "Oh, hell," he confessed ruefully, "I think I'm going to need a few lessons in coping. I'm not doing too well with this. Maddie . . ."

"Yes?"

"I've reserved a taxi to drive us out to the airport in the morning."

"Us?"

"I couldn't stand at the front entrance here and watch you get on the airport bus," he told her. "I don't know how I'm going to watch you get on the plane. I keep wanting to grab the clock and push the hands back."

"I know. Believe me, I know."

His eyes darkened. "We haven't talked about after tomorrow," he pointed out.

"Yes . . . I know that, too."

"This can't be the end for us. I have to see you when we get back to the States."

When she didn't immediately answer, Chris turned away from her and looked out into the darkness. "Maddie, you don't want it to end tomorrow, do you?"

She shook her head, and the words came tumbling out. "No, darling. Of course I don't want it to end tomorrow!"

Chris shuddered and turned back to Madeline. "You had me going for a second there," he confessed. "I start thinking about us, and I become so damned afraid that once you get back to your work our time together will begin to fade away in your memory...until it seems like just another love affair to you."

"Just another love affair?" Madeline repeated, affronted yet touched by his vulnerability. "I've never gone around having love affairs, Christopher Talmadge. In that realm, you're my first."

He'd been rigid but suddenly he appeared to relax. Teasingly he growled, "I hope I'm your last."

Madeline took a step forward, closing the space between them. "My only," she whispered sincerely.

That night Chris and Madeline made passionate love, but again there was an edge of desperation to their lovemaking. They rushed as if they were challenging time, then finally drifted off to sleep, vaguely dissatisfied.

Morning came too soon. Chris left for his own room to shower and change his clothes. Madeline ordered coffee from room service. She had showered and finished packing before the girl arrived.

She took her coffee out on the balcony and tried to imagine what it would be like back in Maine. It was almost impossible to visualize snow and icy winds while gazing out over the languid Caribbean.

The phone's jangle summoned her back inside. It was Chris on the line. "Want to join me in the coffee shop for breakfast?" he asked.

"I had coffee sent up, Chris, and I really don't want anything else just now," she answered. "You know how they feed you on planes."

"Yes, I know, but . . ."

"Yes?"

"Well, I had a crazy idea . . ."

"What?"

"Maddie, couldn't you take another week off and stay here? I think you could change your flight, even now. If you can't . . . hell, I'll book your ticket when I confirm my own. We could fly back as far as Boston together—"

"You don't go to Boston, Chris," Madeline cut in softly.

"I *can* go to Boston."

"Chris, it wouldn't make sense. And even if it did, I can't take another week off. I have patients scheduled for the day after tomorrow, first thing in the morning."

There was a brief silence. Then he said, "Well, it was just a crazy idea—nothing ventured, nothing gained. I can imagine what your schedule is. So, the taxi's coming at ten-thirty. Sure you don't want something to eat before then?"

"I'm sure. I'll meet you in the lobby at a quarter past ten, all right?"

The lobby would offer an impersonal setting, which was what they'd both need to help get through this parting, Madeline told herself as she dressed, put on makeup, and fixed her hair.

She and Chris said very little to each other on the drive out to the airport. Once they arrived Madeline checked her luggage, got her boarding pass, and then discovered there were still forty-five minutes to flight time.

At a loss for words, Chris asked, "How about one last piña colada?"

She shook her head. "I really couldn't."

"And I really shouldn't," he admitted, looking around the lobby as he spoke. "Let's see," he observed. "There's a duty-free liquor store, and a small gift shop. Want to browse in the gift shop?"

"I'll ask them if they have anything made in Aruba," Madeline managed, feeling her throat begin to knot.

They didn't, so she and Chris took seats near the doors that opened out onto the tarmac. The air-conditioning wasn't working very well, and the heat and humidity were creeping in.

Madeline had chosen a sheer wool skirt with a silk blouse, and was carrying the matching wool jacket. She said, "I wish I'd opted for a sleeveless sundress."

"And maybe a fur coat to top it with?" Chris suggested. "You'll freeze in what you've got on once you get to Boston."

"Well, I change planes at Logan, but I think my connecting flight leaves from the same terminal, so I won't have to go outside."

"Is someone meeting you at the airport in Bangor?"

She nodded. "Tom Lucas."

"Your friend at the hospital?"

"That's right. Your memory astonishes me!"

"I have a terrible memory, except where you're concerned." He forced a smile, but it faded fast. "Maddie," he pleaded, "when am I going to see you again? And where? I have to know."

Madeline thought quickly. "I'm going to a conference in New York the middle of April," she said. "I think it's on a Friday, but then I'll have the weekend free. Maybe..."

"No maybes about it," Chris decided. "New York, the middle April. That's a promise, right?"

"Yes," Madeline said. "That's a promise."

But suddenly April—only a few weeks away—seemed many years in the future.

CHAPTER SEVEN

CHRIS DID NOT HAVE the best of homecomings. It was late at night when he flew into Lakeport. His connecting flight had been delayed in New York and, uncertain about his arrival time, he didn't call ahead to ask anyone to meet him.

When he got off the plane he was assaulted by a blast of frigid air blowing in from Lake Champlain. The bitter cold made his leg ache all the more. He took a taxi from the airport into town. He'd done a lot of walking between ticket counters at Kennedy, and he was exhausted.

The big old Talmadge house, in which he'd been living since his divorce, was dark. That was not unexpected. His parents lived in Florida now and came north only occasionally. But he was surprised to see the Parmeter mansion next door without so much as a single light on.

King Faraday had bought the old homestead as a special wedding gift for his wife Claire. She was a Parmeter and had lived in the house during her teens. Renovations on the house had started late last fall, about a month before King and Claire's wedding. Carpenters, plumbers and electricians were still busy at their tasks when Chris left for Aruba. He'd hoped their work would be finished by now, and that King and Claire would be in residence.

The taxi driver carried Chris's luggage onto the porch then waited while Chris unlocked the front door. The thermostat had been turned down leaving just enough heat to prevent the pipes from freezing. It certainly wasn't enough for comfort, Chris thought wryly as he paid the cabbie, then limped around the first floor rooms switching on lights. He pushed the thermostat to seventy-five. After the house warmed up, he could lower it to the usual sixty-eight.

Chris had a cleaning woman who came in once a week. He'd left her some money to stock up on milk, coffee and a few other staples for his return home. Evidently she'd gotten her dates confused. The fridge and the cupboards were bare except for a few canned goods that had been there already.

There was a bottle of scotch in a side cupboard and Chris poured himself a shot and drank it neat. Then he wandered back into the living room, thought about making a fire in the fireplace, but decided against it. Next he thought about trying to start his car and going out to eat. But even though the car was sheltered inside the garage, it wouldn't be easy to get it going in this weather after it had been sitting idle for a month. Anyway, there was always canned soup.

He opted in favor of another drink and, glass in hand, he picked up the kitchen phone and dialed George Faraday's number. Claire and King had been living in King's father's house while the Parmeter mansion was being renovated.

It was good to hear a familiar voice. But Chris felt let down when the elder Dr. Faraday told him that King and Claire had decided to take a two week, spur of the moment vacation in the Virgin Islands, and wouldn't be back for a few more days.

"King had a rare chance to get away," Dr. Faraday explained, "and Claire made arrangements with her partner to handle her art galleries. So they decided to go for it."

"I'm glad they did," Chris managed sincerely, camouflaging his disappointment. Then he politely answered the questions Dr. Faraday posed about Aruba and promised to be in touch.

Once he'd hung up, he sat there, lost in thought and staring at nothing in particular as he finished his scotch. He felt restless, achy, and out of sorts, and wished he had someone to talk to...like Madeline Clarke.

It was amazing how much he missed her. Chris found it hard to believe that being separated from someone he'd known for only two weeks could leave such a void in his life.

He'd phoned Madeline from Aruba the day after she'd left for home, but there'd been no answer at her number. It wasn't until late in the evening that he'd reached her, only to discover that she'd been called into the hospital on an emergency involving one of her patients. She'd sounded tired and tense—and not at all like the Madeline he'd made love with in paradise.

He'd tried her number again the next night, but again to no avail. And when they finally did connect, after two more nights, Chris told her—only half joking—that maybe it would be better if she called him. Madeline admitted she was hard to reach, and gave him her page number at the hospital, just in case.

Just in case of what? Chris asked himself now. What kind of a personal emergency did he need to justify paging her? He dialed her home number and wasn't surprised when it continued to ring unanswered. After a moment's reflection, he decided to risk her possible displeasure, and dialed the hospital. He needed to hear the sound of Madeline's voice. But what he really needed, he thought grimly, was her.

A crisply efficient operator asked for his name, then told him to stay on the line while she paged Dr. Clarke.

He'd teasingly called Madeline Dr. Clarke now and then, but the operator's tone put a professional stamp on her as nothing else had up to now. Although Chris's best friend was a doctor, he'd had so much contact with doctors since his accident, he was slightly weary of the title. The fact that Madeline was also a doctor—and very competent, he was sure—*had* registered. Even so, it gave Chris an odd feeling to picture her in a hospital environment, probably wearing a white coat with a stethoscope dangling around her neck.

"Dr. Clarke," she answered, after what seemed an eternity.

"Madeline, it's Chris," he said, feeling light-years away.

"Chris! Is there something wrong?"

"Yes," he growled, "there's a hell of a lot wrong." He followed that quickly with, "I miss you so damn much, Maddie! That's what's wrong. This distance between us is driving me crazy."

"Where are you?"

"In Lakeport. In a big, cold, empty house."

"When did you get home?"

"About an hour ago, and I wish you were here! I don't see how I can wait another six weeks to see you. That's about what it is till your meeting in New York, isn't it?"

"Yes."

"Couldn't we get together before then?"

Madeline hesitated, and Chris knew he was making things hard for her. She said unhappily, "I don't see how. We're short staffed at the hospital, plus a lot of my patients put things off awaiting my return, so I'm swamped. Until I get my act together here, I wouldn't be very good company."

"To me you would be."

Madeline's laugh was shaky. "Thanks for saying that, but—"

"I'm not trying to put you on the spot," he cut in. "It's just that—"

Madeline's beeper went off before he could finish what he wanted to say. "I have to go, Chris," she told him hastily. "Look, I'll call you tomorrow night."

He had to be satisfied with that. But when she didn't call him the next night he felt more out of sorts than ever. The following evening they finally connected. Madeline explained that when she'd gotten home from the hospital the previous day she'd been so tired she took a nap, then didn't wake up till nearly midnight.

"And I wasn't going to call you that late," she concluded.

Chris was tempted to say it would never be too late to hear from her, but he didn't want to pressure her. It didn't take much intuition to realize that she had a lot on her mind since returning to her practice.

By the time Chris had been back in Lakeport for a couple of days he had a lot on his mind, too. The insurance company finally reached the conclusion that the explosion had been an "Act of God" caused by a violent electrical storm. It was only the amount of the settlement that was still undecided. Before much longer, though, the insurance money would come through. And Chris knew it was imperative for him to make up his mind about just what course he wanted to follow before that happened.

His talks with Madeline in Aruba had revived his interest in the invention he'd come so near to perfecting before his marriage to Sarah. One option open, in line with that, was to go back to school, finish his thesis and get his doctorate, as Madeline had suggested. But as he'd told her, he couldn't see himself doing that. It was late in the day to return to academia.

On the other hand, he doubted if he would truly be satisfied with making plastic vials and the other similar containers for medical purposes that his company had specialized in prior to the explosion.

On several afternoons, Chris drove out to the snow-covered factory site. March had come in like a lion which, according to the old adage, meant it would go out like a lamb. The weather was especially disagreeable, even for late winter in upstate New York. Chris didn't attempt to walk around the grounds as the concrete paths were dangerously ice-glazed. Trying to negotiate them would be a stupid risk. He contented himself instead with sitting in his car and staring out at the desolate winter scene.

There was nothing left of his factory but a concrete foundation. It was difficult to visualize the plant as it had existed last summer—a modern facility with attractive landscaping, working at full capacity. Lakeport needed this kind of light industry, and Chris had employed almost fifty people. He wondered what they were doing now.

The insurance money should give him enough to build a close replica of the destroyed factory. Costs had increased in the interim, of course. Costs were always increasing. But he could finance any additional expense, and even dip into his own capital if necessary. The main problem was to decide exactly what he wanted to do, where he wanted to go from here. And, though Chris tried hard to project his future on those cold March afternoons, inevitably his mind went into a kind of overdrive, and he'd find himself woolgathering about Madeline Clarke.

He'd thought that if he kept busy he wouldn't miss her quite so much. But he missed her more with each passing day. He wished she was around so he could talk plans with her and get her feedback face-to-face. Occasionally he broached the subject on the phone, but that wasn't the same as having her next to him and gazing into her lovely eyes.

Thinking of physical proximity and remembering the love they'd shared inevitably brought on a different kind of longing. His need for her tortured him at those moments. In the middle of the night he'd awaken to find that he'd been reaching for her in his sleep and whispering her name into the darkness.

King and Claire returned from their vacation tanned, healthy and brimming with vitality. They promptly invited Chris over to the Faraday house for dinner and he was glad to accept. But Claire and King were so much in love that watching them was like sitting out in summer sunlight. Chris knew all about the severe emotional problems his two close friends had weathered before they finally came together. He couldn't have been happier for them. But, personally, he'd never felt more lonely.

MADELINE WAS FULLY AWARE of Chris's frustrations. His feelings became more apparent to her every time they talked over the telephone. Each conversation, somewhat paradoxically, was becoming more difficult. By the time they'd mutually agree to hang up, they were reaching for things to say.

Living life on a daily basis was a very different game than vacationing on a tropical island. But there was more to it than that. Madeline discovered that getting back to the reality of her normal way of living meant facing up to more than she'd expected. She became worried that she was the cause of the present strain between Chris and herself. She feared that her love of medicine, and being so locked into her career, could do nothing but aggravate their dilemma.

She reminded herself that Chris had known she was a doctor from the very beginning. But evidently he hadn't fully appreciated what being a dedicated physician entailed. She wasn't sure she'd totally realized it herself—until now.

In Aruba she'd finally begun to emerge as her own person after years of being dominated by Jeffrey. She thanked Chris for that. He'd made her feel more desirable, more wanted, than she'd ever felt before. He'd even gone so far as to fall in love with her—as she had with him.

Was theirs a real love or a temporary infatuation based on the heady chemistry that flowed between them? As much as Madeline wanted to believe it was real love, she had to wonder. She and Chris had both been searching for something in Aruba, although she didn't think either of them could have described what it was.

Had they been looking for soul mates? She had to smile, knowing that it was partially true. They'd both felt a need not only for someone they could "love" and physically enjoy, but also for a kindred spirit with whom they could share the many experiences that needed to be shared, and in whom they could confide.

She believed she'd found that kindred spirit in Chris and she was certain he felt the same way. She just wanted them to be very sure. She didn't want to hurt Chris—he'd had enough hurt to last a lifetime. Nor did she want to be hurt herself.

As their mid-March birthdays approached, Madeline tried to think of something clever to send to Chris. Their phone conversations revealed that he was pretty depressed these days although he went to great lengths to camouflage it.

Madeline sought for a birthday gesture that might cheer him up. They both needed to take life—and each other—a little less seriously just now. She remembered a party she'd been at in Boston some time ago where a belly dancer had suddenly appeared, gyrating wildly in the middle of the birthday person's living room. She wished she could come up with something like that. But she doubted she could find any belly dancers plying their trade in Lakeport!

As she was passing a florist shop in downtown Bangor one afternoon, Madeline saw a display in the window that—while not the perfect solution to her problem—was a lot better than a card plus shaving lotion or a necktie. The display featured a large, gold plastic harp strung with green strings and further ornamented with gold angels, bright green pipes, and even a small green derby. A wide, green satin ribbon proclaimed St. Patrick's Day greetings. Madeline, scanning the absolutely atrocious example of holiday trivia, decided that a green satin ribbon with ''Happy Birthday'' piped in gold could easily be substituted for the St. Patrick's Day message. The florist agreed with her and, for a price, was willing to change his window display, make the suitable alterations on the harp, then ship it off to Lakeport in plenty of time for Chris's birthday.

Chris's gift to her was more traditional—but she loved it. He sent her a dozen exquisite white roses, with six long-stemmed green carnations tucked among them. The birthday card that accompanied the flowers dripped with sentiment and might have seemed maudlin coming from anyone else. Coming from Chris, it brought tears to her eyes.

They made birthday calls to each other on both the sixteenth and the eighteenth, and Chris completely broke up on his birthday, dissolving into laughter as he told her how the cleaning lady had been there when the harp arrived, and couldn't believe what she was seeing. And both King and Claire Faraday, on viewing Madeline's present, had echoed the cleaning lady's sentiments.

When they finished their conversation, Madeline felt warmer and closer to Chris than she had since Aruba.

March edged into April. Even in Maine, a faint hint of spring infiltrated the air. Through phone calls and an occasional letter, Madeline and Chris began finalizing plans for their weekend in New York.

On a bright Friday morning, Chris flew down to the city. Claire Faraday, who had business to attend to at her art gallery, flew down with him. King was on call that weekend at Lakeport General Hospital, so Claire planned to stay in town and visit some friends.

Claire was good company. During the flight, she kept Chris from succumbing to the butterflies fluttering in his stomach at the thought of seeing Madeline again. At Kennedy Airport, he and Claire decided to share a cab into Manhattan. Claire was dropped off first at the condominium in Central Park West she still maintained.

It was only after she'd left him, with a sisterly kiss on the cheek, that Chris began to give in to a bad case of the jitters. As he registered at the desk of the small East Side hotel where he'd booked a suite, he wished he'd flown down the following morning. Then Madeline would have been awaiting him.

As it was, she would be tied up in medical meetings all day. She'd dropped off her luggage at the hotel, but wouldn't be checking in until after a banquet that evening. She'd invited Chris to accompany her, but he'd sidestepped her offer. After this trying interval apart, he wanted to see Madeline alone.

He hadn't counted on the banquet lasting so late. Despite himself, he fell asleep in an armchair—to be awakened by Madeline's kiss!

She'd let herself into their suite with the key she'd picked up from the front desk. When she saw Chris sprawled in the armchair, his sandy hair looking like spun gold in the light of an ivory-shaded lamp, she slipped off her shoes and tiptoed across the room.

Madeline paused for a long moment to look down at Chris, reviewing each of his features as if his face was a text she'd studied a long time ago and wanted to be sure she was recalling correctly. If anything, he was even more handsome than she remembered. And there was a vulnerability to his face when he was asleep that deeply touched her.

As she gazed tenderly at Chris, Madeline's feelings for him, smoldering since Aruba, stirred anew. It was a sensual arousal—he'd always affected her that way. But these feelings dealt more with the culmination of something started then set aside out of necessity.

Madeline admitted, now, that although she'd done a lot of thinking about Chris since her return to Bangor she'd kept her thoughts on a relatively superficial level. She'd even forced him out of her mind more than once, making herself concentrate on some medical matter. She'd tried, without fully realizing what she was doing, to immerse herself in her work so that she wouldn't think too much about Chris. And she'd pondered over his possible attitude toward her career as if she were putting up a safety shield that she could retreat behind if things got too intense. All of this, because she'd been more than a little afraid of what could so easily happen to her where Chris was concerned.

This was a tendency she recognized in herself. When her emotions were deeply stirred, she found a retreat into medicine an easy escape hatch.

She'd virtually thrown herself into her career after Jeffrey's death, working harder than she'd ever worked before. She could feel herself drifting in the same direction now and she vowed she was not going to let herself go that route with Chris.

It was too late anyway! Watching the even rise and fall of his breathing as he slept, retracing the features that already had become incredibly dear to her, Madeline knew—and accepted—the wonderful fact that she'd fallen in love with Chris Talmadge.

LOVE BECAME THE MOTIF between Chris and Madeline that weekend in New York. Love colored every moment they shared.

Madeline knew she'd never forget the expression in Chris's eyes when he looked up at her sleepily after she kissed him that first night. He quickly stirred, reaching for her like a man starved for her touch. Their hunger

for each other became so intense that for several time-
less hours they thought of nothing but satisfying that
desire. Then, in the wake of passion, they explored the
wonder of just being together again. Soft words, soft
caresses, soft kisses...the warm night air became sur-
feited with the elements and gestures of love.

In the morning Chris ordered breakfast through
room service. He was opening the door for the waiter
when Madeline emerged from the bedroom, fresh and
radiant in a yellow silk robe as sunny as the April day.
By her place at the table she found a tiny box with a
single ruby rose beside it.

The flower eloquently spoke of Chris's love for her.
She inhaled its rich fragrance, her senses totally alert.
She could not remember when she'd ever felt so vi-
brantly alive.

Her fingers trembled as she opened the little box
wrapped in rose-patterned paper. Inside she found a
miniature gold unicorn almost identical to the crystal
unicorn Chris had bought for her in Oranjestad.

She looked up, her eyes luminous, her voice catching. "You remembered."

"How could I not remember?" he asked, smiling
tenderly. "I thought the Aruban unicorn might be
lonely."

"The Aruba unicorn has been very lonely."

Chris read her hidden meaning, and dropped all pre-
tenses. "I've been lonely as hell, Maddie," he admitted huskily. "Each day without you has seemed like a
year. I've dragged through the hours. Maddie, I've
missed you so much."

She went into his arms. And by the time they got back
to their breakfast it was cold.

It was a magical day. The morning was reserved solely for lovemaking—for getting to know each other again, as Chris put it. But clasped within the warmth of his arms, Madeline felt that she'd never known him better.

In the early afternoon they left the hotel and walked west to Fifth Avenue, then turned downtown toward Rockefeller Plaza.

Madeline, unable to suppress a professional evaluation, noted that walking was still not easy for Chris. She didn't want to press him, but suspected he'd yet to make an appointment with a therapist. By now he should be on an exercise program. Swimming had been fine therapy in Aruba, but...

"May I ask why you suddenly look so grim?" Chris queried curiously.

"Grim?"

"Okay, then...serious. You look like you just remembered something you don't want to remember."

"Not guilty," Madeline objected. "My shoe is pinching slightly, that's all," she fibbed.

"Women!" Chris groaned. "Come on, let's find a shoe store and buy you a new pair."

"That would be worse, Chris. At least these are almost broken in."

He shook his head and smiled tolerantly as they reached Rockefeller Plaza where the flower beds were abloom with red tulips and yellow daffodils, and the statue of Prometheus proudly basked in the spring sunshine.

"The outdoor café's open," Madeline observed. "Think it would be too chilly?"

Chris didn't answer. And when she looked up at him she saw that it was his turn to look grim. He was viewing the flights of steps leading from the balustrade where they were standing to the large open patio backed by the splashing fountain.

"Or would you rather go to my favorite French restaurant on West 56th Street?" Madeline suggested quickly.

Chris's mouth tightened. He said, "Your diplomacy is showing."

"All right, then. Those are too many steps for you to attempt just yet," Madeline told him.

"Yet...or ever?" Chris muttered. He shook his head and added wryly, "I'm sorry. I'm damned if I'm going to start moaning and groaning about my limitations. But there are moments, and this is one of them, when they fly up and hit me right in the face."

"Let's walk up to the French restaurant and talk, okay? What does your friend King say about you?"

"King's been so busy since he and Claire got back from the Virgin Islands that we haven't seen that much of each other," Chris answered. "Claire flew down with me yesterday, though. She has an art gallery just a few blocks from here."

"I think you mentioned that once."

"Well, if I hadn't been so greedy about keeping you all to myself, I would have suggested we get together with Claire this weekend," Chris admitted. "I want you to meet both Claire and King. They're great people and my best friends. But King has been so damned busy lately. The medical chief of staff has been sick, so King's had to take over some of his responsibilities."

"Have you gone back to the therapist who was treating you at the rehab center?" Madeline asked.

"Angel, please don't play doctor with me! Not that you'd be playing, but I've seen more *physicians*," he emphasized negatively, "than most people see in a life-time. I've told King that, too."

Madeline cleared her throat. "The question, Chris...."

"All right...no, I haven't been back to the therapist and I know that's something I have to put on my agenda. I've just had other things on my mind."

Madeline tried not to let herself be miffed over his statement about doctors. She knew he didn't intend it personally. Even so, it stung. "Have you decided whether or not you're going to rebuild the factory?" she asked.

"No. I've done a lot of thinking about that, but I haven't come to any definite conclusions."

"Chris, I detect a certain lack of enthusiasm when the subject of the factory comes up," Madeline said frankly. "If you don't want to rebuild, you shouldn't."

"It isn't that simple," Chris told her. It was crazy, he thought, but when Madeline was serious about some-thing, as she was now, it made her look younger. She got that intent look on her face that little girls often have when they're playing with dolls.

The little girl look faded as Madeline said, "Few things are simple. In fact, it seems to me that life gets more and more complicated. Then sometimes I won-der if it can be blamed on *life*, or if it's really our own responses to living. I mean, sometimes I think we as-sign the wrong priorities to things."

She looked troubled and Chris wished he could read her mind. He asked gently, "Have you assigned a priority to me, Maddie?"

It was a dangerous question. He knew that as soon as he'd spoken, and found he was holding his breath awaiting her response.

Unexpectedly she flashed him a mischievous grin. "I think I'm going to keep you guessing," she teased.

"Then I'll have to find out for myself, won't I?" Chris teased back. They were walking along West 56th Street, and he smiled down at her. "Just wait until I get you back to the hotel!" he threatened.

"Chris!"

He stopped walking, then reached out and cupped Madeline's chin in his right hand. She tried to get free but he tightened his clasp.

"The original iron fist!" she moaned.

"You'd better believe it," he whispered as he bent down and kissed her squarely on the lips.

It was a tender kiss—unhurried, deep and quintessentially stirring. When Chris released Madeline there was a slightly glazed look in her eyes.

"My God," she murmured. "What you can do to me!"

"Just testing," he told her, unaccountably pleased with himself. "I was checking to see whether or not New Yorkers are really as indifferent to everything going on around them as they're reputed to be." Noticing the turned heads and smiles of passersby, he concluded, "For the sake of the record, they're not. I'd say New Yorkers are as romantic as anyone else. Shall I prove that again?"

"You'd better not." Madeline's smile could not have been more seductive. "I'd rather wait and take the final exam," she told him.

CHAPTER EIGHT

CHRIS AND MADELINE met again in the middle of May, this time in Boston—a good midway point and a relatively short flight from both Lakeport and Bangor. Four weeks had elapsed since they'd shared the weekend in New York. They agreed that it seemed more like four years.

Chris had booked a suite at the Park Plaza and, again, was the first to arrive. The suite was on the tenth floor and overlooked the Public Garden and the adjacent Boston Common. After a long cold spring, the trees, bushes and flowers were budding—the time for new beginnings Chris thought as he waited for Madeline.

He'd made a number of business decisions since their New York interlude. Now he hoped to make a few on the personal front.

They'd been speaking on the phone nearly every day. Sometimes he called her, but more often she called him as he was considerably easier to reach. Chris found their phone conversations wonderful, tantalizing, and sometimes far too stimulating. Thinking of them now, he told himself whimsically that he needed to hold a lot more than a plastic telephone receiver. He needed the warmth and vitality of Madeline herself. He needed the sight of her, the feel of her, the touch of her hand.

When the knock came at the door, he experienced an uncharacteristic moment of pure panic. Was there a chance she'd changed? Not that she, herself, had changed, but that she'd changed her thinking about him?

He opened the door nervously, then stood staring at her for so long that finally Madeline laughed.

"Aren't you going to invite me in?" she teased.

"Of course," Chris retorted hastily. He moved back too quickly and stumbled, then pushed heavily on his cane to regain his balance. He sensed that Madeline was noticing his every move, and guessed she was unconsciously evaluating his progress. At moments like this he almost wished she wasn't a doctor. In truth, his leg had not improved that much, although he'd been going to a therapist and doing the prescribed exercises with a fair degree of faithfulness. This was discouraging, and a subject he really didn't want to discuss. He didn't want to talk about anything that might put a blight on their weekend.

Madeline walked past him into the spacious living room and quickly crossed to the windows. "What a terrific view of Boston!" she exclaimed.

"Thank you. I had the city dusted off and polished just for you," Chris informed her, slowly moving over to join her.

He felt shy with her, and the feeling was strange. He couldn't remember ever having felt like this with anyone else. He gazed down at her profile, loving the way her nose tilted upward, loving the sensuous curve of her mouth, adoring her dark eyelashes.

A bittersweet longing swept over him, a longing so poignant, so intense, that tears stung his eyes. And that, he informed himself, was absolutely crazy! He glanced at Madeline quickly, wondering if she'd noticed his emotional surge. But she was staring out across the park, absorbed with the town houses of Beacon Hill and the gold dome of the State House.

Chris wondered if she was remembering the years when she'd lived in Boston, a time when she'd been married to Jeffrey Clarke and they'd both been practicing medicine here. He'd not thought about her previous associations with this city when he'd suggested their meeting here. Dismayed, he began to fear it had been a bad choice. Then Madeline turned and looked up at him and, in a very revealing moment, Chris knew that it wasn't past memories that were disturbing her—it was the present. She was just as nervous as he was. This tryst meant just as much to her as it did to him. Undoubtedly she'd been experiencing the same anticipation and worrying about the same things.

This knowledge came to him like a personal message, and his heart, which had felt burdened by doubt, lightened remarkably.

He took Madeline in his arms and held her gently, his cheek brushing her soft dark hair. When their lips met, the kiss was incredibly sweet. There was so much pent-up longing in Chris that the sweetness suffused him. He felt giddy, as if he had been drinking too heavily from the nectar of the gods. But he wanted more of that potion, he wanted more of everything. At the same time he wished they could stay exactly as they were—he and Madeline, rooted in this position, embracing each other, with no need to face up to the mounting problems their long-distance relationship was causing...for him, at least.

He whispered, "I love you, Madeline Clarke."

As he spoke he realized that she'd never said those words to him. She'd implied love in her voice and her behavior, and in the glorious messages he so often read in her beautiful turquoise eyes. But she'd never *said* the words.

It wasn't something you could ask someone to say. That declaration had to be voluntary in order to be valid. Knowing that, Chris nuzzled Madeline's forehead with his lips, while his fingers slowly massaged the nape of her neck. Then, no longer able to repress himself, his hands began to roam, as did his mouth, and soon he was covering her cheeks and the tip of her nose and her earlobes with kisses, while that age-old urgency began to possess them both.

When they drifted together toward the bedroom, they were at the brink of passion, reaching and fumbling as clothes were discarded. Their coming together was as natural as the sunrise, and as brilliant as the stars on a clear summer night.

Chris had never felt so physically fulfilled. As Madeline fell asleep in his arms, he shifted his position, watching the steady rise and fall of her breasts. Lovingly, he studied every inch of her face. The dark shadows he saw under her eyes bothered him. She looked tired and, if anything, thinner than she'd been in New York.

He knew she'd gone to Aruba because she'd been working too hard and had actually collapsed at the hospital. He wondered if she was working too hard once again, and the idea worried him.

It hurt to see Madeline appear so tired, and to suspect she was overworked. It especially hurt to know there was so little he could do about it. Chris discovered that he wanted to look after her, care for her, keep her safe from . . . well, from anything that could possibly harm her. This deeply protective feeling was new to him, and a clue to something else.

Chris, who would have sworn only a few weeks earlier that he'd never again get married, knew that more than anything in life he wanted to make Madeline his wife.

That night they had dinner at a Thai restaurant in the Back Bay. Madeline had slept most of the afternoon and she looked more rested. Better, in fact, than Chris did. As the day passed, he'd become increasingly preoccupied with the problems of their relationship, and with the possible solutions.

He'd missed her, wanted her and longed for her ever since they'd parted in Aruba. But instead of fulfilling his needs, these meetings were underlining the inescapable fact that he couldn't imagine the future without her by his side—all of the time.

Watching Chris toy with his food, Madeline frowned. He seemed so preoccupied, so on edge.

"What's the matter, Chris?" she asked softly.

"Hmmm?"

"Please, Chris, what is it?"

"What is what, Maddie?" he asked absently.

"What's the *matter* with you?"

His lopsided grin tugged at her heart. "Am I to answer that in words of one syllable?"

"Is it that bad?"

"Depends on how you define 'bad,' I guess," Chris mumbled, studying his chopsticks morosely. "Look, I'm sorry. I didn't mean to get into anything heavy tonight."

Madeline sighed. "Please...tell me what it is, Chris."

He looked up, his hazel eyes intense. "Okay," he said, "it's us."

"Us?"

"You sound surprised," Chris murmured, "and that surprises me." He paused and, deciding there was no gentle way of putting this, told her, "Maddie...I don't think we can go on this way."

Madeline's eyes widened. "What?"

"It's nothing very complicated, Maddie. I just don't think we can go on this way, that's all."

"Chris, this is only the second time we've met since Aruba."

"Yes." He nodded. "I'm well aware of that. I'm also well aware of every day and hour in between our two times together. And of all the lonely hours to come, if we continue on this course."

"What other course would you have us follow?" Madeline asked, her voice shaking slightly.

He nearly came out and told her that he'd prefer they get married, but he bit back the words. It wasn't the right moment. It wasn't the right place. To make matters worse, he'd gotten into this when she was visibly tired, and he hated knowing that he'd upset her.

He said carefully, "That takes some thinking through."

"I have an odd feeling, knowing you, that you've already thought it through."

Chris shook his head. "No. I'm still groping. But...well, I guess the big question is, where are we going?"

Madeline sighed again, and her thoughts wandered. She'd had a rough week at the hospital. Two of her favorite patients had died. They were elderly and had led good lives. Thanks to the skill of modern medicine they'd both lived longer than the most optimistic of her colleagues had predicted. Even so, she'd found their deaths, within a day of each other, hard to take.

Madeline Clarke, the physician, was a professional who knew all about being objective. But she was also an intensely caring individual, sensitive and empathetic.

Tom Lucas, sipping coffee with her in the doctors' lounge last night, had said, "You can't afford to take things so hard, Madeline. You should know that without me saying it."

"And you never take anything like this hard, Tom?" she'd challenged, because they both knew the opposite was true.

"All right." Tom had grinned, conceding her point. "We're a couple of softies. Look, I'm glad you're going to get away for the weekend. Forget about everything except having fun, promise?"

She'd promised. Now she thought about that promise and wished she could keep it. She wanted so much to simply relax with Chris this weekend. She wanted to make wonderful love with him, to share laughter and the beauty of the season.

Instead Chris seemed determined to get into areas she just wasn't ready for. Not now. A survival instinct in her simply refused to allow any serious subject to intrude, such as exactly where she and Chris were going. The fact that they *were* was enough.

She knew her face was reflecting some of her feelings because Chris's expression subtly changed. At once she became aware that she'd disappointed him, perhaps even hurt him, and that was the last thing she'd wanted to do. He was still smiling, but it was a shuttered smile, masking pain.

They didn't say much on the way back to the hotel. Chris was keeping a careful emotional distance from Madeline as they walked into the suite. She got the message and felt her frustration mounting. With so little time together it seemed unfair to be getting into deep areas they couldn't possibly wade through during the course of a single weekend.

"Want to watch some television?" Chris asked. "Or would you rather go down to the cocktail lounge and have a drink? Come to think of it, maybe there's some sort of entertainment. I didn't check."

Until tonight they'd never needed outside diversion. From their first encounter in Aruba, just being together had been enough. But Madeline now faced the opening of an invisible gap, and said directly, "I don't want to go anywhere, Chris. I want to be with you. That's why I'm here."

Why did he look so skeptical? His expression struck her with added force when he countered, "Can I believe that?"

"You know very well you can!" Madeline snapped, feeling herself losing control. After the traumas of the past week she needed understanding, not doubt.

"Damn it, Chris!" she began. Then the tears brimmed and she couldn't keep them back. "Don't you know...that all I want is you?" she gasped between sobs, clenching her fists. "I probably haven't shown it, but it's true."

For the moment, that was more than enough. Chris crossed the space between them and took her in his arms, crooning soft words of comfort in her ear. She was exhausted, he could see now. He accused himself of being selfish and blind to her needs. He should have put her first, but he hadn't.

They'd been so quick to make love today, and certainly he wouldn't have changed that. But now Chris realized he could very well have taken time out to ask Madeline how things were going for her, and how she was getting on. They had so much to share, but he tended to forget there were moments when the sharing should come ahead of the lovemaking.

They moved over to the window, arms entwined as they gazed out over Boston. The nighttime lights were beautiful, and the city sounds somehow soothing. Chris held Madeline close and wiped the tears from her cheeks.

"Thank you for being with me," he whispered in her ear. "And for giving so much of yourself."

"But I haven't," Madeline protested.

"Yes you have, Maddie," Chris told her gently. "You've made me feel alive again."

After a while, they moved into the bedroom and slowly undressed. They got under the covers, but not to make love. Rather, they embraced each other, longing for comfort and warmth, and fell asleep within the confines of each other's arms, evoking a very special kind of closeness.

ON SUNDAY NIGHT Chris flew back to Lakeport. The next morning he had an appointment with his lawyer, Bill Edgerly. His association with Bill went back a long way. He and Bill—along with King, Claire and Claire's cousin Ellie—had gone to high school together. Ellie and Bill had gotten married just after Labor Day last summer, and now Ellie was expecting their first child.

Bill was satisfied with the way the insurance settlement was working out, to Chris's great relief. Once he had the claim check in hand, it would force him to make the decision about whether or not to rebuild his factory.

Leaving Bill's office, Chris drove to the post office and bought stamps. He had a number of letters to write in the next couple of days.

He was heading back to his car when he heard his name being called, and he swung around to see Lorna Henderson hurrying his way. This was the first time he'd run into Lorna since his return from Aruba, and her expressive dark eyes were glowing as she confronted him. Suddenly, to his astonishment, she raised herself up on her tiptoes and kissed him on the cheek.

Chris smiled sheepishly. Lorna was a very pretty girl, and her obvious pleasure at this reunion was flattering.

Sweeping his face with her eyes, Lorna said, "I've been wondering where you've been keeping yourself. I never see you around town."

"I've been busy trying to get a lot of things straightened out, so I've been holed up at the house," Chris explained.

"I can imagine. There's been some talk around the hospital. You know, the usual scuttlebutt. Someone said you're going to sell the land to a group that wants to build a medical clinic."

"Someone's wrong," Chris answered promptly. This rumor had drifted back to him, too. So had the rumor that he was going to donate the land to the town for a new library, though he couldn't imagine why anyone would think a library should be built at the outer edge of Lakeport, several miles from the center of town.

"Well, you know the way people talk," Lorna stated.

"Do they ever," he agreed, unconsciously surveying her. She was wearing a bright green skirt, an ivory sweater and pretty gold earrings. "So you're still working at Lakeport General?"

"Quite often for your friend Dr. Faraday," Lorna said. "He seems to like having me on his surgical cases, which is great with me. That's special duty and the pay's great."

"I imagine King's a good person to work for, isn't he?"

Lorna laughed. "He can be a regular martinet, Chris. Or should I say Mr. Talmadge?"

"You should say Chris. You know that."

"I'm on duty tonight," Lorna went on, "but I don't have to be at the hospital for an hour and a half. It's so great to see you, I wondered . . ."

"Yes?"

"Do you suppose we could have a cup of coffee or something?"

Chris didn't know why her simple request should make him uneasy. Actually it was flattering—just as her kiss had been.

"Why not?" he agreed.

As he and Lorna settled into a booth in a nearby coffee shop, Chris was chuckling inwardly. He couldn't help feeling that he was out with a favorite niece or a younger cousin. He estimated Lorna's age at twenty-two, maybe twenty-three. She was not quite young enough to be his daughter, but nevertheless he felt almost paternal toward her.

During the time he'd been a patient at Lakeport General, he'd wondered how long Lorna would stay at the hospital. She was pretty and vivacious, and so eager to expand her horizons. Judging from the things she'd told him, it was easy to think she'd want to move on to a more exciting life.

She'd often stopped in his room as she was leaving work, lingering for a half hour or more just to talk with him. Chris had put this down to kindness on her part because he'd been a patient for so many weeks. He'd asked her more than once if she didn't have a date to rush off to. She'd always said, rather vaguely, that her boyfriend was in the air force and currently stationed in Texas.

That memory prompted Chris to ask, "Still going around with the same guy, Lorna?"

She seemed startled by the question. "You mean Tim?"

"I don't think you ever told me his name."

"Tim O'Brien," she said, stirring sugar into her coffee. "It's funny you should mention him. I mean . . . he just came back east recently. Now he's stationed at the S.A.C. base in Plattsburg."

Plattsburg was also on the shores of Lake Champlain, about ten miles north of Lakeport. The large Strategic Air Command base was at the southern end of the town.

"Well," Chris said, "looks like there'll be some romance brewing."

Lorna frowned slightly and said, somewhat abruptly, "I don't know about that."

"I thought you were in love," Chris teased.

She looked up sharply. "I never said that."

"No, I guess you never did. I just thought—"

"Tim's from here," Lorna cut in. "We went through school together. Then he joined the air force right after graduation. That was nearly five years ago. He's been all over the world and...well, I guess I'm not very good at waiting."

"He wanted you to wait for him?"

"Yes, he did. Now he wants me to marry him."

"How do you feel about that?"

Lorna shrugged slightly. "I like what I'm doing, I like nursing, and I'm not ready to get married yet. That's what I keep telling Tim. It's hard, though, now that he's back here. He can be awfully persistent. It's one thing with letters and phone calls, but in person it's altogether different."

Chris thought of his own attempts at persistence with Madeline in Boston. They hadn't worked, and he felt a stirring of sympathy toward Airman Tim O'Brien.

"Doesn't Dr. Faraday live right next door to you?" Lorna asked suddenly.

"Yes and no," Chris replied. "We'll be neighbors before long, but the house isn't quite finished yet."

"That's right—I'd forgotten. That's the old Parmeter mansion. I took piano lessons there from Miss Delia Parmeter."

Chris chuckled. "So did I."

"My mother used to tell me Miss Delia would slap my fingers with a ruler if I didn't practice."

"And did you?"

"Not like I should have."

"Did Miss Delia slap your fingers?"

"No." Lorna giggled infectiously. "One time she picked up a ruler and I thought I was going to get whacked. I started playing like mad...and I think it was the best I ever did. I'll never forget how surprised she looked."

"I can imagine," Chris said dryly.

His memories of Delia Parmeter were vivid. He remembered all the Parmeters clearly. They'd all been musicians and fascinating characters as well.

Lorna walked Chris to his car. "It's really been great to see you," she said, lingering. "You look terrific. And...well, I hope you don't mind my bringing it up, but I think you're getting around very well. Dr. Faraday must be pleased about that."

Chris's smile was rueful. "I still can't toss the cane in the garbage," he confessed. "I wish I could."

"So what's a cane?" Lorna asked. She giggled again and he had to smile. When she laughed like that it was downright contagious. "I think having a cane makes you look distinguished."

As he drove home, Chris envisioned himself going through life leaning on his cane, looking distinguished. It was a picture he didn't especially relish.

He let himself into the house and, for the first time since his accident, he approached the old piano in the corner of the library. It was a baby grand that had seen better days, but it still had an excellent tone and was surprisingly in tune.

Chris ran his fingers over the keyboard nostalgically. Then he sat down on the bench and attempted a piece that, in days gone by, he'd played reasonably well under Delia Parmeter's guidance.

He quickly discovered how out of practice he was. Tomorrow, he decided wistfully, he'd get out some of his old music books and plug away. Anything, he realized sadly, to fill his hours apart from Madeline.

CHAPTER NINE

MADELINE AND CHRIS SAT at an outdoor café in Boston's Quincy Market. Flowers bloomed around them in pushcarts and outdoor greenhouses, creating a profusion of intoxicating color. The air was touched with the tang of the sea. A passing breeze toyed with tendrils of Madeline's dark hair that had escaped from the chignon twisted at the nape of her neck, while the sun brought a flush of color to her cheeks.

She was wearing a deep turquoise dress that matched her eyes, and Chris thought she'd never looked more beautiful. For the first time since Aruba, she also looked rested.

"I'd say you've been getting your beauty sleep lately," he observed.

"I have." She smiled. "Things are going well at the hospital—at least for my patients. I've only been called in at night twice in the past ten days. A new record!"

"Not working nights becomes you, Maddie."

"Thank you," Madeline said shyly.

For a moment Chris was content just to look at her. Then he said, "It's so terrific to see you, I can't believe we're really here. Do you realize it's been five weeks?"

Madeline nodded. "Yes, I know."

They'd not intended to let so much time go by without seeing each other. But they'd both had their own, though differing, workloads. Chris had been deeply involved in the planning of his new factory building and in getting together the needed people to do the job for him. And Madeline had never been busier at the hospital. So the weeks had simply escaped. Already it was late June.

Chris had again taken a suite at the Park Plaza, but this time Madeline had arrived first. Chris had walked through the door and into her arms, and the feeling had been beyond description. He tried to imagine what it would be like to come home every night and find her waiting for him. Heaven on earth, to say the very least.

"Share with me, will you?" Madeline prodded, her eyes aglow.

"Share what, Maddie?"

"You're smiling and I don't know why."

Chris quickly decided that he didn't want to tell her. This lady with whom he was so deeply in love was a hard-working physician, and there wasn't a chance in hell she'd be waiting *every* night when he came home from his factory—and his research lab, he amended, realizing she didn't know about the lab yet.

"We have a few things to catch up on," he informed her.

Madeline was watching him very closely. "Want to be more specific?" she suggested.

"Well...I wanted to save this till I could tell you face-to-face," Chris began. "You know I'm rebuilding the plant, of course. But that's not all."

"You're mystifying me, darling."

He smiled. "I'm building a research lab," he confessed, his pride surging. "It'll be an annex behind the main plant. Small, but with room for expansion later, if things work out."

Madeline sat up straight. "Your invention?" she asked, reaching for his hand.

"Yes," he said, nodding.

"Oh, Chris... that's terrific!"

"Yes, it is," he agreed, entwining his fingers in hers. "A few weeks ago I decided to talk to King about it, as you'd suggested. I unearthed all my old sketches and plans and worked them over from a fresh viewpoint. Anyway, King and I concluded that what I have in mind can work, possibly very successfully, in coronary surgery."

Madeline's eyes were shining. "That's absolutely wonderful!" Almost shyly she admitted, "I haven't wanted to push you, but I can't begin to tell you how much I've hoped you'd get back into something you feel is truly challenging and rewarding. Not that running a company isn't challenging, but..."

"This will only be a step," Chris warned.

"A step in the right direction. That's what counts."

Her enthusiasm was exactly what Chris needed. They'd ordered *café con leche*, which reminded them both of Aruba. As they sipped, Chris sketched out his ideas and Madeline listened, posing an occasional question that showed him how precisely she grasped his concepts.

That weekend—like the other weekends they'd spent together—flew by much too quickly. Sunday evening they took a taxi out to Logan Airport, then parted to catch their separate flights. Once again Chris felt he was losing a chunk of himself. Without Madeline he was incomplete.

THE MIDDLE OF THE NEXT WEEK, Madeline's beeper went off as she was making her morning rounds.

Preoccupied with a problem involving the patient she'd just left, she picked up the nearest house phone. "Yes?" she asked abruptly, neglecting to identify herself.

There was a brief silence at the other end of the line. Then Chris said, "Maddie? Evidently I've called at a bad time."

"No, Chris . . . it's all right."

"It can't be all right when you sound that impatient."

"I'm sorry," Madeline told him sincerely. "I was thinking about this cancer patient I just saw."

"That makes what I was going to tell you seem pretty trivial," Chris replied heavily.

"What were you going to tell me?"

"Well, King and Claire are moving into the Parmeter mansion in a couple of days, and they want to have a big bash on the Fourth of July. I wondered if you could make it?"

"To Lakeport?"

"It's not the end of the world, Maddie."

"I didn't mean that."

She'd never invited Chris to Bangor, and he'd never asked her to come to Lakeport. They'd met in New York because of her medical convention there. Subsequently they'd chosen Boston because it was convenient for both of them. It was also a city where they could be almost as anonymous as they'd been in Aruba.

Madeline hadn't consciously realized this until now. But in choosing meeting places away from Bangor and Lakeport, their motivations seemed pretty clear. They'd wanted to be alone with each other without outside distractions and other people. They'd needed that kind of time and space.

Chris asked, "Are you still there?"

"Yes."

"Maddie, what's the problem?"

The problem was that they'd be opening the gates and letting the world in if she went to Lakeport. Madeline wasn't sure she was ready for that.

She said carefully, "There's no real problem, but..."

"But?" Chris echoed darkly. A strained silence followed before he added, his annoyance barely camouflaged, "Maybe I'd better call you at home tonight."

"I'll call you," she promised. "Is around eight okay?"

"I'll be there."

CHRIS ANSWERED on the first ring and Madeline felt a knot in her throat. She knew he'd been sitting right by the phone, waiting for her call. She'd tried to find time during the day to think about going to Lakeport and meeting his friends, and couldn't imagine why she should feel reluctant about doing so. But unfortunately this had been the busiest day she'd had at the hospital in a long while, and she hadn't been able to get home until nearly seven-thirty.

Clutching her receiver, she thought about Chris sitting in his big empty house, waiting for her to call. It made a disturbing picture.

He came to the point quickly, and said, "Look, Maddie... if you don't want to come, just say so!"

She'd been feeling sorry for him, imagining his loneliness plus the problems he still had with his leg. He'd not fully come to grips with his handicap and she wondered if he ever would. His impairment kept him from doing so many things he loved, and he'd yet to discover any compensating activities.

Her reverie came to a screeching halt. Startled by the abruptness of his question, she said defensively, "Chris, you sprang it on me so quickly this morning that I couldn't give you an instant answer."

"I think I already apologized for calling you at the hospital," he returned stiffly. "It won't happen again."

"Please, Chris. You're being childish."

"Childish, now?"

"Yes, damn it!" she bristled. "I was making rounds and concentrating on my patients. When you work, don't you focus on what you're doing?"

Chris concentrated very deeply when he worked. Lately he'd been putting in long hours working on his invention. In fact, plans and papers were strewn all over his dining room table. He'd gone out for a quick supper, then spent another hour with those plans after getting home. If it hadn't been for Madeline's promised phone call, he'd still be poring over the details of his design.

He let her question go and said softly, "Seriously, Madeline...I shouldn't have called you at the hospital. It could have waited till tonight. I'd been talking with King, that's all, and he told me about this party Claire's planning. He suggested that I invite you."

"I see," Madeline returned rather stiffly.

"Sweetheart," Chris said, laughing, "don't sound so miffed! I'm afraid I tend to ramble on about you sometimes," he confessed, "and...well, King and Claire want very much to meet you. I want you to meet them, too, Maddie, because you and I..."

"Yes?"

"Our lives are too separated," Chris told her simply. "And we've got to do something about that."

MADELINE FLEW INTO LAKEPORT two days before the Fourth of July and Chris met her at the airport. He was wearing a short-sleeved white sports shirt and he looked bronzed and healthy. And his limp seemed less pronounced, Madeline noticed as they walked together toward his car.

They drove by the factory construction site on the way into town and Chris admitted ruefully, "I'd hoped to have more to show you, but the work on the new building is going slowly."

"But at least it's going," Madeline said encouragingly.

"Very true," Chris agreed, slanting her an appreciative smile.

Madeline knew that he lived in an old family homestead, the deed to which had been turned over to him when his parents moved to Florida. Still, she hadn't expected the house to be so big. It was an enormous Victorian structure, set well back from the broad, elm-shaded street. A hedge separated it from the imposing house next door, which Chris pointed out as the Parmeter mansion.

It was a hot afternoon, but the high-ceilinged rooms inside Chris's house were cool and shady. The decor was rather dark and formal, and Madeline found herself thinking that if this were her house she'd lighten things up considerably. New drapes, new slipcovers—she laughed at herself as her mind raced through the changes she'd make. She had to admit that this feminine response gave her a good feeling.

Chris said, "Monica, my cleaning lady, prepared the upstairs front bedroom for you. Her sense of propriety, I guess," he added, grinning wickedly.

"Where do you sleep?"

"I've converted a small room here on the first floor my mother used as a sewing room," Chris told her. "It has an adjoining bath with fixtures so old they've become chic."

Madeline had noticed the long staircase in the front hall and had wondered how he managed so many steps. The answer, she saw, was that he didn't.

Chris made iced tea and they sat at the kitchen table, talking more animatedly every minute. Then he took Madeline outside and showed her the garden. It was a long tract of land, impressively planted with perennials and shrubs. Beautiful pink and white peonies were blooming, catching Madeline's attention.

"Those bring back memories," she confessed, bending to sniff the fragrance of the flowers. "We had peonies in Scranton when I was a child."

"These have been here as long as I can remember," Chris recalled, feasting his eyes on Madeline as he spoke.

"This must have been a wonderful place to grow up. Did you have a lot of playmates?"

"Enough," Chris told her. "Though I never minded being by myself."

"What was it like, being an only child?"

His expression changed. "I actually wasn't an only child, Maddie."

Madeline was perplexed. "I would have sworn that when we were in Aruba you told me you were an only child."

"I did," Chris admitted. "It . . . it's something I've gotten in the habit of saying, to avoid the whole truth."

"What are you talking about, Chris?"

Even now, after so many years, Chris swallowed hard, thinking back. "I had a brother who was three years younger than I was," he said. "My folks used to have a camp on Valcour Island—that's out in Lake Champlain. When Stephen and I were little we used to go over there on the weekends. My father kept a small outboard down at the town dock . . ."

He paused, the memory as clear as yesterday. Then he continued, "The year I was six—Stephen was three—we were over there one afternoon and Stephen started playing in someone's skiff. Just a little dinghy, really. I . . . well, somehow I managed to push it out into the water. There was quite a strong wind blowing and the boat drifted with it. Stephen started yelling. I tried to swim after him, but I wasn't that good a swimmer. I ran up to the camp and got my father. But by the time we got back down to the beach Stephen had fallen overboard."

Chris's face was bleak. "My father swam out to the boat and dove down many times. It seemed like forever. But . . . he couldn't find him. Two days later Stephen's body floated ashore on the opposite side of the island."

"I'm so sorry," Madeline managed brokenly. "God, it must have been terrible for you."

"My parents never blamed me," Chris said steadily. "At least, they never came out and said anything. For a long time, though, I felt that every time my mother looked at me she was thinking about Stephen. We . . . we never went back to the island."

Tears filled Madeline's eyes. "If I'd had any idea, Chris," she whispered, "I would never have brought it up."

Chris folded his arms around her and held her very close. "I never felt the moment was right to tell you," he said, his voice a caress. "I don't want us to have any secrets from each other, Maddie. I want us to know the good and the bad.''

He laughed tenderly. ''Now for some of the good,'' he told her, running his fingers through her hair. ''King is very enthusiastic about the valve design. He's passed it on to several cardiac surgeons, and they share his enthusiasm. Once I get the lab built, it looks like it'll be all systems go.''

It was a relief for both of them to change the subject and talk about Chris's plans for making a working prototype of his synthetic heart valve. Later King and his colleagues could study and test the device in hopes of getting it federally approved.

Madeline met the Faradays that evening. She and Chris joined King and Claire for dinner at an old inn on Lake Champlain. Afterward they returned to Chris's house for a liqueur. It was a warm evening and they sat on the screened back porch, watching fireflies flicker through the bushes and listening to the steady drone of the cicadas.

King and Madeline touched only lightly on their medical careers. Mostly the group talked of the long ago time when King, Claire and Chris had all been in school together. King and Chris had actually gone to kindergarten together, Madeline discovered. Claire had entered the picture years later, when she moved to Lakeport as a teenager after the deaths of her parents.

King told several amusing stories about Chris, and Chris countered with a few of his own about Claire. By the time the Faradays left, toward midnight, Madeline felt she'd known them for ages. It was easy to understand why Chris considered them his best friends.

''They're great,'' she told Chris once they were alone.

"I knew you'd like each other." He was obviously pleased. "It was nice of you to volunteer to help Claire make things for her party, too."

Madeline smiled. "I'm not much of a cook, generally speaking, but I do know how to turn out a few mean hors d'oeuvres!"

"I wish you knew a few magic tricks," Chris countered enigmatically.

"Magic tricks?"

He smiled wryly. "I wished you knew how to convert a cot into something fit for dual habitation. When I moved my sleeping quarters downstairs, I wasn't thinking of sharing space with anybody," he elaborated.

It was a more revealing statement than he'd intended, Madeline thought, and she couldn't help but laugh.

"It really isn't very funny," Chris reproved.

"I don't know about that," she teased.

"You don't? Look, lady..."

"I'm looking," Madeline said wickedly, "and I like everything I see. Do you know you look absolutely terrific? What have you been doing with yourself?"

"If you're speaking of my tan, I've been getting out into the sun, both in the backyard and on the beach. I've also been getting in as much swimming as possible. The lake's still pretty cold—" He broke off, then complained, "But none of this has anything to do with our bed dilemma!"

Madeline smiled demurely. "We'll make the best of things, I'm sure."

They did exactly that, and found that even a narrow cot could be surprisingly adequate for lovemaking filled with tenderness and caring. The same sweet passion surfaced between them again, punctuated by fiery moments of sensual delight.

In the early hours of the morning, though, Madeline began to get a cramp in her leg, and gently extricated herself from Chris's embrace. He was sleeping soundly, one arm thrown across her shoulder, and didn't even move as she slipped out of bed.

She headed upstairs to her room, a Victorian delight with pink rosebuds scattered over the wallpaper, a four-poster, and a marble-topped dresser. A white candle-wick spread covered the bed, and a pink comforter was folded at the foot. Madeline climbed between the crisp percale sheets, and pulled the comforter up over her.

Though it was July, the night air was cool and she fell asleep almost immediately. It wasn't until dawn's light filtered through the curtains that she came awake and drowsily realized there was someone standing by her bed.

In the dim light she recognized Chris. Still half asleep but awake enough to wonder about it, she asked, "How did you get up here?"

Chris smiled. "It wasn't that hard, really. I guess I found out where there's a will there can sometimes be a way." So saying, he slid into bed next to her.

They made blissful love together, then fell asleep in each other's arms. And for Madeline there was a difference to waking up a few hours later and finding Chris by her side. There'd been other times in other places, but now she was deeply conscious of the fact that she was in Chris's home.

She glanced at him, and a slight smile curved her lips. Watching him sleep she thought about what a continuity there was to this house for Chris. With the exception of the time when he'd been married and had lived in New York City, this wonderful old house had been his home all his life.

Madeline knew many people who were hidebound by roots and traditions, and was often grateful that she wasn't steeped in her own past. Chris was the perfect example of someone with a strong heritage who was not introverted in the way "home" and "family" sometimes induced.

It had been many years since she'd had a real home herself. Her mother sold the house in Scranton less than a year after her father's death, and moved the family to Endicott, New York, where Madeline's uncle worked for IBM.

She and her mother had lived in a small furnished apartment, while her two older brothers were either working, or at college—she couldn't remember which. After a time, her mother had met John Rollins, who also worked for IBM. A few months later they were married.

Her stepfather was a short, slight man with thinning red hair and freckles. He wore glasses with thick lenses that distorted his eyes and, to a child like Madeline, lent him an almost sinister appearance. She remembered seeing an actor in spy movies who'd always reminded her of her stepfather. Even now, whenever this actor appeared on the screen, Madeline inevitably cringed.

There was no logical reason for her reaction, she admitted. John Rollins had always been kind to her, although there'd never been any rapport between them. A longtime bachelor—he was close to fifty when he married her mother—he'd never had any experience with little girls, and had no concept of how to go about winning her affection.

IBM had transferred her stepfather to an office in Kansas City, and they'd moved there when she was thirteen. A couple of years later they'd moved back east, this time to the Albany area. Madeline had finished high school in Albany, and she couldn't wait to get away to college.

College had been an escape for her, and she'd done very well. She won scholarships, and eventually was accepted by the Boston University School of Medicine. By then she'd been on her own for years.

Aside from memories of the house in Scranton, where she'd spent what she considered the most stable years of her childhood, Madeline had never known a place she could really call home. It had been so different for Chris, she mused, watching him sleep, her love for him surfacing. Suddenly she wished she could meet his parents.

That morning, Madeline was especially thoughtful. It was the day before the Fourth of July, and she was glad to go next door and help Claire fix tidbits for the cookout.

The Parmeter mansion, as everyone called it, was a fantastic old house, and had been beautifully redecorated. Claire took Madeline through the numerous rooms, then led her out into the garden and along the path that paralleled Chris's property. At the end of the path she showed Madeline the little house—the "doll house," she called it—that long ago had been a fantasy hideaway for her and her cousin Ellie.

Claire was such a warm and genuine person that it was hard to picture her as a successful New York City businesswoman. But Claire was also that, Madeline knew. Chris had told her how Claire had inherited the New York and Florida art galleries from her first husband, and had not only maintained, but enhanced, their world-famous reputation.

When she returned to Chris's house late that afternoon, Madeline was thinking about how Claire appeared to be doing a marvelous job of juggling a career and a marriage. Until now, Madeline had wondered if any woman could do that with such a degree of success.

On the Fourth of July morning, Madeline awakened to the patter of rain on the roof. Chris had shared the four-poster with her, and was still asleep as she slipped carefully out from under the sheets and tiptoed over to the window. The rain was coming down in torrents and looked like the all-day variety.

Later, as Madeline and Chris were having breakfast, she surveyed the scene outside again and asked, "I wonder what Claire's going to do about her cookout. I'd think she'd have to call it off."

Claire had a better idea. The large room known as the Orchestra Room—once used for rehearsals of the Lakeport Symphony—had been refurbished as a "summer room," and was perfect for a party. Claire decorated the room like an impromptu café, by asking everyone she'd invited to bring card tables with them. The tables were covered with quickly purchased white paper cloths, and set with red and blue paper napkins to carry out the Fourth of July motif. Finally, the center floor was left clear for dancing and charcoal grills were set up on the covered patio just outside.

The party went off far better than anyone could have planned and, in the final hours of the holiday, couples drifted dreamily to music supplied by King over an excellent sound system.

Madeline again felt Chris's chagrin because he couldn't dance with her. This time, though, he was diverted by his many friends who promptly joined him every time someone whisked her out onto the floor of the make-believe ballroom.

King danced with Madeline twice. He kept their conversation casual during the first dance but during the second one he suddenly whispered in her ear, "I just hope you're half as much in love with Chris as he is with you."

She was so startled she missed a step. Rallying, she gazed up into King's intently serious deep blue eyes.

King said quickly, "Believe me, I know it's none of my business. But Chris is as close to me as a brother. Otherwise, I certainly wouldn't rush in where angels fear to tread."

When Madeline didn't answer, he said in an even lower voice, "He's been through a hell of a lot. It'll be a year ago tomorrow since the explosion, you know."

"I knew it was in the summer," Madeline fumbled. "I didn't realize that it was right after the holiday."

King nodded. "I've seen a lot, and so have you," he said. "But I'll never forget the sight of Chris when they brought him into the emergency room. I don't think anyone in the hospital thought he could make it through the night, let alone walk again. So ... I'm pretty proud of him."

Madeline smiled tenderly. "So am I," she whispered. "And ... just for the sake of the record, doctor, I love your friend Chris very, very much."

CHAPTER TEN

MADELINE RARELY WENT to the movies. It wasn't that she didn't like movies, she just never had time. But when Tom Lucas asked her to go with him to a popular new comedy at a downtown Bangor theater one Friday night in mid-July, she accepted eagerly.

Tom's wife, Valerie, and their six-year-old daughter, Gloria, were visiting Valerie's parents in Nova Scotia. Tom had been wandering around the hospital like a lost soul for the past couple of days, moaning that he wasn't cut out to be a bachelor. Madeline could empathize with him. Since her trip to Lakeport, living alone had started to seem pretty bleak.

The movie she and Tom saw provided some much needed laughter. Afterward they stopped for a drink and, in the course of conversation, Tom brought up a subject he'd broached on several other occasions. Madeline remembered the last time clearly. It was a week before she'd vacationed in Aruba.

Contemplating his scotch and soda, Tom said suddenly, "You know, Madeline, I can't help but wonder what's holding you here."

"In Bangor?"

"Yes. I mean . . . there's nothing wrong with Bangor. Matter of fact, as soon as Valerie gets back we're going to start hunting for a house to buy. I like living here, and

I like what I'm doing at the medical center. But it doesn't strike me as the right place for you.''

She smiled. ''I seem to remember your saying that before.''

''You're damned right I have, and I'll probably say it again. I'm very fond of you, which means I'm concerned about you.'' Tom grinned. ''You know, Valerie was jealous as hell of you for a while.''

''You've got to be kidding!'' Madeline protested.

''No, I'm not. And convincing her she's the only woman in my life required some rather long night sessions, if you get my meaning.''

''Valerie should hear you!''

''It's a good thing she can't,'' Tom agreed. ''But to get back to you, Madeline . . . am I wrong in assuming you're carrying a torch for that guy you met in Aruba?''

Had it been anyone other than Tom, Madeline would have made a quick conversational switch. She liked her privacy. She and Tom, though, had met during their medical school years, and had kept in touch ever since. And it was Tom who'd put in a word for her at Eastern Maine Medical Center, not long after Jeffrey's death.

Now she said, rather reluctantly, ''You're not wrong. You're just too perceptive.''

''That's why I'm such a good doctor!'' Tom beamed, reminding Madeline of the Cheshire cat in *Alice In Wonderland*. ''To tell you the truth,'' he admitted, ''Valerie got the vibes before I did. Remember that night a while back when you came over for Sunday night supper with us? She told me later there was something different about you. Specifically, she diagnosed love.''

''I think you're putting me on, Thomas Lucas,'' Madeline objected.

"Nope, I'm telling you the way it is. So...I've got to meet this guy and test him out to make sure he's right for you."

Madeline laughed. "You're too much, Tom," she said.

"Maybe," he conceded, "but we just want to see you half as happy as we are. The way you looked when you came back after visiting this guy—" Seeing the astonished expression on her face he broke off, then said, "Valerie's not the only psychic, you know. When you got back from Aruba, I knew you'd met someone."

"Gad!" Madeline exclaimed. "I had no idea I was so transparent."

"You're not. I probably should have been a psychiatrist, that's all." He chuckled, and added, "Maybe I would have been, if Freud and Jung and all those other old guys hadn't done their thing with the human psyche first."

"Honestly, Tom!"

"So why are you hanging on, Madeline? Is this really where you want to be?"

They didn't linger on the question. And Madeline couldn't have provided an adequate answer anyway. It was a subject she'd been addressing to herself—and getting absolutely nowhere with.

Chris had never come right out and asked her to join her life with his. Yet each of their partings had been more traumatic than the one before. There was little if any doubt of how much they wanted to be with each other.

As she went about her work at the hospital the next couple of days, Madeline did some brooding about Chris and herself and their chance for a mutual future.

The picture seemed ringed by big questions marks and, contemplating them, Madeline wondered why.

Was Chris afraid of asking her to share her life with him? Was that it? Was he thinking of her commitment to her career? Or was it that nagging complex about his leg that stood in his way?

From everything she'd observed about him, Chris was one of the strongest and most courageous men she'd ever met. King Faraday's comments about him the night they'd danced together had reinforced her own feelings in that respect. It seemed odd to think that a man like Chris should be hesitant about taking the next step in their relationship when he'd capably faced up to so many other things. Especially when he made no secret at all of his love for her.

Under other circumstances she might have decided that Chris felt burned by the failure of his first marriage to the point where he didn't want to take another serious chance with a woman. But she was sure that wasn't the case. From everything she could judge, Chris had come to terms with his divorce just as he'd come to terms with the destruction of his business, and as he would eventually come to terms with the handicap that still hindered him.

He was rebuilding the factory, and making good progress with his prototype synthetic heart valves. But when they'd parted at the Lakeport airport two days after the Fourth of July, he'd merely said he'd call her the next night. As he had, and did, almost every night since.

One afternoon Madeline came to the rueful conclusion that if Muhammad wasn't going to come to the mountain, the mountain would have to go to Muhammad. She made up her mind that when Chris called that night she'd invite him to Bangor the following weekend. Valerie Lucas would be back from Nova Scotia, and she'd ask Valerie and Tom for dinner Saturday night to meet Chris. Then on Sunday she would take the bull by the horns.

She didn't know exactly what to suggest. She only knew that she and Chris were going to have to work out something so they could be together much more often. It wasn't just a question of lovemaking, much as she desired Chris physically. Rather, it was a need to be with him completely.

When the telephone rang that night, Madeline was so sure it was Chris she picked up the receiver and promptly said, "Hello, darling."

She heard a masculine chuckle. Then a soft, low-pitched voice drawled, "Well, that's a nice greeting, I must say."

Flustered, Madeline stuttered, "I...didn't. That's to say, I mean...who is this?"

"King Faraday," came the answer. "And this is Dr. Clarke, isn't it?"

Both by training and instinct, Madeline was not one to panic. But all she could think of when she heard King Faraday identify himself was that something—something terrible—must have happened to Chris. Why else would Chris's best friend be phoning her?

Her knees went weak, and she sagged on the edge of the couch. "Yes, King...it's Madeline," she managed to say shakily. "Is Chris all right?"

"Of course," King stated. "Why do you ask?"

"Well, because..." she began, then stopped.

Into the ensuing silence, King said, "I'm not calling you about Chris, Madeline, but believe me...he's fine. Sorry I scared you."

"That's okay," Madeline assured him, catching her breath.

There was a pause before King said, "Anyway, this is a medical matter I'm calling about."

"A medical matter?" she echoed.

"Yes. Lakeport General," he went on, "is a relatively small hospital, judging by the standards to which you're accustomed. But we're a complete facility, and we serve quite an extensive area. I'm the surgical chief of staff, and then there's a medical chief of staff—John Danforth."

Madeline's nerves were steadying as she listened to King, and she wondered what his point was.

"Well, John has recently undergone cancer surgery," King stated. "He's making a good recovery, and his prognosis is excellent. But...he's pushing sixty. He's been practicing medicine for a long time and, at this point, he's contemplating retiring. I can't blame him."

"I see," Madeline murmured, still unclear about what all this had to do with her.

"He hasn't made a definite decision, and I don't think he should be asked to, especially now," King continued. "But we're going to be without his services for several months, at a minimum. My guess is that he's going to enjoy puttering around and doing the things he hasn't had time to do all his life. In short, that he won't want to come back. I'd imagine that's the way I'd feel, if I were in his shoes. So, there's a problem."

"You need someone to step in on a temporary basis, is that it?" Madeline asked.

"Precisely. And finding that person isn't going to be easy. A year from now they might have to relinquish the position, depending on how things are going with John. They might even be out of a job altogether. But if Danforth decides to retire, I'd like to think the person who takes his place now might seriously consider staying with us."

"I see," Madeline said slowly, racking her brains for the name of someone she could suggest to King. "Well, I can ask around here, and I also have a lot of contacts in Boston. There may very well be someone who'd like to exchange the city scene for a nice town like Lakeport—"

"I was thinking of you," King cut in.

Madeline was dumbfounded. She'd been shocked to hear from King Faraday in the first place, and now this lightning bolt offer astounded her. He didn't even know that much about her medical background.

He said, as if reading her thoughts, "Chris has filled me in about you, to quite an extent. For your information, he doesn't know I'm making this call. I didn't want to tell him because he'd be bitterly disappointed if you said no—a fact, incidentally, which should have no bearing on your decision."

Madeline was well aware that she should take any number of professional factors into consideration before giving her answer. King was right. That the man she loved happened to live in the town where she was being offered a job shouldn't weigh as heavily as many other things. Regardless, she clung to King's statement.

"You think Chris would be that bitterly disappointed?" she asked cautiously.

"I don't think it, I know it. Right now, Chris is living only half a life. And from what I've been observing and hearing, you're the only person who could ever make his life complete." King chuckled. "But he's the one who should be telling you that, not I."

"Well, he hasn't."

"I know," King told her. "Chris ... well, you didn't know him before his accident, so it's harder for you to judge. But he still hasn't come back all the way, Madeline. I'm sure you're aware of that. He has a lot of self-doubts, and I think maybe he's unsure he could measure up to everything you'd want in a husband."

"Please, King!" Madeline urged, then attempted a laugh. "Aren't you rushing things?"

"Maybe," he conceded. "But that's still the ultimate goal when two people feel about each other as I think you and Chris do." King paused, then continued in a lighter tone, "Someday I'll tell you about Claire and myself. I lost her for fourteen years, and when I had the chance to get her back, I nearly blew it. Then one day I ran head on into the fact that the only thing that really mattered to me was marrying Claire and spending the rest of my life with her."

"Chris never said anything about that," Madeline murmured.

"Chris wouldn't. Chris is very loyal to his friends, and very close-mouthed, as well. Because of that facet in his character, he tends to keep the things he feels most deeply locked up inside."

"I suppose you're right."

"I know I'm right. But ... I'm not going to pressure you. It's up to you to think this offer out, and decide what it might or might not do for your career. Okay?"

"Okay," she agreed, beginning to feel mind-boggled by the whole thing.

"I'll call you back in a couple of days," King told her. "Meantime, if you have any questions, don't hesitate to get in touch."

"Okay," Madeline said again before King rang off.

The next day it took all of Madeline's professional objectivity to concentrate on her work. She kept wondering exactly what Fate had dropped in her lap. Joining the staff at Lakeport General would mean living where Chris was living. Then again, she'd have her hands full at the hospital. Many times the demands of her work would have to come first, and she wondered how Chris would react to that.

If they were ever going to have a completely meaningful relationship, though, he would have to learn, sooner or later, what it meant to be involved with a doctor.

Chris hadn't called last night. And even though King had said Chris knew nothing about their "business" call, Madeline wondered if he'd somehow found out, and was shying away from discussing the issue.

She warned herself that she was being overly imaginative, and tried as hard as she could to look at King's offer objectively. By midafternoon, after juggling the various pros and cons, she concluded that the Lakeport General position was a definite step up for her, and that Muhammad could now go to the mountain without any sacrifice whatsoever.

She wandered into the doctors' lounge, which fortunately was empty, and dialed Chris's Lakeport number, expecting he'd be home at this hour of the day. But he wasn't. Most likely he was out at the construction site, she decided, and as far as she knew, there was no way he could be reached by phone there.

Madeline was glad to get out of the hospital that day. It was late afternoon and an orange sun descending in the west presaged another hot day tomorrow. Driving along the Penobscot River, she passed the bridge that led to the Old Town Indian Reservation. She'd moonlighted at the small dispensary there, and told herself whimsically that if everything fell apart between Chris and herself she could quit Lakeport and petition the Bureau of Indian Affairs to hire her.

She chided herself for being so gloomy all of a sudden about the situation between Chris and herself, and knew that what she needed was to talk to him and explore his feelings about King's offer.

As soon as she reached her apartment, Madeline dialed Chris's number. But again there was no answer.

Feeling frustrated and restless, she made herself some iced coffee and settled down to watch TV until she could reach him.

THAT AFTERNOON Chris was in a small bar and grill in a town about ten miles south of Lakeport. It was the last place he'd planned to be. And Lorna Henderson was the last person he'd expected to be with. Especially as this was their second meeting in twenty-four hours.

Late yesterday, he'd stopped by the hospital with some data he wanted to give King Faraday regarding his design. King was going to an important medical meeting in Albany in a few days, and planned to present some detailed information about the synthetic valves to his colleagues.

King had been in surgery when Chris arrived at the hospital. It was an emergency case, Chris was told, and King could be tied up for quite some time. So he left his material with an O.R. nurse he knew very well—one of many people he knew very well at the hospital, he thought ruefully.

He'd parked his car in the back lot, avoiding, as always, the Reserved for Handicapped spaces. Nor had he applied for a handicapped license plate. Negating these visible signs was, he supposed, refusing to face up to the truth, but he still did it. He just couldn't accept the fact that his leg was permanently lame.

It had been a hot and humid day. Walking out to his car, Chris was thinking about getting home and drinking a cold beer. He'd decided to conjure up a salad for his supper, then settle down in front of the TV until it was time to call Madeline.

He was nearly at his car when he heard his name being called, and he turned to see Lorna Henderson hurrying across the parking lot. She was in uniform, and the sight of her white dress, white stockings, and white shoes brought back sharp memories. Lorna had been his special nurse for a long time—starting just about a year ago, he realized. She'd been very good to him, and very patient.

Once Claire Faraday had half-teased that Lorna was falling in love with him. At that time, he was still in a wheelchair with months of rehabilitation therapy ahead. He'd scoffed at Claire's suggestion, putting it down to a morale-building attempt on her part. Even though Lorna was a very pretty girl and he had a normal male response to her, she didn't appeal to him on more important levels.

Lorna was a good nurse and knew how to put up a professional facade. But she was too young and immature for him. During the long hours they'd spent together, Chris's occasional glimpses behind her facade had shown him how easily she could be provoked to either laughter or tears. She was a very intense young lady.

There'd been moments when he'd awakened to find her sitting quietly by his bed, watching him. Admittedly, seeing the expression on her face had sometimes given him a funny feeling. Still, he'd been so preoccupied with his physical problems at that point he'd never dwelled too much on Lorna's potential infatuation with him, though he would have been an idiot not to realize she was attracted to him.

As the weeks had passed, he'd encouraged her to talk about herself. She came from a large family, and her parents—plus several brothers and sisters—lived on a farm at the foothills of the Adirondacks. She had a boyfriend, although she never actually mentioned his name. But she'd shown Chris a snapshot of a tall, rather gangling young man in an air force uniform, and Chris had been comfortable with the thought that, in due course, this airman would come back to Lakeport for Lorna, and that they'd marry and live happily ever after.

It was at King and Claire's wedding that he'd first felt apprehensive about Lorna. He was getting around on crutches by then, but it was difficult going. Lorna had watched over him like a mother hen at the reception, and had insisted on plying him with champagne and tidbits of food.

He remembered Claire, and also her cousin Ellie, teasing him about Lorna's attentions. But again he'd put their quips down to morale building.

The wedding had been held in the hospital chapel, primarily for his benefit. He wasn't up to much traveling at that point. And as the guests drifted away from the small reception, held in the boardroom, Lorna took it upon herself to escort Chris back to his room, and assist him into bed.

She'd looked absolutely stunning that day. She'd worn a bright green dress that set off her dramatic brunette beauty. Even now Chris remembered the scent of her perfume wafting across his nostrils, and how he'd felt a genuine surge of desire. He was sure any man would have felt the same way—especially someone who'd been confined to a hospital bed as long as he had and was only now beginning to feel human again.

When she'd closed the door of his room behind them, it had been natural, almost inevitable, to take her in his arms. Their kiss had been mutually passionate, but Chris's brakes had slammed on a few seconds later, and he'd tried to make light of what had just happened.

Not too long after that, he'd been transferred from the hospital to a nearby rehabilitation center. In the interim, he'd been cautious to keep things light with Lorna. And he'd presumed that maybe her boyfriend had come back to marry her.

The day he met her at the post office, she'd brought him up to date, of course. But looking back, he had to admit he'd seen that same disturbing look in her eyes, even when she was talking about her potential husband.

Now she caught up to him. She was smiling, and her jet hair and pretty face were bathed in the old-gold radiance of the sun's long rays.

"I was afraid you were going to get away before I could see you," she said. "I was just getting off my shift when Cora told me you were in the building."

Cora, Chris recalled, was one of the older nurses.

"How are you, Lorna?" Chris managed to ask, feeling strangely awkward.

"Fine, just fine. I've been wanting so much to see you again, though, since that day we met in town. Actually, I've phoned you a couple of times."

"I've been out a lot," Chris allowed, which was true.

Lorna glanced at her white-banded wristwatch. "It's nearly six," she observed. "Look . . . I need to go home and change, but then how about the two of us having dinner together?"

The invitation was so unexpected that Chris was caught completely off guard. An hour later, as he was driving over to Lorna's apartment to pick her up, he cursed himself for not having thought of a quick but plausible excuse.

The idea of having dinner with her was pleasant enough—it wasn't that. Rather, it was that peculiar uneasiness Chris felt whenever they were alone, because Lorna might think he was leading her on.

He tried to laugh, and reminded himself that certainly he was old enough and, hopefully, wise enough to handle any situation she might provoke. He and Lorna had, after all, shared a lot of time together, and there was no reason why they couldn't be friends.

But if Lorna wanted more than friendship?

She'd dressed last night in shocking pink. As they drove away from her apartment, Chris somewhat nervously realized she was not a person one could hide in a crowded room. She wasn't exactly flamboyant, but she certainly was colorful.

It was she who'd suggested they drive to a lakeside restaurant in another town for dinner, giving Chris the impression that she wasn't anxious to have anyone see them together. This was slightly puzzling, but he didn't dwell on it.

As it turned out, she was a very pleasant dinner companion. Afterward, they went to a small nightclub that featured a comic floor show. Still later, when Chris dropped Lorna off at her apartment, he had to admit that she'd been extremely undemanding. To his relief, she didn't ask him to come in. But she did lean over and kiss him lightly on the cheek as she whispered good-night.

He was smiling as he drove home, telling himself that he'd built up the whole situation out of proportion. What a relief to come to that conclusion!

It had been after midnight when he'd gotten home—too late to call Madeline. He went to bed with a sense of something missing, then realized it was because a day had passed without his hearing Madeline's voice. Just the sound of her voice had come to be tremendously important to him.

He'd thought, today, of paging her at the hospital, but decided against it. And as he'd let himself into his house and gotten a beer, he'd decided to try her home. Just then, the phone had rung. But it hadn't been Madeline at the other end of the line. It was Lorna, sobbing.

"I have to see you, Chris," she'd said frantically. Then she'd suggested that they meet at a small road-side bar and grill, a good ten miles out of town.

She'd hung up before Chris could tell her he couldn't possibly make this rendezvous. She'd sounded ex-tremely agitated even for Lorna, whose emotional thermometer, he suspected, was capable of rising very quickly.

He was tempted to call the place she'd set for their meeting and tell whomever answered the phone to lo-cate Lorna and he'd explain he couldn't make it. But he didn't. The memory of the care Lorna had given him during his long hospitalization swept back. Aside from this stupid infatuation, which he was finally having to accept, she had been wonderful.

A WAY TO REMEMBER 169

Chris was deeply disturbed as he drove out of town. And he was even more disturbed when he walked into the small roadside tavern to find Lorna seated in a corner booth, her eyes swollen and puffy, a half-empty glass of beer in front of her.

Her greeting did nothing to help the situation.

As he sat down opposite her, Lorna twisted a paper napkin between her fingers and blurted, "Thank God you've come, Chris. Tim has found out about us!"

CHAPTER ELEVEN

CHRIS ORDERED a bottle of Heineken and mentally counted to ten before he answered Lorna. Then he said quietly, "I don't know what you're driving at."

"Us," Lorna repeated. Her beautiful black eyes pleaded with him to understand. "We were seen last night, Chris," she announced dramatically.

"I presume you're talking about when we were having dinner together in a fairly crowded restaurant?"

She shook her head. "No, it was later, when we were in the nightclub. A friend of Tim's was there with his girlfriend. He saw us. When he got back to the base he told Tim."

"What if he did?" Chris queried.

"What if he did?" Lorna echoed, her eyes widening.

"Lorna," Chris said patiently, "you're acting as if we've committed some crime. We're friends, you and I...but we both know that's all there is to it." Chris was determined to make *that* statement. "We went out to dinner together, we took in a floor show together, as friends. Give me Tim's phone number and I'll call him and straighten this out."

"No," Lorna retorted.

Chris's eyebrows rose. "What do you mean, no?"

"Just that. It would only make it worse to have you talk to Tim."

Chris took a long draught of his beer. He told himself he should have heeded the signposts he'd noticed a long time ago but didn't really want to see. He should have recognized both Lorna's dramatic, impetuous nature and this crazy infatuation she had for him. Sarah had been very much like her—in the beginning.

He said wearily, "Come on. That's the most ridiculous thing I've ever heard. Even if you and Tim were already married, there'd be nothing wrong about what we did last night. You know that and so do I, and there's no reason for him not to believe us when we tell him so."

Lorna took a lace-edged handkerchief out of her handbag and dabbed at her eyes. Without looking at Chris directly, she said, "Tim is jealous of you. He's been jealous of you for a long time."

"Why should that be?"

"Last year, when you were in the hospital, I wrote him about you. He . . . he knew how I felt about you. I never tried to hide it, Chris."

"Lorna, please!" Chris wished he could vanish and reappear a hundred miles away. He didn't want to hear this!

"I fell in love with you the first night I was assigned to your case," Lorna stated. "I—I've never changed about that, Chris."

He tried to smile. There was a chance that, if he kept this light, they could both wriggle their way out. "How many of your patients have you fallen in love with, Lorna?" he quipped.

Her dark eyes smoldered. "Only you!"

"Well," he said, "I must admit that all the while I was in the hospital my heart skipped a few beats every time a pretty nurse walked by. And there were quite a few pretty nurses."

"I don't believe that."

Her expression told him that a touch of humor wasn't going to work. He said carefully, "Lorna, you're flattering me with the things you're saying. But I don't think you're being fair to me, or to Tim, or to yourself. You used to talk to me about Tim, remember?"

"Vaguely," she admitted grudgingly.

"I had the impression you cared for him—and had, ever since you were kids in school together. If that's the case, it would be foolish to toss away what you and Tim may have together for just a fleeting fancy. Anyway, Lorna . . . there is someone else in my life."

"I don't believe that, either."

"Well, there is. Someone with whom I'm very deeply in love."

"Claire Faraday," she accused.

"My God, no," Chris protested, honestly shocked. "You are *way* off base. The woman I love doesn't live in Lakeport."

As he said this a deep longing for Madeline swept over Chris. And he had a sudden need to be in touch with her, even if all he could do about *that* at this particular moment was talk to her on the phone.

As he drove home, half an hour later, Chris wanted Madeline so much he physically ached. As he let himself into the house, the phone was ringing. But by the time he picked up the receiver, he heard only a dial tone.

He sat down and dialed Madeline's number, and tried not to think about how he'd feel if she wasn't home. He was tempted to drive straight to Bangor and storm her apartment!

He smiled wryly at the thought of bursting into Madeline's living room . . . using his cane as a weapon. Fortunately she answered on the second ring.

"Mental telepathy," she said promptly when she heard his voice.

"Did you call just a minute ago?"

"Yes, and I won't count the times I tried to get you earlier."

Chris drew a deep breath. "Something pretty crazy happened."

"Both last night and tonight?"

"Last night I got home so late I was afraid I'd wake you if I phoned."

"Oh?" The small word thudded between them and, in its wake, Madeline felt surprisingly despondent.

To her surprise, Chris chuckled. "I like your reaction," he admitted.

"What's that supposed to mean?"

"That maybe you missed my call last night."

He said it teasingly, but suddenly none of this was very funny. Tears stung Madeline's eyes, and her voice choked as she sputtered, "You're damned right I missed your call."

"Maddie, what's the matter?" Chris demanded quickly.

"Oh . . . I don't know. I wanted to talk to you, that's all. King Faraday called me. Did he tell you that?"

The words tumbled out, and Chris tried to digest them.

Puzzled, he repeated, "King? No, he didn't tell me. But then we haven't been in touch for a few days. Why did he call you?"

"It seems that the chief of the medical staff at Lakeport General is bowing out, at least temporarily."

"John Danforth? I know he had surgery recently."

"Yes. Successful surgery, as I understand it, but he wants to take a long leave of absence. King thinks that at the end of it he may decide to retire. Meanwhile, there's a vacancy to be filled."

The world stopped still. Then, as it began to revolve again, Chris asked very cautiously, "Are you suggesting you might be the person to fill it?"

"Well... King Faraday did."

"And you... how do you feel about it, Maddie?"

"Half an hour ago," Madeline said shakily, "I called King and said yes."

MADELINE FLEW TO LAKEPORT in early August for a meeting with King Faraday and the hospital's board of directors. To Chris's chagrin—and considerable annoyance—she booked a room at the Château Champlain, a big new hotel right on the lake.

Chris met her at the airport, his annoyance obvious. "It's absolutely ridiculous, your staying at a hotel," he announced as soon as they were alone in his car. "I only have a fourteen room house," he added sarcastically.

"Look," Madeline explained, "some of the board members may want to contact me. I thought it might appear rather... obvious, if I was staying at your house."

Chris favored her with a withering glance. "Don't you think you're being somewhat quaint?" he challenged. "Anyway, you stayed at my place the last time you were here. The *only* time you've been here," he added.

"The only time you've invited me," Madeline countered quickly. She sighed. "This isn't a very good way

to start what might be my long-time residency in Lakeport," she pointed out.

"Am I to infer that if you decide to join the hospital
staff you'll continue to live at the hotel? Or are you
thinking of buying a condo or a house of your own?"

"Sarcasm really doesn't become you, Chris," Madeline commented. "You're not a cynical type by nature."

"I'd like to know why the hell I shouldn't be!" he
snapped.

"It's not like you to sound as if you're feeling sorry
for yourself, either," Madeline retorted.

Chris pulled over to the side of the road, parked, and
turned toward her tight-lipped, his anger brimming. It
wasn't the first time he and Madeline had drawn sparks
with each other, but it was the first time he'd felt angry
with her all the way through.

She turned away from him and stared out the window, so that Chris was left looking at her lovely profile. Her chin tilted defiantly as if she was ready to
counter anything he might say, and her French twist was
slightly disheveled. This, he'd noted, often happened
with Madeline's glossy hair. Just now the small lapse
from perfection in her coiffure seemed like a key to her
personality.

She was a cool professional, to be sure. She was also
warm and vulnerable—and, at moments, still a little girl
at heart. Chris wanted to sweep her into his embrace
and to be loving and gentle at first. Then passion could
take over and he would make love to her until they both
were exhausted and fell asleep in each other's arms.

"And how the hell can I do that in the Château
Champlain?" he muttered half under his breath.

Madeline turned. "What did you say?" she asked suspiciously.

Despite himself, Chris grinned. "I wouldn't want to repeat it."

"Christopher Talmadge!" She looked tired, on edge, and thoroughly impatient. "I don't see what you can find that's funny about this!"

"Us," Chris answered simply. "We're so crazy about each other we can hardly keep our hands to ourselves, right?"

He saw her lips quiver and plunged on. "If you insist, I'll take you to your damned hotel. But that can come later. First, we're going to my house. To my bed, damn it!"

He watched Madeline's face undergo a remarkable transformation. Despite herself she started to smile, and then they were both laughing together. Laughing, and clasping each other as well as two people can manage in a car with bucket seats. But when their lips met the kiss was an electric promise of all to come.

They made love that summer afternoon. Passionate love first. Then, after Madeline called the hotel to say she'd be checking in late, they made wonderfully languorous love.

Early in the evening, Chris scrambled eggs and heated muffins for an impromptu supper. Then they drove out to Baskin's Beach on Lake Champlain. The secluded property was privately owned, but accessible to friends of the family.

"The Baskins also own that big farm we passed along the road," Chris said as they walked down a bramble-lined path onto a stretch of rock-studded sand. "Either they just don't like the water or they never have time to go swimming themselves. About the only other people I ever meet out here are Claire and King."

The Faradays were not in evidence that evening. So Chris and Madeline swam together at sunset, while the sun gilded both the crystal waters of Lake Champlain and their bodies in bronzed splendor.

Later, as Chris drove Madeline to the hotel, she said, "This has been so glorious, so wonderful. It's going to be hard to get down to reality tomorrow morning."

"What time are you meeting with the board?"

"Ten o'clock," Madeline said. "King doesn't have any surgery scheduled in the morning so, unless there's an emergency, that should work out for him."

Chris glanced at her quizzically. "You sound nervous about this," he commented.

"I am. It's an important job. I hope I'm up to it."

He was surprised. "You're being overly modest, Maddie. Good God, you worked in Boston. Lakeport should be a breeze in comparison."

"I wouldn't say that," she corrected. "I'm being offered a job as chief of the medical staff, remember? It's been held by a physician who is a lot older and more experienced than I am."

"If King wasn't confident that you could fill John Danforth's shoes, he wouldn't be offering you the post," Chris stated resolutely.

She smiled. "You don't know very much about me as a doctor, Chris," she reminded him.

Stung, he retorted, "Sometimes I don't think I know anything about you as a woman. Sometimes I think you're part chameleon."

"You find me so changeable?"

"Yes, I do." As he said this, Chris sensed the danger of their getting into another argument, and he didn't want that. He added quickly, "But it only makes you incredibly alluring. Seriously...maybe I don't know much about you as a doctor, Maddie, but I know King Faraday very well. I'm sure that no matter how much I've raved about you, he thoroughly delved into your background before he made that call to Bangor. So relax."

At the hotel, Chris insisted on carrying Madeline's suitcase for her. He did so, juggling it somewhat awkwardly, then waited as she registered.

It gave him a strange feeling to watch her standing at the desk, signing her name to the register while he stood aside. It made Chris all the more aware that he didn't want to be on the sidelines in Madeline's life. He wanted to share the mainstream of life with her and, for perhaps the thousandth time, he wondered if he was up to it.

Almost from the beginning he'd had this nagging doubt that if she was to become too deeply involved with him he might hold her back. Although she was right about him not knowing the specifics of her medical career, Chris sensed that Madeline was a very good doctor, and could probably go as far as she wanted in her field. Now he wondered if Lakeport General, in the final analysis, would be enough of a challenge for her.

Sometimes he marveled that King continued to stay in Lakeport. He knew King had had offers to go elsewhere, to bigger hospitals. Once he'd mentioned that to King, and King had turned the query aside with a smile, stating succinctly, "Bigger is not necessarily better."

Would Madeline feel the same way?

A bellboy came to take Madeline's suitcase, and she smiled up at Chris. "Will you be home around lunchtime tomorrow?" she asked, "or is there someplace I could reach you? I'm going to want to tell you what happens as soon as I know myself.''

He scowled. ''I was thinking, Dr. Clarke, of inviting you to have lunch with me...if that would fit into your scheme of things.''

''It would.''

''Meantime, am I going to be permitted a chaste good-night kiss?''

''You men are all alike,'' she whispered teasingly.

He kissed her lightly on the lips, but even that slight contact was like striking a match to tinder. ''Damn,'' he muttered under his breath.

Madeline shook her head reprovingly. ''Till tomorrow,'' she promised.

MADELINE HAD an attractive lakefront room in the Château Champlain. She was sure that in the daytime the view would be spectacular. She also knew she wasn't going to be satisfied with a spectacular view. She wanted Chris at her side. She'd left him only minutes ago, but she wanted him with her right now!

Alone in her room, she began to feel foolish about having booked herself into this hotel. As she unpacked, she was tempted to thrust her things back into her suitcase, call a cab, and race over to Chris's house.

It wasn't an easy temptation to resist.

As she showered, Madeline tried to sort out her reasons for making a hotel reservation without consulting Chris first. She could think only that it was, in its way, a kind of declaration of independence on her part— something that had not come home to her until now.

So much of her career life had been spent not exactly in Jeffrey's shadow, but certainly under his auspices.

For such a long time he'd called all the shots for her, both professionally and personally.

She knew Chris was an entirely different type of man. He was much more *contemporary* than Jeffrey'd been—a funny word, but the description fit. Jeffrey, she remembered wryly, had clung to a number of outdated macho concepts, even while encouraging her in medicine.

She wasn't sure how Chris felt about her career. He hadn't really come to terms with it yet, despite his brief brushes with reality most of the times he tried to call her. If she met the criteria for this job in Lakeport and took it, Chris would have to face up to the fact that, quite often, her time was not her own.

King Faraday was a very close friend. That should help Chris understand the demands of a doctor's life. He was familiar with King's schedule. But understanding something and living with the same could be two very different kinds of drumbeat.

Living with the same? Madeline smiled sadly. For all of their caring, she and Chris had yet to express that kind of commitment openly.

This afternoon and tonight, they'd been so wrapped up in each other they'd not really discussed, to any great extent, either his work or hers. Nor had they talked about the future. They'd been too involved in the present, which included her nervousness about her upcoming interview. And that bit of dialogue hadn't gone over too well!

From their phone conversations, though, Madeline knew that Chris hoped to open his factory by October, and that King and his colleagues were giving him the green light with his invention, which was the most terrific news of all.

Madeline turned on the radio, then climbed into bed to the strains of soft music. A cool breeze wafted through the windows, making the night good for sleeping. But sleep refused to come.

Restless, she got up and went to the window. The moon was nearly full, drenching Lake Champlain's dark surface with silver. Watching the shimmering water, Madeline ached terribly for Chris's love.

THE NEXT MORNING, Madeline was relieved to find King already present when she walked into the hospital boardroom. There were four men and two women on the board, and King performed the introductions. The only name familiar to Madeline was that of Bill Edgerly. She knew he was an attorney and that he'd represented Chris in his dealings with the insurance company. Chris had also told her that Bill was married to Claire Faraday's cousin Ellie. And, if she remembered rightly, he'd only recently become the proud father of a baby girl.

Madeline wondered if John Danforth might attend the meeting, but he didn't. King explained to the board members that the medical chief of staff had left with his wife for a vacation in the Thousand Islands on the St. Lawrence River.

As the meeting progressed, Madeline discovered that Chris had been right in his evaluation of King Faraday. King had obviously done his homework on her. This she judged not only from the folder of correspondence he thumbed through, but by the astute questions he asked.

The board members let King do most of the questioning, posing queries of their own just occasionally. Madeline caught the women, especially, glancing at her rather quizzically, and she had the uneasy feeling that maybe they considered her too young and inexperienced for this post.

It was nearly noon when the meeting broke up. The directors had taken advantage of the meeting to ask King a few questions about other hospital matters, all of them relatively simple, which King quickly answered to their satisfaction. The atmosphere was definitely amicable. Still, as King walked out into the corridor with her, Madeline had no idea whether or not she'd passed the test.

King said, "I'd suggest we have lunch together, but I only have time to grab something in the cafeteria. I have a gall bladder operation scheduled for two o'clock."

Madeline nodded, her mind still on her interview. She'd tried to answer every question as comprehensively as possible, without overstating her case. Now she wished she'd said a few things differently.

King walked to the main entrance with her, then out to the top of the steps that overlooked the parking lot. "What a gorgeous day!" he observed. "What I'd *like* to do this afternoon is to head down to Baskin's Beach and get in some windsurfing. Have you ever tried it?"

Madeline shook her head. "I've limited my water sports to swimming."

"What about other sports?"

"Well, I ski . . . and ice-skate some," she said. "I've never had time for golf. At one point I took a few tennis lessons, but I never kept with it. However, I do play a wicked game of Ping-Pong!"

"There's a room down in the basement here set up with a table," King told her. "A grateful patient donated it so the staff could whack out some of their frustrations from time to time, but it doesn't get as much use as it should. Sometime, I'll challenge you to a game.''

"You're on," Madeline said, then caught her breath.

Did King's statement imply what she thought?

She didn't want to come out and ask him directly, because she was beginning to appreciate how crushed she'd feel if the reply was negative.

Madeline wanted this job at Lakeport General, wanted it more than she'd realized. Her reasons, to be sure, were not entirely medical. The challenge of being chief of the medical staff was exciting, but the idea of having Chris so close by made her heart pound. It would give them a real opportunity to find out if their futures could mesh.

She became aware of King smiling down at her tolerantly and, as she met his eyes, he laughed. "Why don't you just ask me?" he teased.

He was incredibly good looking. His hair was pure gold in the sunlight, and she'd never seen such deep blue eyes. He and Chris were equally handsome, though in distinctly different ways. Madeline could imagine what a pair they must have made in those days when they'd been able to do so many things together that Chris could no longer do, like windsurfing.

Madeline smiled back at King, and said frankly. "I'm afraid to."

"Afraid?"

"Scared to death," she confessed.

"You want the job that much? I wondered about that," he admitted. "You present quite a cool facade, Madeline."

"Training," she managed weakly.

"I commend you for it," King said, still smiling. "And...may I welcome you to the staff at Lakeport General, Dr. Clarke?"

She stared at him, remembering the board. They'd been polite in their farewells, but she'd gotten no vibes from them whatsoever.

"Are you sure about this, King?" she asked. "I mean...I'm meeting Chris for lunch and I'd hate to tell him the answer is yes if it turns out to be no."

"I know those people," King said. "If their feelings about you had been negative, I would have been aware of it, believe me. But if you have any doubts, why not hold off telling Chris?" He glanced at his watch. "I have the gall bladder at two," he said, "and a consultation after that. I *should* be able to get out of here fairly early, though. Claire's in New York, but why don't you and Chris stop by the house for a drink around five? If by any chance I get hung up, I'll call you at Chris's."

Madeline wished she could be as sure about King's pronouncement as he was. All afternoon she kept wondering if maybe he'd made a mistake in his estimation of the board's reaction to her. She remembered those questioning glances the women had given her. And one of the older men, too, she recalled. In fact, he'd said something rather chivalrous about lady doctors getting younger and prettier all the time. She'd accepted the statement as a compliment, but now she wondered if maybe he, also, had thought she was too young for the job.

She was preoccupied during lunch, and when Chris asked if she'd like to go out to Baskin's Beach for a swim, she shook her head. They were driving away from the restaurant when Chris looked across at her, his face mirroring his concern. "Is there something you're not telling me, Maddie?" he asked.

"No. Why?"

"Because you haven't been with me, oh . . . for about the last hour. If they turned you down, I wish you'd come out with it."

Had they turned her down? Madeline tried to focus on King's optimism, but she still couldn't be sure. She said, unhappily, "I don't know what the verdict is."

She was beginning to feel that she'd actually been on trial this morning, and was about to be found either innocent or guilty!

"Maddie . . . I think you must have an idea of how much I want you here in Lakeport," Chris said carefully. "But if for some reason I can't even begin to imagine, you don't get the job, it's not the end of the world."

She nodded in silence, hoping he meant that. And when he unexpectedly suggested they take in an afternoon movie, she agreed. Anything to take up time, she thought nervously. Still, she only managed to give the picture a fraction of her attention, and later couldn't remember more than a vestige of the plot.

Finally it was five, and Chris was ringing the doorbell at the old Parmeter mansion and King was opening the door.

He looked at Chris and Madeline standing on the threshold, and burst out laughing. "I've never seen two people with such enormous question marks in their eyes," he teased.

"Damn it, King, we're both about to lose our minds!" Chris retorted.

"Then I'd better save your sanity, hadn't I?"

Neither Chris nor Madeline could speak.

"Just before I left the hospital," King told them, "Bill Edgerly called me. For the record, the board of directors of Lakeport General Hospital is delighted that Dr. Madeline Clarke has applied to fill Dr. John Danforth's position in his absence."

King reached out, and enveloped Madeline in a bear hug. "Welcome aboard!" he beamed.

CHAPTER TWELVE

"MADELINE, is there a chance you could skip down to the cafeteria in a little while and have a cup of coffee with me?" King Faraday, wearing his operating room greens, stood in the doorway of Madeline's office.

Madeline had just finished dictating a report about an elderly patient of hers whom King had recently operated on. She still had a lot of paperwork to get through, but if King wanted to meet with her, that took precedence. "Give me about ten minutes," she told him.

On her way down to the cafeteria, Madeline wondered if there was a specific reason why King wanted to see her, or if he merely needed to share a cup of coffee with someone to whom he could talk shop. She knew he'd had a very busy morning in surgery.

The elevator stopped at the second floor, and an orderly got on, pushing a stainless steel hospital cart. He favored Madeline with a smile and a "Hi there, doctor," and she smiled back. She'd only been in Lakeport two weeks, and already she had a very warm feeling about Lakeport General.

This was due primarily to King. Not only had he introduced her to almost all of the personnel, he'd helped her learn every fiber of the hospital ropes. Thanks to King, the staff had accepted her very quickly. Thus far, she had a good rapport with everyone.

She had an interesting, and frequently challenging, caseload. More than once already, she'd made a diagnostic decision that had brought plaudits from her new colleagues. It was satisfying to feel that she was justifying her appointment.

She arrived in the cafeteria before King and carried her coffee to a table in a far corner of the room. She chose the table because it was by a window that looked out over the hospital garden.

King had proudly told her that, until very recently, this back area had been a litter haven. Then members of the Lakeport Garden Club had adopted the civic project of converting the seedy area into a beauty spot. They'd succeeded admirably, and the garden was a visual delight. There were plans afoot to build a patio next year, and maybe add a path with benches where staff members and visitors alike could enjoy a few minutes of quiet.

Feasting her eyes on masses of bright zinnias, marigolds and cosmos, it never occurred to Madeline that anyone might look upon her choice of table as a bid for privacy.

King strode across the cafeteria carrying a tray, and settled down comfortably in the chair opposite Madeline's. In addition to coffee, he'd bought a piece of blueberry pie topped with a huge mound of ice cream. "Don't you want to indulge?" he asked, grinning boyishly.

"Thanks, but no thanks," Madeline said, shaking her head. "Mostly due to Chris, I eat twice as much now as I did in Bangor. Soon I won't be able to fit into my clothes."

"Speaking of Chris ... for a long time I've wanted to thank you for getting him back into the field where he belongs," King said. "This device he's working on could be quite significant." He added confidentially, "You know, Madeline, I'd like to see Chris go for his doctorate, primarily because tacking those letters after one's name often lends an automatic validity in the eyes of a lot of people who don't know any better but still have influence to wield. Maybe you can push him to finish the thesis he started way back when."

"Maybe," Madeline agreed. "I've talked to him about it, but he thinks he's too decrepit to go back to school."

"You know what I could say to that," King volunteered as he attacked his pie. "A more immediate concern to me is that I think Chris is shortchanging himself with the lab facility he's building. He's treating it as not much more than a side shed to the main plant."

"Have you told him that?"

"Not in so many words," King admitted. "I know I should try, but Chris can be as stubborn as a team of mules. You, Lady Luck, are the one person who can sway him."

Lady Luck. She gazed at King wonderingly, the nickname stirring memories of Aruba.

"Surprised at my knowing Chris's secret name for you?" King teased. "We *are* old friends, Madeline . . . and I don't think anyone appreciates more than I do how much Chris needed some luck in his life. When it came to him in the form of a beautiful woman . . . well I, for one, couldn't be more pleased."

"Come on, King," Madeline demurred, feeling herself flush.

King leaned closer and almost whispered, "Madeline, my friend Chris is very much in love with you. I know I'm not letting any secrets out of the bag when I tell you that. You see, the reason I'm bringing it up—or it certainly wouldn't be any of my business—is that there's absolutely no need for you to continue living at the Château Champlain for the sake of appearances. That's what has been on my mind, and why I wanted to talk to you today."

Madeline felt a lump in her throat and quickly glanced away, trying to get a grip on her composure. Instead she found herself meeting the intent gaze of a beautiful girl in a nurse's uniform who was sitting by herself in the opposite corner of the room.

She froze. There was dislike in those dark eyes— strong enough to send vibes all the way across the cafeteria. And there was something else. Disapproval?

There was something oddly familiar about this nurse and, momentarily baffled, Madeline combed her memory, wondering where she could have seen her before. Then it came back to her. This was the girl standing by Chris's side in the picture taken at King and Claire's wedding.

King asked swiftly, "What is it, Madeline? Have I shocked you?"

"No, no, it isn't that," she protested quickly. "King, when you get a chance, glance behind you. There's a girl sitting at a table against the wall on the other side of the room. A nurse. I'd like to know who she is."

King raised a curious eyebrow, but made no comment. A moment later he stood up, reached over to the next table and procured the sugar bowl. "Here," he said then, in a voice loud enough to carry. Handing the bowl to Madeline, he added, "There's some of that diet stuff in this one."

Lowering his voice, he reported, "That's Lorna Henderson. She's been on vacation the past couple of weeks. Matter of fact, she just came back on duty to-day, which is why you haven't met her. Anyway, why such a reaction?''

"It was the way she was looking at me," Madeline replied, deeply puzzled. "Maybe it's just my imagination, but . . ."

"Come on," King urged. "You can confide in me."

"I know I can. It sounds so foolish on my part, that's all." Madeline shrugged. "Let's forget it."

"I'd rather not," King said quietly. "I've only worked with you for a little while, Madeline, but we've already shared some hairy moments. You're not shaken easily, and you were just now."

"I was startled," Madeline corrected.

"By the way Lorna was looking at you?"

"Yes. As you said, she and I haven't met yet, but . . . she looked at me like she recognized me."

"You're pretty well known around here, Dr. Clarke," King pointed out.

"Maybe," Madeline conceded. "What bothers me, King, is that I'd say she actively dislikes me. Maybe that makes sense to you. It doesn't to me."

King considered this, then said cautiously, "It makes a little sense to me, yes. It could be that Lorna's somewhat put off by you because of Chris."

"Why should that be?"

"Hmmm," King mused. He smiled across at Madeline ruefully. "Claire warned me way back that she thought Lorna had a crush on Chris," he said. "I didn't take it too seriously. When Chris was a patient here, I put Lorna on his case because she's an extremely good nurse. She devoted a lot of time and attention to him, but I never gave it too much thought. Even if I had, I probably would have concluded that Lorna was doing her job. Taking care of Chris wasn't such a bad deal, after all. Let's face it, he's relatively young and attractive."

"Tell me about it."

King smiled. "Well, I know that when Chris was transferred to the rehab center Lorna visited him a few times, but I didn't think too much of that, either. It's natural sometimes for both nurses and doctors to follow up on a patient of such long standing, especially when they've been keenly interested in his case."

"I suspect Lorna was very much interested in Chris's case," Madeline observed dryly.

"You sound like Claire. Okay, I guess I should have been more alert. From now on, I will be. That kind of patient-nurse involvement isn't a good idea unless—as sometimes does happen—the attraction is mutually genuine."

"You don't think Chris responded . . . to Lorna's interest?" Madeline floundered.

"Fishing, doctor?" King teased.

"Yep," she admitted grinning.

"No, Chris was as oblivious to Lorna's interest in him as I was," King stated. "I'd swear to that. So relax. I can assure you I've never seen Christopher Talmadge look at any woman the way he looks at you!"

Madeline thought about that remark as she left the hospital later. King wasn't one to say such things lightly. She already knew him well enough to be sure of that. So the memory of his words gave her a warm glow.

She and Chris were meeting for dinner, but she had a couple of hours to kill before he would pick her up at the hotel. She felt she needed some exercise, needed to flex her muscles. She'd done more desk work than usual the past couple of days. She went for a swim in the ho-

tel pool and did laps until she began to feel physically
tired. Then she stretched out in the late afternoon sun
for a while and tried to relax her mind.

All the time she was thinking about King's assurance
that people wouldn't raise their eyebrows too much if
she decided to move in with Chris. And those that might
didn't really matter.

"We may be a small town, relatively speaking," King
had said. "But I like to think that a lot of us don't suffer from the so-called small town mentality."

She'd laughed at that, saying quickly, "Well, I'm sure
you don't. But some of the board members looked
pretty straitlaced."

"As some of them are," King had agreed. "But they
hired you for your ability, Madeline. I think in your
short time here you've proved they made the right decision. Your private life is your own business. Anyway,
in the echelon here I happen to rank first, with Danforth on the shelf. So technically speaking, I slightly
outrank you."

"I love the way you put that," she had murmured.

King had looked uncomfortable, but he'd only
shrugged and said, "As far as I'm concerned it's a
technicality, nothing more. I bring it up because complaints would be directed at me before they ever reached
you. There haven't been any complaints, and believe
me, if there ever are any, I'll deal with them. You've
become a valuable addition here. So...*pax vobiscum*,
okay?"

"Okay," Madeline had agreed, but then cautioned,
"Don't expect me to move in with Chris tomorrow,
though. We have a few things to work out."

King didn't query her about those "few things." And he wouldn't, Madeline knew, as she dressed for her dinner date with Chris.

She didn't bring up her discussion with King while she was with Chris that night. The right moment just didn't arise.

Before taking her to the country inn he'd chosen for dinner, Chris drove her out to the factory so she could see the progress being made. There was still plenty of daylight left and, as they walked around the modern facility, he gave her a graphic idea of how each space would be used.

"We'll have a considerably expanded capability for production," he said. "I'm glad of that because it means I'll be able to employ more people. There are better job opportunities around Lakeport these days because of the new light industry that's been moving into the area. Still, some of the people who worked for me either haven't been able to find jobs, or have preferred to stay on unemployment compensation because the other places don't meet my wage scale."

As Chris talked about the future of his company, Madeline knew he cared about his employees, cared about them deeply. This radiated from him, and she instinctively squeezed his hand.

"What was that about?" he asked, taken aback.

"I love you, that's all," Madeline told him unsteadily.

Chris stopped, and his hazel eyes were suddenly moist. "That's *all*?" he asked incredulously. "Maddie, would it be important if the sun didn't come up tomorrow morning?"

"I imagine the world would end, wouldn't it?"

"It wouldn't last long. And that," Chris said slowly, "is what your love means to me."

She nearly mentioned her talk with King, but Chris was urging her on, anxious to show her something else.

When they were back in the car and driving away, Madeline almost brought up another subject she and King had discussed—the way Chris was shortchanging himself with the space he'd allotted for his lab.

He was, definitely. She'd seen the plans before, and this was not the only time they'd visited the site, but it was the first time the construction had been advanced enough for Madeline to get a clear idea of the overall layout. King was right. Chris not only deserved, but needed, much more in the way of a research area.

She was on the verge of saying this but she thought twice. It would be wiser, she decided, to have King present this subject, regardless of the things he'd said about her influence with Chris.

She remembered King saying, "It pays to think big, and I wish we could convince Chris of that. Right here in this hospital, almost every day, I see what happens when people haven't thought in realistic terms about the future. Our 'new' wing is only twelve years old, but already we're cramped for space. One of these days we're going to have to mount a fund drive. Believe me, that's something I dread getting into. People are always seeking money for a variety of causes and, even though some of them are very worthy, appeals get pretty redundant."

Madeline remembered those words as she and Chris enjoyed an intimate dinner. And she hoped there would still be time for Chris to amend his plans, if she and King could convince him to do so.

As it was, she had to tell him that she'd be on call at the hospital this coming weekend. The staff rotated emergency room duties and it was her turn. If she'd been around longer she might have considered trying to trade time with another physician, but she didn't feel she could do that. Unfortunately, Chris had planned a drive up to Montreal on Saturday, where they could spend the night. They both needed the change of scene. But now...

Breaking the news to Chris about the weekend would be bad enough without also revealing that she and King had been discussing him behind his back.

Thinking about this, Madeline had a vision of the dislike she'd seen smoldering in Lorna Henderson's dark eyes.

IF MADELINE had suspected Lakeport General's emergency room facilities were overcrowded before her first weekend on call, she was thoroughly convinced of this by the end of Saturday night.

The emergency room simply wasn't adequate for the patient load. People who needed attention had to be kept waiting because there literally wasn't the space in which to treat them. It wasn't a question of a personnel shortage nearly so much as the lack of a modern, well-planned facility.

Madeline spent both Saturday and Sunday on call in the emergency room, snatching what sleep she could in a small cubicle reserved for staff use. When the weekend was over, she could have counted the hours of actual sleep she'd been able to get on the fingers of one hand. But that wasn't what mattered. The patient load, and the lack of space, did.

"Where do they all come from?" she asked Harry Kroeger, a young surgeon on duty with her, during a temporary lull.

Kroeger was a Lakeport native who had come back to establish a surgical practice in town after finishing his residency requirements in a Syracuse hospital. He shrugged and said, "Times have changed. After your friend Chris Talmadge built his plastics factory, other companies moved into this area. Not entirely with the blessings of the town fathers, I might add. Though they haven't given the newer enterprises the grief they gave Talmadge."

Madeline had been stifling a yawn, but Harry Kroeger's statement thoroughly alerted her. She asked swiftly, "Why is that?"

"Well, the conservationists put up a big hue and cry about the plastics plant for a variety of reasons. They thought the smoke would pollute the air, for one thing, but that didn't prove to be true. Still, once a rumor like that gets around, it's hard to erase the impression it makes."

"I can imagine," Madeline said.

"To get back to why the patient load has increased so much," Harry Kroeger continued, "people have moved to the Lakeport area to work in the new plants. Naturally they bring their families with them. I wouldn't say the population has mushroomed, but it has grown considerably, and it's still growing."

He sighed and, watching him, Madeline wondered if she looked as tired as he did.

Rubbing a weary hand across the back of his neck, he said, "We need more breathing space in this hospital. Or better yet, a clinic on the outskirts of town that could handle walk-ins and emergencies."

"Has anyone else thought of that?"

"Dr. Faraday, for one," Harry Kroeger said promptly. "And a few other farseeing individuals as well, I'm sure. But sometimes I think most towns like Lakeport are stuck with ostriches for councilmen. And do they ever keep their heads stuck in the sand!"

They became busy again immediately after this conversation, and stayed busy. And Madeline didn't really recall her conversation with Harry Kroeger until two afternoons later when, toward sunset, she and Chris were again swimming in the cool, beautiful waters of Lake Champlain.

Chris had been understanding about her having to call off their trip to Montreal. But she knew he'd been disappointed and had silently struggled through a lonely weekend. At this moment, she was sure the last thing he'd want to discuss with her was a problem dealing with medical logistics. They needed, right now, to be absorbed only in each other.

She was tempted to tell Chris what King had said about their living together. But she still wasn't sure how he'd react, even though King was his best friend. Living together would be a *very* personal involvement—something that should originate between Chris and herself. He'd been annoyed at her taking a hotel room when she'd arrived in Lakeport, but he'd yet to say a word about her moving out.

Was he waiting for her to bring up the subject? Madeline wondered. And...why didn't she? Was she still hesitant about committing herself to a man—even a man she loved as much as Chris—on a twenty-four-hour basis? Were memories of Jeffrey making her fearful of losing the independence she'd fully attained not that long ago?

Floating beside her, Chris said, "You're tired out, aren't you, sweetheart?"

He spoke so tenderly Madeline's eyes misted.

"King is working you too hard," Chris growled.

"No, Chris. We all share the load."

"Sometimes," he said savagely, "I hate having to share you with anyone or anything."

His was a passing mood, Madeline realized, engendered by their separation over the weekend. Yet it was the wrong thing for him to say at that precise moment. If theirs was to be the forever relationship she wanted, they would both have to compromise.

She closed her eyes wearily, wondering how to tell Chris this. Then suddenly she felt water spattering her face. Shocked, she looked up to see Chris grinning mischievously as he scooped up a handful of water and threatened to splash her again.

"Don't you dare!" she shrieked.

But he did dare. And a moment later they were tumbling together in the water, playing like a couple of children sired by Neptune and a mermaid. Madeline's tension drained away, and only love was left. Love to be shared and enhanced by passion as they went back to Chris's house and, through the night, came together with their special blend of fire and tenderness.

The next day, Madeline wandered into the hospital cafeteria around two in the afternoon. She'd put in a full morning, and had worked through the normal lunch hour.

She was carrying her sandwich and coffee across the room when King hailed her. He and Harry Kroeger were having their own late lunches and they asked her to join them.

Harry Kroeger left a few minutes later, and King, after a moment's reflection, decided he wanted some dessert. He strolled over to the food counter and came back with a dish of chocolate pudding.

Watching him, Madeline had to laugh. "How do you ever keep your figure?" she asked.

"*You* can ask that?" he mocked. "Like yourself, dear lady, I work off most of the calories. Even when I'm not slaving away here in the hospital, I get plenty of exercise. I lured Claire into trying windsurfing a while back, and she loves it. You ought to try it. Either Claire or I would be happy to teach you."

"I'd like that," Madeline admitted. "But to tell you the truth, I'm afraid it would point out to Chris just one more thing he can no longer do."

King considered this. Then he said reflectively, "Handling a sailboard does require a certain balance. But Chris might well be able to get it back. He has the advantage of having been very proficient not that long ago. Matter of fact, I should encourage him to come out with me one day. The worst that could happen is he'd get a good dunking."

After a moment King continued, "Harry said you had a constant full house in the E.R. over the weekend."

"That," Madeline opined, munching her tuna salad sandwich, "is the understatement of the century. The place was a zoo."

"He also said he mentioned our idea of a clinic, separate from the hospital."

"Yes, he did."

"He's right, of course," King averred. "And the funny thing is that someone very close to us owns the land that would make a perfect location for such a place."

"Chris?"

"You guessed it," King said. "I don't know how many acres Chris has out at the factory, but it's a considerable number. Years ago, when land around here was dirt cheap, his grandfather bought up every inch he could get his hands on. Old man Talmadge was crafty, to put it mildly. Today there just isn't that much available space left, unless you go way out of town. Within the confines of Lakeport itself there's nothing for sale that would be suitable."

"You sound as if you've pioneered this."

"I have," King admitted. "A while back, Harry and I started scouting around for sites. We thought if we had a definite plan in mind it would be easier to drum up public support. Anyway, we were daunted not only by the scarcity of suitable land, but by the price people wanted for what they were willing to sell. To date, that's as far as we've gotten. But as you saw for yourself, something has to be done. The situation is fast approaching the critical state."

Madeline thought for a moment, then said, "In urban areas, King, you find walk-in medical clinics in all sorts of places. Many aren't any bigger than a convenience store, so why couldn't there be an in-town clinic here?"

"There could be," King agreed. "And I'd say there should be, at some point in the future. But what we need now is a facility considerably more extensive than the usual Doc-in-a-Box. Not a full-fledged hospital, but something big enough so that ten years down the pike it won't be totally obsolete."

"So there'd have to be several acres involved?"

"The more the better—" King nodded "—to allow for expansion." He polished off the rest of his pudding, then observed, "I know that some of the land Chris owns is swampy, and some is thick, second-growth timber. It's too bad really. If things had been planned differently, there would have been room for a clinic, a real lab for Chris, and the plastics factory, too. As it is, Chris has placed his plant in the dead center, which precludes any other major construction, as far as I can see."

King shrugged. "At this point in time, there's no use getting into the clinic concept with Chris," he said frankly. "The lab... well, that's something else again. I still wish he'd take a second look at what he's doing."

"I'm afraid it's too late for that," Madeline said sadly. "It's all systems go with Chris and the factory right now. If he finds he can put more time into his research ideas, and they begin to succeed, I suppose he *could* expand at a later date."

"Probably," King conceded, "but it would be more costly, of course."

They switched subjects then, but King's words nagged Madeline for the rest of the day. The trouble was, he was right, and yet how could she get the message across to Chris? He had so much on his mind, she hated to add to it. There were endless details in connection with his business, for one thing.

Also, when he'd gone for a checkup with his physical therapist recently, he had been chastised roundly for not keeping up with the exercise program that had been mapped out for him. He'd reluctantly told Madeline this while they were lying in bed together in his house on the morning of her day off. "The therapist says I can't expect to ever get rid of the cane unless I shape up,'' Chris had admitted.

"That makes me feel like an idiot,'' Madeline had muttered remorsefully. "Here I am a doctor. The least I could do is keep breathing down your neck!''

"Why don't you start doing that right now?'' Chris had suggested.

Madeline had glanced at him suspiciously, and saw the laughter in his eyes. Laughter, and something else. That wonderful desire that magically bonded them together.

"You!'' she'd exploded.

But hers had been an explosion sparked with passion. And as she'd reached out and savored Chris's touch, and mumbled love words in his ear, her concerns had flown far away.

Now it seemed they were back....

CHAPTER THIRTEEN

WHEN CLAIRE FARADAY started planning a Labor Day picnic, both Madeline and King laughingly crossed their fingers.

Claire announced her plans several days before the holiday, when she, King, Madeline and Chris were sitting out in Chris's garden early one evening enjoying mint juleps that Chris had proudly made from his own homegrown mint.

Claire said, "We could go out to Baskin's Beach and swim and windsurf. You know, just laze around, eat and drink and..." She ran out of breath.

"You're seriously expecting both Madeline and me to be in attendance?" King asked her, half teasingly.

"I should certainly hope so. It's the last big holiday of the season, in case you haven't been checking your calendar lately."

"What's your on-call schedule?" King asked Madeline.

"I can't quite believe it, but I'm off on Labor Day."

"So am I. Harry Kroeger has been nominated to handle surgical E.R. cases—that Monday, at least."

"I think Terry Evans is on call for the medical cases," Madeline remembered.

"Shall we accept this as a gift from Fate?"

"Why not? Who are we to question Fate, doctor?"

"Who indeed, doctor?"

Claire looked from her husband to Madeline, then back to her husband again. "Does that mean I can go ahead and plan what kind of sandwiches to make?" she queried with deceptive innocence.

"Don't opt for any fillings that are too perishable," King warned. "I'll be very surprised if both Madeline and I manage to stay off the hook."

"I learned long ago to hold the mayonnaise until the last minute," Claire reminded him.

It was a beautiful end of a summer evening. Fireflies flickered through the bushes. The trees were dark silhouettes in the last light of dusk, and the moon was harvest gold.

"Makes me feel like building a campfire and toasting marshmallows and singing songs," Claire mused, glancing toward the moon. "Do you two guys remember when we used to do that this time of year? We'd be thinking about going back to school in a few more days and we'd milk every last ounce out of what was left of summer vacation."

"I remember," Chris nodded dreamily.

"You were in love with Katie Mueller," Claire reminded him.

"And who was Katie Mueller?" Madeline asked archly.

"The class beauty, naturally," King answered promptly. "Except for Claire, of course."

"Except for Claire!" Claire scoffed. "Katie Mueller was voted Miss Lakeport Regional High," she told Madeline. "The senior class even had a pageant for her...remember, King? Most of the kids thought Katie would sail right on to Atlantic City and become Miss America. She was tall and willowy, with gorgeous red hair and blue eyes that made yours look pale in comparison.''

Claire continued, her eyes sparkling with mischief, ''Let's see...what else was there about Katie? She could sing—you must remember that husky, sexy voice, Chris? And every boy in the senior class had a crush on her, but she only had eyes for Chris.''

''I didn't have a crush on her,'' King protested.

''Really? That's not the way I remember it.'' It was Chris's turn to tease. ''My recollection is that you followed Katie around that night of the senior prom begging her to save you just one dance.''

''Come on,'' King groaned. ''Everyone knows I was head over heels for Claire.''

''True, but your peripheral vision didn't suffer any for it,'' Chris taunted.

They laughed, then Madeline asked, ''What happened to Katie Mueller?''

''She got married to Tink Brigham a couple of months after we graduated.''

''*Tink* Brigham?''

''I think his real name is Archibald, but everyone around town called him Tink because he's always had this habit of tinkering with things. Sort of a Mr. Fix-It,'' Chris explained. ''It paid off, because now he owns the big hardware store down on the corner of Main Street and Pine. Anyway, Katie married him—he was a good ten years older than she was—and they had five or six kids. I lost count after a while. She's no longer tall and willowy, incidentally. She's tall and scrawny, and...''

King managed an exaggerated sigh. ''So,'' he commented dryly, ''the dreams of adolescence do vanish, eh, Chris? Or should I say that our high school sweethearts seldom make it as perennial valentines.''

"Wait a minute!" Claire warned.

"Present company excepted," King apologized, giving Claire a look that was enough to show the world there was no other woman for him.

Watching the two of them, Madeline felt a bittersweet pleasure. Claire and King were so much in love. Being with them was always a heartwarming experience, but it also made her wistful. She wanted King and Claire's kind of rapport for Chris and herself, and thus far they hadn't managed it. They were in love with each other, gloriously so. And yet there were undeniable obstacles.

Claire and King, she knew, had had their share of obstacles. They'd weathered their storm and triumphed, and were completely themselves around each other. Claire had her own, successful career and so, certainly, did King. They'd come to terms with each other's work, as well as with each other, and the result was something terrific to witness.

Madeline hoped it could work out like that for Chris and herself. It required a lot of juggling to combine two careers with a successful marriage, but King and Claire were proof that it could be done. She and Chris were not King and Claire, however. Would they be equally tolerant of each other once they'd gotten a little farther down the road? And equally mindful of each other's rights?

She still hadn't told Chris what King had said about her moving into this house with him. True, only a few days had passed, but Madeline was chagrined with herself for stalling. She supposed that deep in her heart she hoped Chris would suddenly implore her to come live with him. But she couldn't blame him if he didn't. It was she, after all, who'd set the course of things when she'd taken the room at the Château Champlain. Now she bemoaned her own lack of insight because she hadn't realized how that must have hurt Chris's pride.

It was up to her to make the next gesture. She knew that, and the crazy thing was that she wanted desperately to make it, yet she kept holding back. Was she afraid that, if she *did* move in with Chris, it might prove too quickly whether or not they could make it together forever. Was she subconsciously fearing that they couldn't?

Madeline was accusing herself of being a coward when they heard the phone ring. King rose and said, "I'll get it. It's probably the hospital for either thee or me, Madeline."

"I hope not," Claire muttered.

"I second that," Madeline agreed promptly.

She glanced across at Chris. She didn't want to leave him tonight. She wanted to spend the night with him in the big old four-poster up in the front bedroom. She wanted to wake up tomorrow morning snuggled in his arms. Damn it, that's the way she wanted to wake up every morning.

Madeline was making up her mind that before they went to bed together tonight she was going to tell Chris that she wanted to move in with him, when King appeared in the doorway. Seeing the stricken expression on his face, her thoughts dissolved as apprehension clutched her.

It was Claire who cried out, "My God, King, what is it?"

King bypassed Claire's agonized query to zero in on Chris. "That was the fire chief on the phone," he said, his face taut, his blue eyes blazing. "They received a call about fifteen minutes ago that someone saw flames out at the plant. By the time they got there, the whole building was engulfed. There's a fair bit of wind, tonight...and the chief doubts they'll be able to save very much.''

By MIDNIGHT, there was nothing left. Nothing, except a skeleton of girders, framework and embers that glowed in the night like thousands of evil eyes.

The fire chief, looking ancient, stated, ''It was arson this time. Arson pure and simple.'' He sipped steaming coffee from a thermos cup as his brooding eyes surveyed the smoldering ruins of what was to have been Chris's new factory.

Chris's face was an ash gray. He looked so terrible that Madeline's fear was a constant, throbbing pain. All she could think of was that few people were too young to have a coronary, and right now Chris looked on the verge of one.

''Who could do something like that?'' he muttered, staring at the devastated scene in front of him, bathed in the macabre pale light of the moon. ''Why?''

''It beats me,'' the chief mumbled. ''But a hell of a lot of the things people do nowadays beats me.''

The chief wandered off to give final instructions to his men, and Madeline tugged at Chris's shirt sleeve. ''Darling,'' she urged, ''let's get out of here.''

''Where the hell is there to go, Madeline?'' he asked bleakly. Shuddering, he added, ''I think I'm living in a nightmare.''

''I know,'' Madeline murmured gently, ''but it's not doing you any good to stay here.'' She hesitated, then told him, ''Let's go home, Chris.''

He looked at her, still dazed, and she knew he wasn't getting the import of what she'd just said. How could she expect him to? She ached for him, but she'd seldom in her life felt more helpless. "Darling, please," she urged.

King came up to them. "Can you give Claire a ride back to the house?" he asked.

"Sure," Chris said absently, his eyes still fixed straight ahead.

"I'm going to the hospital," King stated.

Madeline caught something in his tone and asked quickly, "There wasn't anyone in the building, was there?"

"No."

"I should have hired a security guard to stand watch around the clock," Chris muttered bitterly.

Madeline was watching King closely. "Was someone hurt?" she queried.

He nodded. "One of the firemen. I don't think it's too bad, mostly smoke inhalation. But I want to check on him myself."

"I'll come with you," Chris said quickly, snapping to.

"There's no point in your doing that, Chris. I'll phone you as soon as I've checked him over. It'll be of more help to me, frankly, if you'd take care of our two girls."

Chris didn't pursue the matter, and Madeline knew he was deeply absorbed in his own thoughts. Automatically, he headed for the driver's side of the car, but she intercepted him. She could only dimly imagine the horror of what he'd just been through and she knew he must also be reliving the first terrible fire, only fourteen months in the past. It was no time for him to be driving!

She was prepared to make a stand about this, but after a mumbled protest Chris subsided into silence and let her take the wheel. Claire nodded approvingly as she climbed into the back seat.

After a silent drive back into town, Madeline pulled up at the curb in front of the Parmeter house. Claire said quickly, "Please... just go on into Chris's driveway, unless the two of you want to come in for a nightcap?"

"Thanks," Chris said, "but I think I, at least, will pass on that for the moment, Claire."

Madeline turned into the driveway, then stopped to let Claire off at the edge of the sidewalk. She was aware of Claire's anxious glances toward Chris, and of the concern in her voice as she said, "Keep in touch. If I hear anything from King before you do, I'll phone."

"Thanks," Madeline said gratefully.

A few seconds later she brought the car to a stop in front of the garage and turned to see Chris glowering at her.

"The two of you don't have to treat me as if I've suddenly turned into the village idiot," he told her irritably.

"I wasn't aware we were."

"Well, just now Claire acted like I was on a leave of absence. She was talking around me, not to me."

"She was talking to me, damn it!" Madeline retorted. There was an edge to her voice as she added, "Please, Chris... don't make mountains out of nonexistent molehills."

"I'm not trying to."

They slowly made their way up the path to the house. It was only when they reached the back door that Chris said suddenly, "I'm sorry, I guess I should have taken you straight to the hotel."

Madeline glared at him. "Maybe you are out of your mind, after all."

He smiled awkwardly. "I've had the feeling the rest of you think I am."

She ignored that. "Can you seriously suggest I'd even consider going back to the hotel tonight?" she asked, stabbed with hurt to imagine he'd think such a thing.

Chris said quietly, "You do live there, you know."

"Not any more, I don't."

"What's that supposed to mean?"

"All I have to do is pack my suitcase," she answered, then added, her voice shaking, "If you want me."

Chris stood still as stone, staring down at her, then slowly shook his head. "That has to be the stupidest question in the history of man."

He reached out for her and Madeline went into his arms, clinging to him tightly, wanting this togetherness more than anything else in her life.

Inside the house, Chris switched on the kitchen light. Madeline was shocked when she got a really good look at him. His pallor was frightening.

"Do you have any brandy?" she asked.

"Yes. Why?"

"As a doctor, I'm prescribing you a double shot."

"As a doctor, yet?" he asked, pretending to be impressed.

"Chris, you look like hell."

His smile widened. "Do you talk to all your patients like that?"

"I'm serious."

"Dearest, I don't need brandy..."

"You don't need me right now, not in *that* way," Madeline interrupted. "To be frank, we're both too done in for our lovemaking to be any good."

"Oh, really? Would you care to make a little bet?"

She marveled that Chris could retain his sense of humor in the face of what had happened tonight, and was aware more than ever of his hidden strength. Chris was pure steel when it counted.

He said, "Okay, I'll go for your brandy—provided you join me. If you'd consult a mirror, Dr. Clarke, I think you'd find you don't look so hot yourself." He added, "I'd tuck you into bed, *sans* sex for tonight, except King might be calling."

"Yes, I know."

"God, I hope that fireman wasn't severely hurt," Chris brooded. "I'm beginning to think the factory's jinxed."

He pulled out a chair at the kitchen table and sat down. "The brandy's in the dining room cupboard," he told Madeline wearily. "For once, I'll yield to my aching leg and let you get it."

Madeline brought the bottle back to the kitchen and poured a liberal quantity of the amber liquid into two snifters. As she watched Chris swirl his brandy around before he tasted it, she had an almost overpowering desire to fold him in her arms and hug him. A maternal impulse? she queried, scoffing silently at the idea.

Someday maybe there would be someone for her to mother, Madeline thought suddenly. Occasionally she'd wondered if it was unnatural that she'd never really yearned to have children as so many of her female friends did. But the thought of having a child of Chris's now filled her with an entirely new emotion. A child in their image would be so incredibly wonderful....

He looked at her and smiled. "I'd swear you have stars in your eyes, Maddie."

"I think maybe I do."

"Kind of a funny time to, don't you think?"

"Yes, I know. But I wasn't thinking about now."

"What were you thinking about?"

Madeline smiled wistfully. "You, and us...and something much later on."

The phone chose that moment to ring. At the other end of the line, King told them that the injured fireman would be okay.

"A few superficial burns and some smoke inhalation," he reported. "We're going to keep him here for a couple of days to be sure his lungs are clear."

"Thank God," Chris said simply.

Madeline knew he was again reliving his tragic fire of last summer when five people had died and several others were injured, most notably himself. She was thankful that history had not entirely repeated itself.

A PRIORITY FOR CHRIS the next day was a visit to the fireman who had been injured the previous night.

Throughout the morning he was busy with telephone calls involving police and fire officials, insurance people, and a curious media. So it was midafternoon when he finally pulled into the hospital parking lot. He was feeling the weight of a number of things as he reached for his cane and climbed out of the car. It was as if everything he'd been working for since his return from Aruba had been wiped out—literally blacked out—by a single stroke of Fate.

He tried to shake off an encroaching mood of depression as he entered the hospital lobby and made his way toward the reception desk to check on the room number of the injured fireman. Then, as he was turning toward the elevator, he heard his name being called and saw Lorna Henderson hurrying toward him.

He swore under his breath. He couldn't think of anyone he wanted to see less just now.

Her lovely face mirrored her concern as she reached out and clutched his coat sleeve. "Chris," she said, managing to put a volume of meaning into his name. "I'm just getting off work and I was hoping to get in touch with you. I feel so terrible about the fire."

"Thanks, Lorna," Chris answered uncomfortably, vividly remembering the last time he'd seen her. He'd left her outside the roadhouse where she'd asked him to meet her. It hadn't been a good parting.

She looked up at him, her dark eyes full of compassion. "This is such rotten luck for you," she moaned.

"Yes," he agreed, his impatience with her starting to brim. "Well...right now I'm going to pay a quick visit to the fireman who was injured last night. Then I have an appointment with the chief of police."

"I see."

She was literally standing in his path. Chris began, "Lorna, if you'll excuse me..."

"I have to talk to you, Chris."

The intensity of her words made him flinch. The last thing he needed was a confrontation of any sort with her. God knows he'd been firm at the roadhouse. How could she have failed to get his message?

"I mean it," she insisted. "There's something going on that you should know about. I've wanted to call you but ... to be honest, I didn't know how to tell you."

"What are you talking about, Lorna?"

"Dr. Faraday and Dr. Clarke."

"What about Dr. Faraday and Dr. Clarke?"

"Well...there's something going on between the two of them. At least, that's the word that's going around the hospital. And, I've seen them myself...."

"What the hell do you mean by that?"

Chris didn't realize he'd raised his voice and was standing over Lorna, glaring down at her, until she backed away and said nervously, "Please! People are watching."

"So they're watching!" Chris replied roughly. Lowering his voice, he demanded, "Just what have you drummed up this time?"

"I haven't drummed up anything."

She glanced toward a small reception room off the lobby. "Please," she urged, "why don't we go in there? We're making a scene."

He shrugged and followed her, deciding wearily that his best course was to hear her out.

As soon as they were inside he said impatiently, "Look, I have a million things to handle today. So come out with it, okay?"

Her lips trembled. "You don't have to be so nasty to me," she murmured. "I was only thinking of you."

"I doubt that," Chris said dryly. "Regardless...what's 'going around' about King Faraday and Madeline Clarke?"

"People are saying they're having an affair."

Chris stared at her. "Come off it, Lorna!" he snapped.

"I've seen them myself, in the coffee shop."

"In the coffee shop?" He forced himself to laugh. "Is that where people around here hold their secret rendezvous?"

"Chris," she implored, "like I said, I'm only thinking of you."

"What about Tim?"

"What?"

"What about Tim O'Brien? Or have you ditched him since I last saw you?"

Lorna's voice was suddenly very small as she said, "No, I haven't ditched Tim." She held out her left hand. A small diamond sparkled on her ring finger. "I took a two week vacation a little while back, and I spent most of it with Tim," she informed Chris. "So...we're engaged."

"Well, congratulations." His skepticism must have been even more obvious than he'd intended because Lorna flushed.

"I'm sincere about Tim," she stated defiantly.

"I hope you are," Chris rejoined, thinking wryly that she couldn't possibly know how much he hoped that was true!

Lorna anxiously scanned Chris's face. Then, unexpectedly, she blurted, "I've been so mixed up lately. I mean...I love nursing, and I like it here at Lakeport General. And this is my home town. My family still live near here...."

"Lorna, please! Come to the point."

"I don't want to leave, Chris. That's been part of the problem with Tim, don't you see?"

"Lorna, I honestly don't have time to go into this."

"Chris, you know how torn I've been between you and Tim. And Tim's in the air force, which means I'd have to leave at some point if I married him and travel wherever he goes. Can't you see? I can't bear the thought of leaving Lakeport and..."

He was afraid she was going to say "and you." But she didn't.

"Has something changed?" he asked carefully.

"No, but Tim says he'll resign from the air force if I want him to."

Chris shook his head. "He's making it his career, isn't he? That's what he wants?"

"Yes," she admitted reluctantly. "That's what he wants."

"And you'd ask him to give that up and stay here?"

"He could get a job. Maybe in your factory."

"Are you trying to be funny?" Chris demanded sharply. "I have no factory."

"But you will."

"I'm not so sure of that." He glanced at his watch. "Look, I have to go."

"I'm supposed to meet Tim, anyway," Lorna told him.

On his way through the lobby, Chris nearly ran into a nice looking young man wearing an airman's uniform. He suspected that this must be Tim, and a backward glance over his shoulder showed he was right. Lorna and her fiancé were walking toward the exit together.

He tried to dismiss Lorna's pronouncement as idle gossip or, even more probably, a figment of her active imagination. But his thoughts were chaotic, and it took all his self-control to pull himself together and say the right things to the injured fireman a few minutes later.

At that point, Chris felt a sudden need to see King. Just to see him, talk to him, and let matters swing back into sane perspective.

Hoping that the O.R. schedule had been completed for the day, Chris headed for King's office. There were few people around this hospital who didn't know him because of his long residence as a patient. When King's secretary saw him, she smiled a warm greeting. But then she told him that Dr. Faraday was down in the cafeteria and, despite himself, he winced. Could it be possible that King and Madeline were having one of those "rendezvous" Lorna had talked about?

That morning Madeline had arrived at the hospital at seven o'clock, feeling both physically and emotionally exhausted. She'd wanted desperately to stay home with Chris, but there'd been no way to get the day off. Her caseload was too heavy. She had a colonoscopy scheduled for eight o'clock, and a very full agenda thereafter.

It was nearly four before she could escape to the cafeteria for a bite to eat. She saw King Faraday standing in front of the steam table surveying what food there was left and she surmised correctly, that he'd been putting in the same kind of day she had.

King settled for a sandwich and Madeline followed his example. Then, by mutual accord, they carried their trays to the same table. They were lingering over second cups of coffee, discussing their respective patients and the day's happenings, when they looked up to see Chris standing beside them.

Chris had been handling things very well when Madeline had left him that morning. She'd marveled at his resilience. But now he looked harried, and he was frowning as he asked abruptly, "Would I be interrupting something if I joined you?"

"Of course not," King answered promptly before Madeline could speak. "What can I get you?" he added as Chris pulled out a chair and sat down. "The pickings are on the lean side but the brownies aren't too bad, and of course there's always coffee."

Chris's eyes met Madeline's briefly before he answered, and she flinched at what she saw in them. Hostility? Dislike? She tried to analyze Chris's quick gaze, and couldn't understand why there should be anything negative between Chris and herself.

"I ate earlier," Chris told King tautly. "Anyway, I'm meeting with the chief of police in half an hour. I came over here first to visit with the fireman who was injured last night."

"I'm sure he appreciated that," King approved. "For the record, he's doing fine. I plan to discharge him tomorrow morning."

"So he indicated."

"I gather if you're meeting with the chief of police there's not much doubt about the fire being arson."

"No doubt at all," Chris answered. "The chief said they found an empty kerosene can tossed in the woods nearby. Also, a couple of the workmen he's questioned told him they've noticed an orange pickup truck around the site a lot lately. Evidently someone's been parking on the property and just sitting there and watching."

"That sounds pretty weird," Madeline put in.

Chris nodded, then continued in a weary but exasperated tone, "Yes. I wish to God they'd said something to me about it. They thought it was just a guy with a fascination for watching things being built."

Madeline was sharply aware that Chris actually had avoided her eyes as he spoke. And from then on he addressed his remarks to King.

When he left them a few minutes later, Madeline felt at an unexpected loss. She had the feeling that Chris was deeply troubled over something concerning her—something that had nothing whatsoever to do with last night's fire.

CHAPTER FOURTEEN

CHRIS STOPPED just inside the front door and set Madeline's suitcase against the wall. He turned to her, smiling, his heart in his eyes. "I'm remembering something from my high school Spanish class," he said. "When you welcome someone into your home you say *es su casa*. This *is* your home, Madeline. Forever, I hope."

Madeline's heart was pounding and tears filled her eyes. She said softly, "So do I, Chris."

He held out his arms to her. His embrace felt strong and warm and wonderful. He smelled clean and masculine, almost woodsy, and Madeline laughed shakily. "That after-shave lotion you're using could double as an aphrodisiac."

It was ten o'clock Sunday morning. Holding her out at arm's length, Chris surveyed her with mock disapproval. "At this hour of the day, on the Sabbath?"

"At any hour, on any day."

"Is that an invitation?"

She shook her head. "I still have a couple of tote bags full of stuff in the car," she said and added hastily, "I'll bring them in. Then let's have some coffee."

"How prosaic," Chris groaned, his eyebrows eloquently upraised. "And how frustrating!"

Madeline smiled. "I need to get my feet on the ground," she confessed.

This was true. She was taking a giant step on this early September morning. Until she'd walked through Chris's front door just now and realized that, henceforth, this lovely old house was going to be her home, she hadn't realized just how profoundly she'd be affected.

It was one thing to love someone, and she loved Chris very much. It was something else entirely to make the commitment of living with them. The only other man she'd ever lived with was Jeffrey Clarke.

Heading back up Chris's front walk, carrying a tote bag in each hand, Madeline couldn't imagine two more dissimilar men than Jeffrey and Chris. She knew, without doubt, that she'd never loved Jeffrey as she loved Chris, but Jeffrey had conditioned her feelings about sharing space with a man. For the most part, their home had always been Jeffrey's—and always would have been, had Jeffrey lived.

Chris was different in that respect. He was far more flexible because he'd learned how to roll with the unexpected punches life sometimes threw. Madeline knew in her heart that Chris wanted to make a go of living together as much as she did. If they could successfully share their lives within the confines of his home, it would mark the true beginning of their future together.

She wanted that future.

Chris had gone out to the kitchen and, as Madeline walked down the hall, she caught the delicious aroma of brewing coffee. She glanced into the various rooms she passed and couldn't help but think, once again, that the furnishings were rather formal for her taste. Still, many of the pieces were quite beautiful, and the possibilities for brightening up the decor were endless.

She'd never really had the chance to play interior decorator, and the idea was exciting. But she was in absolutely no hurry to start. She and Chris, and their adjustment to each other on a twenty-four-hour basis, came first.

As she entered the kitchen, she noticed the bouquet of yellow chrysanthemums that Chris had placed in the middle of the kitchen table. The sight of the flowers tugged at her heart, and Madeline could feel herself at the edge of tears again—tears of happiness this time. His small gesture was much more poignant than if he'd ordered a vanload of blossoms from a florist.

She looked across the room at him and said simply, "I love you, you know."

Their gazes met, and an emotion Madeline couldn't identify flickered in Chris's hazel eyes. He said unsteadily, "I hope you do. It's the one thing in life I need to be sure of, Maddie." He meant it.

Searching his face, Madeline was shocked. "My God," she sputtered thickly, "do you doubt me?"

Did he doubt her? Watching her, Chris thought he'd never in his life seen anyone lovelier than Madeline right now. She was wearing a deep rose dress that set off her beautiful coloring, and her silky hair swept her shoulders in a dark swirl. And although they hadn't spent very much time at Baskin's Beach lately, her face was flushed with a sun-kissed blush.

In the next instant his thoughts swerved savagely to Lorna Henderson. Damn her! He knew he couldn't blame these recent twinges of jealousy entirely on Lorna, but she'd unlocked the door of suspicion. Regardless, he was the one who'd walked through that door and, in a revealing moment, he blamed himself bitterly for doing so.

He'd hesitated in answering Madeline and the damage had been done. The bleakness in her eyes was testimony to that as she said, "If you doubt my love for you, Chris, I shouldn't be here."

Watching her, Chris felt that he'd been living in the center of a gray fog. Suddenly the fog had vanished, and the smile he gave Madeline was dazzling. "Dearest," he said softly. He sighed, adding wryly, "My problem is that I can't believe Lady Luck has come to stay in my life."

His admission had the effect of unlocking a gate between them. The gate opened and they forgot about coffee. They forgot about everything except each other.

The arrival of Monday morning broke this wonderful spell of togetherness and, with great reluctance, Madeline wrenched herself away from Chris and went to work. As she drove to the hospital she wished she and Chris could have arranged to meet somewhere for lunch, but it wasn't practical for her to make such a suggestion until she knew what sort of day she was apt to have.

As it was, Chris had an appointment with Bill Edgerly. Again, the question of insurance had to be dealt with, and Madeline hoped he wasn't going to face the long battle he'd fought his way through the first time around. Chris's peace of mind was disturbed enough just wondering who'd started the fire in the first place—and why.

The police were convinced it was a case of arson. Thus far they'd tracked down three orange pickup trucks in the area, but each owner had an alibi for the time of the fire.

As she parked her borrowed car in her reserved space, Madeline realized ruefully that she and Chris both had a lot of loose ends to tie up. His were not of his own making, but hers were—the result of more or less living out of suitcases ever since Jeffrey's death.

She still had furniture and other personal belongings in Boston, hastily placed in storage when Tom Lucas had called her about coming to Eastern Maine Medical Center. Even if she'd gone somewhere else, she would have handled things that way. She'd unloaded the condo she'd shared with Jeffrey at far less than the market value, simply to absolve herself of its rather oppressive memory.

In Bangor she'd rented a furnished apartment, not wanting to be tied down by house ownership. But when she'd flown to Lakeport last month she'd left other personal belongings there, plus her secondhand car, parked on the street. The car she was driving now had belonged to Chris's parents. They'd given it to him when they moved to Florida, and he'd kept it in good condition.

Madeline decided she'd probably sell her car in Bangor. But whatever she did, it was going to mean a trip back to Maine.

Suddenly that seemed like a good idea. She promised herself she'd work out a schedule with King as soon as possible whereby she could take three or four days off. She and Chris could drive to Maine together and stay at her apartment while she finalized things. At the same time she could introduce Chris to Tom and Valerie Lucas, and show him off a little!

Madeline had a relatively easy schedule that Monday morning and at eleven she called Chris and caught him at home. When she suggested that he drive over and have lunch with her at the hospital, he seemed quite taken aback. Then he quipped, "Well, I guess there's a first time for everything."

"And it won't be the last," she promised. She liked hearing the sound of his voice while knowing this was a local call. It gave her a good feeling to think that Chris was only a few miles away. As she hung up Madeline sat back at her desk, pleased with the way things were going between them.

Ironically, as she and Chris were walking along the corridor to the cafeteria that noon, Lorna Henderson came toward them, evidently having just finished her lunch.

Lorna muttered a greeting to Chris and would have passed right by, but Chris reached out and took hold of her arm.

"Wait up there, Lorna," he told her, and there was something about his tone that alerted Madeline to the fact this was no ordinary meeting. "You know Dr. Clarke, don't you?"

"We haven't been introduced," Lorna said stiffly.

"I'm glad to meet you, Miss Henderson," Madeline said quickly, but coolly. "I've seen you around, of course."

"I've noticed you, too."

Madeline wondered if the beautiful young nurse was deliberately avoiding meeting her eyes, or if she was being overly imaginative. A vision of the photo of Lorna and Chris flashed in front of her and, with it, a funny pang that she promptly diagnosed as jealousy.

Well, it would be easy enough to be jealous of Lorna. She was staring up into Chris's eyes, and Madeline would have sworn she still had a crush on him.

This conviction stayed in her mind as she and Chris were eating lunch, and finally the bubble burst.

"Chris," she demanded stubbornly, "was there ever anything between you and Lorna?"

He couldn't have looked more astonished. Then his eyes started to twinkle and he actually grinned. "Just what are you asking me, Maddie?" he challenged.

Madeline felt her cheeks getting hot. "All right," she said tightly. "Did you have an affair with her?"

"While I was bound up in plaster, or in the wheelchair?"

"You're not answering my question."

Chris snickered. And while Madeline smoldered, he vented his amusement, then caressed her eyes with an expression so tender and loving, she knew it would be impossible to remain angry with him.

"That's the funniest thing I've ever heard! It's also a real ego boost, and those you hand out rather sparingly. I can't believe this."

"What are you talking about, Chris Talmadge?"

"Maddie, you sound like you're jealous of Lorna Henderson!"

"Maybe I am."

Now it was Madeline's turn to avoid meeting someone else's eyes. After a moment she added, "I certainly could be, if I had any reason to think that you and Lorna—"

"Excuse me," Chris cut in, his merriment resurfacing. He actually held his napkin to his face, trying to camouflage his laughter. Then he said, "Dearest, you don't know what you've done for me. I've been jealous as hell lately, even though I've been reminding myself every hour on the hour what a damned fool I could so easily make of myself."

"Now what are you talking about?"

"You and King?"

"What?"

"All right, Madeline, I don't blame you for looking that way," Chris conceded. "But a few days ago Lorna indicated there was some scuttlebutt going around the hospital about you and King. She also said she'd seen you two sharing a table in here, talking in a *very* intimate way."

Madeline muttered a word she rarely used, and couldn't have looked more disgusted.

"Look, I don't want you to take this the wrong way, but the day I was here visiting that fireman, and I spotted you and King . . . well, I almost thought I was interrupting something myself," Chris admitted.

"So that's why you acted so strange!" Madeline stared at Chris in disbelief.

"I can't believe you'd be jealous of Lorna, either," Chris countered, grinning wickedly.

Still annoyed with him, Madeline retorted, "I don't see why you should be so damned happy about this."

"In part, because it's like looking in a mirror," he told her. "I was very close to losing it myself, for reasons as entirely unfounded as yours are. It wasn't that I ever suspected you and King of anything, it was just the way Lorna put it."

"Okay, let's blame it on Lorna," Madeline decided dryly.

Chris smiled tenderly. "Maybe you'll take this the wrong way, Maddie. But it's fantastic to know that you can actually be jealous of me," he confessed softly.

"Do you think I'm made of stone?" Madeline demanded. "Do you really think I keep my emotions locked up in a vault, and draw them out only when I want to?"

Chris smiled widely. Watching him, Madeline felt as if the sun had come out from behind the clouds and was shining golden light directly upon her.

"I know a fair bit about what you do with your emotions, Maddie."

"I hope so, because jealousy is very negative, even though it's also pretty human. You appear to be blissfully unaware of the fact that you're a very attractive man. I seem to remember telling you that before."

"I know...and I thank you, Maddie," he said sincerely.

"Your modesty is equally appealing," she continued. "You know, Chris, I realize other women are bound to be attracted to you, or worse...fall in love with you. But don't expect me to be impervious to it."

An odd expression flashed in Chris's eyes and he asked, "This isn't a morale builder, is it?"

"Of course not, and don't look so skeptical."

"I guess I can't help being skeptical," Chris told her. "You're giving me those kinds of grades...lame leg and all?"

"Yes, darling," Madeline said huskily. "Lame leg and all."

Chris's eyes darkened as he murmured, "God, you can't imagine how much I want you right now."

"And you can't imagine how much I want you," she whispered back.

The subject of Lorna Henderson was temporarily forgotten. That night, though, as they were getting ready for bed, Madeline said carefully, "I don't mean to belabor this, but didn't you ever encourage Lorna at all?"

He was unbuttoning his shirt. Tossing it on a nearby chair, he looked over his shoulder and teased, "Is she still on your mind, Maddie?"

"It really isn't funny, Chris. She could be dangerous, if she goes to the lengths of inventing things like she did about King and me."

"I think maybe that was sort of a desperation move."

"So you admit she's desperate about you?"

"I didn't mean that, exactly," he groaned. "To tell you the truth, I think Lorna's come to a crossroads in her life, and she doesn't know which way to go."

"How so?"

"Well, her boyfriend's in the air force, for one thing. They were high school sweethearts, but then he joined the service and got shuffled around, per usual. Since the beginning of summer, though, he's been stationed back in Plattsburg. And he's still very interested in Lorna, judging from the engagement ring he gave her."

"Since she took the ring, it would seem she must have settled at least one thing in her mind, wouldn't you say?"

"I don't know. She told me she loves Lakeport, and loves working at the hospital. If she marries Tim, she'll probably have to leave here because of his career. She also said Tim's willing to resign from the air force if it'll make her happy, even though he'd planned to make a career at whatever it is he's doing."

"It would be pretty selfish of her to let him do that!"

"Maybe," Chris said, and added slowly, "but I guess one person usually has to give a little more in most relationships. In Lorna's case, I think she's mixed up. But if she didn't really care about Tim, she would have ditched him long before now. I'm guessing she's that type."

"I can imagine."

"Hold it!" Chris teased, "I'm the sarcastic one, remember?" He held up his hand, and added, "Seriously, I don't think Lorna has really grown up yet. She still has her fantasies..."

"Many women have their fantasies all their lives," Madeline interposed. "Sometimes they get them confused with reality. But if they're practical, they keep the two separate and play out their fantasies in other ways."

"Sounds interesting," Chris mused.

Madeline ignored that, and asked instead, "Are you saying that in Lorna's case she's still waiting for her knight in shining armor to come riding along on his big white horse?"

"I think she was," Chris admitted.

"And you became her knight?"

"I certainly didn't realize it at the time. But I guess a few other people did. Claire Faraday, for one. I'm still not convinced, myself, except that... well, Lorna isn't exactly letting go."

"I could do with an explanation of that last statement," Madeline said, pulling back the bedcovers. She slid beneath the sheets, then propped her head up on a pillow and gazed at Chris.

He sat down on the edge of the bed, his smile rueful, and Madeline listened intently as he told her about everything that had passed between Lorna and himself since his return from Aruba.

When he'd finished, she said, "You almost make me feel sorry for her. The little witch!"

"I guess that's my problem. I can't help but feel sorry for her myself."

They let it go at that. But a couple of weekends later, when Madeline was again on call in the emergency room, she discovered Lorna Henderson would be working with her, and she instinctively put herself on alert.

They had a very busy night and at its conclusion Madeline had to admit that whatever Lorna's shortcomings might be, she was an excellent nurse. There wasn't a single aspect of nursing that she could be faulted on. Her skills, attitude and cooperation all rated an A.

Madeline was greatly relieved to discover this. It would have been difficult if Lorna had reached the point of trying to take out any hostilities toward her in a way that might have affected one of their patients.

Fortunately Lorna was a total pro, Madeline decided thankfully as, sometime after midnight, she stretched out on the cot in the little cubicle provided for doctors on call.

She'd hoped to get some sleep, but that hope was short-lived. An accident on the Northway, the main highway between New York and Montreal, sent four seriously injured people to Lakeport General at three o'clock in the morning. By the time they'd all been treated and admitted—two in critical condition—the sun was rising over Lake Champlain.

Madeline was so exhausted at the end of her shift that she decided she'd better stop at the cafeteria for a cup of black coffee. It would revive her enough to make the drive home without falling asleep.

She immediately spied Lorna sitting alone at a table near the door. On impulse she took her coffee over to the table, and asked, "Mind if I join you?"

Lorna was visibly startled. "Why...no," she stammered.

Madeline sat down wearily. "A long night, wasn't it?" she commented.

"Yes, it was."

"By the way, I appreciate the way you worked. It takes an efficient team to get the job done . . . especially under circumstances like those."

"Thank you."

Madeline realized Lorna had her guard up and she wondered if Lorna knew she was actually living in Chris's house. Feeling that she was treading on thin ice, she nevertheless asked, "I understand you became engaged recently."

Lorna unconsciously fingered the diamond on her left hand. "That's right."

"Are wedding bells in the offing soon?" The question sounded smug to Madeline the second she'd posed it, and she mentally pinched herself.

"Maybe around Thanksgiving, but I don't know yet," Lorna said, looking somewhat perplexed at the turn this conversation was taking. She asked suddenly, "You came from another hospital, didn't you?"

Surprised, Madeline nodded. "The Eastern Maine Medical Center in Bangor," she said.

"Do you miss being there?"

"No," she said honestly. "I enjoyed my work, and the staff was terrific—as they are here. I miss a few people in particular, but Bangor isn't that far away. We'll stay in touch, I'm sure."

"How would you feel if you left Lakeport?"

Madeline felt as if she'd been issued a challenge, and finished her coffee before she gave her answer. Then slowly and deliberately she said, "I wouldn't want to leave Lakeport, Lorna. My reasons for coming here in the first place had a lot to do with my personal life, as I think you know.''

Lorna didn't answer. And, after a moment, Madeline rose and said, "If you'll excuse me..."

"Certainly, Dr. Clarke," Lorna nodded dully, then added, "Goodbye."

"Goodbye," Madeline managed, wondering whether she'd done the right thing by bringing the subject of Chris out into the open. She hadn't mentioned his name, but the implication was obvious. And she felt sure Lorna had gotten her message.

Outside the hospital, halfway across the parking lot, she met King Faraday.

"Coming to work early, aren't you?" she asked him.

"Going home so soon?" he countered. Surveying her more closely, he said, "You really look bushed. Rough night?"

"Very," Madeline told him. "Four people from an accident on the Northway, two of them critical. That was just a couple of hours ago." She shrugged. "There couldn't have been very many cars on the road at that hour," she said. "How do people mess up like that?"

"I don't know," King told her. "But they always have, and they always will. Speaking of which, are you okay to drive home?"

Madeline smiled. "I'll be fine, King. Thanks."

"Well, hopefully one day we'll have specialists running the emergency room. Then the staff physicians like yourself can concern themselves with what they do best—and maintain a reasonably normal schedule. Of course, if we had that clinic you and I were talking about..."

Madeline nodded. "Very true," she said.

King fell silent. Then he asked abruptly, "Has Chris said anything about what he's going to do this time?"

Madeline was so weary it took a moment for the question to register. "You mean about rebuilding?"

"Yes."

"Not really. He's been conferring with Bill Edgerly quite a bit lately. We stopped at Bill and Ellie's for a drink the other evening, incidentally. Their baby is adorable."

"Yes," King agreed, "and they're going to be terrific parents. I don't think any woman's ever wanted a baby more than Ellie. But to get back to Chris..."

"Chris will definitely start again," Madeline reported, "though it does occur to me that maybe he could do things differently this time."

"That thought has crossed my mind, too," King admitted. "I know it's costly to have an architect's plan drawn up and Chris has already paid for one, but remember what I said about the possibilities he'd overlooked?"

Madeline shook her head. "I'm too fuzzy right now to think this out clearly," she confessed.

"I shouldn't have brought it up," King apologized. He patted her shoulder. "Go home and get some sleep."

Madeline entered the house in a daze, but Chris was out. She trudged directly upstairs, drew down the shades in the bedroom, undressed and got into bed. She was so exhausted she fell asleep almost immediately.

When she awakened, hours later, the house was completely quiet. And there was something about the quiet that made her instinctively sure she was alone.

She padded to the window and glanced out at the sunny day. As she turned, her gaze was caught by the two little unicorns on top of the dresser. She picked up the crystal unicorn Chris had gotten for her in Aruba, and a gentle smile curved her lips. To her this small glass animal was symbolical of so many good things . . . even more than the little gold counterpart he'd given her later to keep the first unicorn company. Though she loved that one, too.

Still smiling, she slipped on a dressing gown and went downstairs. It was strange how empty a house could be when the person you loved, the person you wanted to be with at that exact moment, was not in it.

Chris had left a note on the kitchen table. "'You were sleeping so soundly I didn't have the heart to wake you,'" she read aloud. "'I'm meeting with Bill at two-thirty and with the police chief after that. Be back as soon as I can.'"

A glance at the kitchen wall clock showed that it was nearly five, but Madeline was hardly surprised that she'd slept the day away. She went back upstairs and showered, anxious to feel refreshed and look presentable when Chris got home. She slipped on gray slacks and a bright blue top and, for the sake of coolness, fastened her hair into a swirling bun on top of her head.

Time passed and the stillness around her began to gnaw at her nerves. She didn't feel like watching television, or reading a book, or doing much of anything. What she wanted was to see Chris.

This wanting made her wonder how he'd felt yesterday and last night when she'd been working at the hospital. She'd only managed to call him once. Even then their conversation had been brief, shortened by the sudden need for her services.

Funny, she thought, how easy it was not to look on the opposite side of the coin. Yesterday must have been equally lonely for Chris. Probably he'd spent the evening by himself, here in the house—unless he'd gone next door for dinner with Claire and King.

She had no idea what demands Chris's business might have on his future, but she was certain his work could be as endless and time-consuming as her own, though in an entirely different way. And if his invention became successful? That, too, might change the entire complexion of his life-style. There might be conventions, and sales trips, and long lonely nights in far off hotels....

Madeline sighed. She was still tired and, recognizing that, made allowances for the way her introspection was going. People all over the world juggled their careers and free time in order to make relationships work. If the love between two people was strong enough, temporary setbacks would never affect the overall picture.

If their love was strong enough? She tossed the phrase around in her mind as she paced the big front parlor, glancing anxiously out the window for a sign of Chris. And when he finally turned into the driveway, her heart gave her the answer.

Madeline flew out the front door and down the steps to meet him. She threw herself into his arms with a fervor that nearly knocked him off balance.

Chris gazed anxiously into her eyes and asked, "Maddie, is something wrong?"

"No," she said, her voice little more than a whisper. She nestled her head against his shoulder and embraced him very tightly. "Please, Chris," she breathed, "don't ever leave me. Don't ever let me go."

CHAPTER FIFTEEN

IT WAS LATE SEPTEMBER before Madeline and Chris found a time slot in which they could make the trip to Bangor. The foliage was changing in northern New England, and the blend of blazing colors was spectacular.

"The air's like wine, and the colors are intoxicating," Madeline exclaimed rapturously. "I could get drunk just looking at everything."

She and Chris, having spent the night at Franconia Notch in New Hampshire's White Mountains, were driving east along a winding two-lane road where every bend opened upon a magnificent vista.

"I get drunk looking at you," Chris observed with a tantalizing smile.

"And I get drunk looking at you, too," Madeline answered. "But that's a different kind of intoxication."

"You're not thinking of joining AA because of it, are you?"

"Not a chance! I intend to remain inebriated forever, as far as you're concerned."

"Likewise," Chris told her. He diverted his eyes from the road just long enough to brush her face with an intent, caressing gaze. "It's odd to think that a year ago no one could have convinced me to believe in Lady Luck."

Madeline knew that a year ago he'd been in a wheel-chair, and there'd been a good chance he'd never be able to walk again. She said, a catch in her voice, "Please always believe in this Lady Luck, okay?"

"Always," he promised.

Madeline's landlady in Bangor, knowing she was coming, had dusted the apartment and opened a few windows to let in the fresh autumn air. She'd even placed a large vase of colorful dahlias on the coffee table in the living room.

Remembering how alone she'd felt when she'd first moved here—and how unsure of her footing, without Jeffrey—Madeline said softly, "Bangor was good to me, Chris. I'll never forget this place. The people were kind and friendly. Mrs. LeFevre cleaning up and leaving flowers is a typical example."

"Yes, that was very nice of her."

"They welcomed me at the medical center, too."

"Hey," Chris protested. "You're going to make me feel you're sorry you left."

Madeline smiled impishly. "Do you really think that?"

"It would be nice if you'd prove I'm wrong," he muttered.

Madeline pretended to give the matter deep thought. Then she said, "We don't have to be at Tom and Valerie's for dinner until seven. I'd say that gives me plenty of time."

Later they spent a delightful evening with Madeline's friends, the Lucases. As they were leaving, Tom drew Madeline aside, and said in a low voice, "There's one more thing I wanted to tell you, Dr. Clarke."

"Yes?"

Valerie and Chris were standing at the front door, talking animatedly, as though they'd been friends for a long time. In fact, Chris had hit it off with both Valerie and her husband.

Tom leaned close to Madeline's ear, his voice barely a whisper. "I *had* to look him over," he confessed. "If you hadn't brought him to Bangor, Valerie and I would have made the trek to Lakeport before much longer."

"How about making it anyway?"

"We just might do that. What I wanted to say, though, is that he passes on all counts, Madeline. He's a terrific guy, a genuinely terrific guy. And he loves you. It's written all over him. Valerie's going to go into such a romantic reverie once the two of you get out of here I'm not sure I'll be able to fulfill her fantasies."

Madeline laughed. "I think you'll manage, Tom."

"I'll give it my damnedest try," he said, grinning. He kissed her lightly on the cheek and counseled, "Stay happy."

"That's your prescription?"

"Definitely. No limit on the refills, either."

On their way back to her apartment, Chris looked at Madeline curiously and commented, "That was an interesting little final scene between you and Tom. Am I wrong in suspecting it involved me?"

"Excellent diagnosis," Madeline approved. "It was all about you, darling."

"Are you going to let me in on the verdict?"

Madeline noted the anxiety that crept into his voice and shook her head. "One of these days you're going to have to shed the last of that inferiority complex, Christopher Talmadge," she chided.

"I wasn't aware I was suffering from one."

"People often aren't aware of their complexes, but yours is fading nicely."

"That's a professional evaluation?"

"I don't know about its being professional, but it certainly is a personal one," she teased.

"Maddie?"

"Yes?"

"Seriously, what did Tom say about me?"

"He thinks I've found the perfect man," Madeline beamed, unprepared for the spasm of pain that flitted across Chris's face.

"I don't think that's very funny," he said unevenly.

"I wasn't being funny, Chris. That's what Tom really thinks. He and Valerie couldn't be happier for me. As," she finished quietly, "I am for myself."

Madeline would recall that admission many times as the fall progressed.

About a week after the Bangor trip, the various possessions Madeline had had in the apartment arrived by truck. A week after that, Tom wrote that he'd sold her car. He also enclosed a check.

"Let's take this and splurge," Madeline suggested to Chris, holding it up gleefully. "We've been wanting to go to Montreal for ages. Let's go this weekend."

Chris readily agreed, but once again their Montreal getaway didn't materialize. On Friday night King performed an emergency appendectomy on the young doctor who'd been scheduled to handle the emergency room duty that weekend. As luck would have it, Madeline was the only other physician available to take his place.

She went to the hospital Saturday morning, and didn't get off until Sunday evening. It was another very busy weekend. The patient volume made her more aware than ever of the urgent need for a walk-in clinic in the Lakeport area.

When she finally got home, she made up her mind that, as soon as she'd had some rest, she would bring the matter up with Chris. Then the two of them could talk to King.

It didn't work out that way, though. Madeline slept poorly that night and, because she had Monday off, Chris decided to let her sleep later than she normally liked. It was after ten when she opened her eyes, and she was still groggy as she went downstairs a short time later.

She found Chris in the kitchen, talking on the telephone. Even if she hadn't seen his taut face and blazing eyes, the carefully controlled fury in his voice would have warned her there was something very wrong.

Gripped by apprehension, she poured herself a cup of coffee and took it over to the kitchen table.

At last Chris snapped, "I'll get back to you later," and hung up the receiver. He turned to Madeline, his face a mask of bitterness.

"What is it?" she gasped.

Chris swore so violently, she was shocked.

She let his fiery outburst drift away before she repeated, "Chris, what *is* it?"

"Some damned do-gooders," Chris blurted. He limped to the kitchen table, pulled out a chair, and sat down heavily. "I can't believe this!" he groaned.

"Can't believe *what*?"

"Some of Lakeport's leading citizens have formed a committee to protest my rebuilding the factory."

"Why?"

Chris glared at her. "Hell," he said. Then, as if explaining something to a rather slow child he continued.

"You must know by now that a lot of people around town never liked the idea of my starting a plastics factory here in the first place. Some damned fool advanced the theory that dealing with plastics could be dangerous. The rumor got around that there was a high explosive risk, not to mention the danger of air pollution. When there actually *was* an explosion, you can imagine how those people reacted. It was difficult to make them believe that what happened literally was an act of God, as we finally proved. In other words, there would have been the same result, once lightning struck, no matter what I'd been making there."

"Certainly they can't say the same thing about this latest fire?"

"I don't know what the hell they're saying. No, they can't say the same thing. Whatever, there's a chance that the people opposing me can actually get a state injunction to delay my doing anything. And you know what that could mean. The whole thing could drag on for months, even years, while I go right down the financial drain."

"How could anyone get an injunction like that?" Madeline demanded. "It's your land."

"True, but some of it's swampland. The factory site doesn't even touch on that area, but the conservationists are crying that I'm going to destroy the environment if I build again. Then there's the forest. I'm not touching that, either, but there's another argument that I'll be destroying valuable timber if I do." He laughed bitterly. "I wish it was valuable timber," he said. "At this point, I'd chop down every tree and profit!"

Madeline knew he didn't mean that, so she let his remark pass. "Who were you talking to?" she asked.

"Huh? Oh, that was Bill Edgerly. He was trying to assure me I have plenty of legal legs to stand on. Nevertheless, there's going to be a public hearing on this at the high school Wednesday night. The opposition will be there to speak their various pieces, you can be sure. And I'll have to state my case, of course," Chris said grimly, then swore again.

He turned to face Madeline, then continued, "Bill says he thinks what they want is for me to sell the land to the town at a minimum price. They want it converted into a park of some sort. Nice, eh? I can only lose my shirt with a deal like that."

The rest of Monday didn't get any better. Chris spent most of his time at a desk in the library, going over a stack of material dealing with the plans for his factory. Bill Edgerly came by late in the afternoon, and they were closeted together for over an hour.

Madeline soon knew there was no point in her bringing up the question of putting the land to the multiple uses King envisioned. Chris was in much too bad a mood to listen. Determined to fight his opponents head on, he stubbornly insisted he would rebuild exactly the same structures in exactly the same places he'd planned all along.

Shortly after Bill left, Claire Faraday called. When she heard Claire's voice on the phone, Madeline instantly suspected that Bill had stopped by the Parmeter mansion, and had filled King and Claire in on what was going on.

Claire said, "Seems to me the two of you could do with a slight change of scene. How about coming over in an hour or so and taking potluck with us?"

"I'd love to," Madeline said honestly, "but I don't know if I'll be able to budge Chris from his desk."

"Want King's help? King can be pretty forceful."

"Thanks, but let me try first."

When Madeline issued the invitation to Chris, she met with even more resistance than she'd expected. He looked at her blearily, his eyes red-rimmed from poring over so many facts and figures. "You go," he told her impatiently. "I'm not hungry."

"Whether or not you're hungry doesn't have much to do with it," Madeline pointed out calmly. "You need to get away from all of that." She nodded toward the papers stacked on his desk.

"By Wednesday night," Chris replied, "I'll have to be able to face my critics. That's going to take a fair bit of preparation."

"I disagree," she said bluntly. "You know everything there is to know about your planning. It's all right in the front of your mind, and at your fingertips. You're not going to forget what you already know if you take a break for an hour, are you? When you get back, you'll be able to put things in better perspective, that's all."

Chris looked up warily. "You think I need to put things in a better perspective?" he asked sarcastically. "Well, I think I see the picture pretty clearly. I admit, Maddie, I'm mad as hell. But I'm going to fight, damn it! And until this is over, I don't want to go to King and Claire's, or anywhere else. So, you go," he repeated defiantly.

Madeline faced him, equally defiant. "All right," she sputtered, "I will."

King smiled wryly as he greeted her. "I gather you couldn't move the lion from his den," he observed.

"Precisely," Madeline said, her ire still showing.

"Could you use a drink, doctor?"

"A strong one, please."

"How about one of my fantastic martinis?"

She nodded. "I could do with that."

By the time Madeline was on the second of King's fantastic martinis, she was wondering if she'd made a wise choice. She was tired, physically and emotionally, and the gin was getting to her.

She said as much, and King answered easily, "No problem. You're with friends, Lady Luck. Claire and I can carry you home, if necessary. Try to relax, will you?"

"You know how much good it does telling people to relax, Dr. Faraday!"

"Don't I though. I thought you might be different, that's all." He grinned at her fondly. "Claire, shall we tell Madeline what we were talking about when she came in?"

"I suppose we might as well," Claire decided. "I'd told King I didn't think it was such a great idea to bring it up just now, but on the other hand..."

"Bring what up?" Madeline asked. The gin was making her foggy enough. She didn't need to be mystified as well.

"Bill stopped by after he was at your house," King said, confirming Madeline's earlier suspicion. "So we have an idea of what the score is."

"Yes?"

"You know, Madeline, there's a real need for a park out in that part of town," King said quietly. "Apparently there's talk of a recreation complex, too."

She was amazed. "Are you saying that Chris should sell his land to the town for practically nothing, and give up on the plans for his factory and his lab?"

"Not at all," King assured her. "What I'm saying is that Chris owns a lot of land out there. Over a hundred acres, I found out. He pays a low tax rate on all of it, comparatively speaking, and an especially low rate on the swampland and the forest, if you can call it that. In time, it could become a forest again, if the trees were carefully culled. And that could be done—if some of the land was given over for a park."

King paused and sipped his drink. "What I'm saying," he continued, "is that I think a lot could be accomplished with Chris's acreage, for the benefit of all."

"Do I read clinic into that?"

"Yes, you do. To my way of thinking, there's space for a factory, a separate lab for Chris, an adequate clinic with room to expand, and a park, including a recreation center."

"That sounds like a very tall order, King."

"I know, but Bill agrees with me. Bill says the problem is that right now Chris is seeing red, and who can blame him? But if he's insistent about following his present course, his vision may be too shortsighted to win very many points at the hearing."

"Chris hasn't really been speaking to me today," Madeline admitted. "Mostly, he's been swearing and grumbling to himself. Frankly, King, it was rotten luck that I had to be on call this past weekend."

"I agree."

"I'm not complaining," Madeline continued, "but Chris and I have been hoping to get up to Montreal for a long time now, and it never seems to work out."

"I know how you feel," King empathized.

"Yes, you do. And Chris has been really good about my schedule. I can't fault his attitude there, but . . . I think he did resent this last change of plans, though he didn't come right out and say so. You know how he tends to keep things like that to himself."

"All too well," King said with a nod.

Madeline paused, aware that the gin was loosening her tongue. She didn't want to say anything she might not say otherwise. Still, this was King she was dealing with. King and Claire. If any two people had Chris's interests at heart, they did.

She sighed and said, "On top of everything else, I came home last night, fell right into bed and went out like a light. By the time I got up this morning, Bill already had Chris on the phone. I walked in on the tail end of their conversation. Chris is very bitter about this."

"Not without reason," King said sadly. He looked over at Claire, who'd been sitting quietly in the corner, listening carefully. "Suppose there's a chance you could get Chris on the phone and persuade him to come over here?" he asked.

"I'll try."

Claire left the room. But a moment later, she returned, looking puzzled. "There's no answer," she reported.

Madeline sprang to her feet. "Where could he have gone?" she blurted in alarm.

"Maybe he hasn't gone anywhere," King said calmly. "Maybe he's just in the bathroom, Madeline, so take it easy. We'll call him back in a few minutes. Or, I'll go over."

Fifteen minutes later there was still no response on the phone, so King walked over to Chris's house. He came back to say that Chris's car was not in the garage. Obviously, he'd gone off somewhere.

He smiled at Madeline tolerantly. "Chris is a big boy," he reminded her.

"I know, I know. But...he's so damned vulnerable."

"Not as vulnerable as you might think," King contradicted. "Don't underestimate his strength, Madeline."

"I try not to," she said ruefully.

It was impossible for her to eat any of the delicious supper Claire had prepared. After a time King said perceptively, nodding toward the house next door, "You'd feel better if you went back over there, wouldn't you?"

"Yes," she admitted, "I would."

"Come on, then. I'll walk you home."

There was a chill to the night air, and something ominous about Chris's big house being in total darkness. Madeline shivered as she let herself in while King waited on the porch.

Noticing her reaction, he said quickly, "Look, Chris isn't about to go off the deep end. Stop worrying so much."

"I'll try," Madeline promised. "I just can't seem to help it, that's all."

"So, you love the guy," King nodded understandingly.

She loved Chris very much. But when Madeline heard the sound of his car in the driveway an hour later, she didn't run out to greet him. His attitude had taken its toll on her, and she felt herself slowly burning with frustration.

When she saw him, though, she softened. He looked totally drained as he limped into the front parlor where Madeline had stretched out on the couch. He managed a weary smile and came over to sit down beside her.

"I'm sorry," he said. "I've been behaving like a spoiled bastard. Just this once, don't hold it against me, okay?"

"Just this once," Madeline agreed, pulling him down into her arms and embracing him as lovingly as she could.

THE NEXT DAY, Madeline discovered that Lorna Henderson had been assigned to her service. She sensed that Lorna wasn't too pleased about this, but if she showed it personally the young nurse certainly didn't show it professionally. Again, her performance was faultless.

Lorna looked tired, though, and harried. Surprised at her sympathy for the girl—considering the way Lorna had reacted to *her*—Madeline tried, once or twice, to engage her in dialogue. Lorna, however, sidestepped her attempts.

On Wednesday Madeline made a point of leaving the hospital early, even though she had to defer a fair amount of paperwork in order to do so. She and Chris had made plans to have an early dinner at a Chinese restaurant they both liked. Then they would head directly to the high school where the public hearing was scheduled for seven o'clock.

When they reached the school, the parking lot was so full they had a difficult time trying to find a place to leave their car. And as they walked toward the auditorium, Chris muttered, "I wish I knew whether this show of interest is good or bad."

That was something difficult to estimate. People greeted Chris amicably enough—even those whom he knew were opposing him. Madeline was introduced to the chairman of the town recreation commission, an outspoken advocate of the park-recreation center proposal. Then she met the chairman of the conservation commission, and several other distinguished citizens. Two of the men active in Lakeport's government were also on the hospital board of directors.

Several long tables had been set up on the stage in the auditorium, with a speaker's podium placed in between. Claire and King had saved Madeline a seat in the front row, and she joined them while Chris and Bill Edgerly went to take their places behind the table on the left. The committee chairmen and town councillors sat at the table on the right.

The meeting got underway promptly. The moderator, a local municipal court judge, was obviously bent on handling things efficiently and keeping the emotional level as subdued as possible. Nevertheless, it soon became apparent that emotions were running very high over the issue of what might be done with Chris's land.

As the various town officials rose to state their convictions about the proposal for a park and recreation center, Madeline knew that Chris would have to make a very good case for himself if he wanted to win most of the people in the auditorium over to his side.

A problem, she could see quickly, was that every speaker—and a number of townspeople who spoke from the floor—was making a plea for the general good of the community. It was pointed out that a lot of new housing—condos and small individual homes, for the most part—had recently been built in that outer area of Lakeport near Chris's land. And there was more housing planned, as the population continued to grow.

Madeline feared that Chris's rationale for wanting to rebuild on the same site was going to sound awfully self-interested in contrast to what just about everyone else was advocating. She wished that the meeting could be adjourned until the following evening so Chris could reexamine his thoughts and prepare an airtight case for himself. She wished, even more, that she and King and Claire had spoken to him about their thoughts for a possible compromise.

There were any number of specific ideas put forth, but the one that elicited the most applause featured a park-recreation complex that would contain a public swimming pool and tennis courts, as well as a wooded area for bicycling and picnics. One man also suggested an indoor skating rink that could double as a basket-ball arena. In fact, it increasingly seemed as if every-one had done their homework in record time.

During a momentary lull, King leaned over to Mad-eline and said, "I have to agree with a lot of this. There's a real need here, all right. But we need a health facility even more, though no one's thought to bring that up."

Finally the moment came when it was Chris's turn to state his case. As he awkwardly maneuvered himself over to the podium, Madeline not only sensed his ten-sion, she felt herself sharing it.

Chris, she knew from experience, did not come across especially well when he was tense. He tended to be un-smiling and cool, sometimes to the point of seeming indifferent. As she watched him scan the audience, her heart sank. Chris was projecting none of the charm he possessed in such abundance, and if he were going to make any impact at all on these people he needed to muster up as much of it as he could.

Madeline's fears were verified when Chris started off by stating, simply and succinctly, that in his opinion his factory would offer more to Lakeport than a park complex.

"We're fortunate enough to be located on the shores of Lake Champlain, which is recreational area enough in itself," Chris lectured.

Madeline heard a man behind her mutter, "Yes, for those with the money to own their own boats, or having access to private beaches."

"I brought the first light industry into this town just a few years ago," Chris went on, seemingly oblivious to the critical looks being sent in his direction. "You know that I put people to work who'd been without jobs for a long time. And we were prospering, all of us. Except for a tragic turn of fate, we would have continued to prosper.

"In the interim," Chris continued, "other companies have come to Lakeport, employing even more people. I feel, though, that I was the pioneer who started this trend. And, as you all know, I hoped to be opening my new factory this month. Now fate has intervened once again. But I believe in progress, and I certainly have the right to do with my land what I want."

Hearing this, Madeline blanched. Chris sounded as if he were threatening these people instead of advocating something for their common benefit.

"It's my intention to rebuild the plastics company," he told them. "And this time I will offer not only employment to more of you, but better benefits, more incentive, and a bigger slice of our mutual future." Still unsmiling, he added "Thank you" and turned the podium back to the moderator.

King shook his head in frustration. "Damn it," he said, his voice low, "why didn't he at least smile? That performance was like a cold shower."

The room was buzzing, and everyone seemed to be talking at once. Madeline wished she could zero in on the exact words of each and every conversation. Inwardly, she was cringing. Judging from the vibes alone, Chris had made a bad impression.

She knew how much this meant to Chris and, fundamentally, she was with him every step of the way. Yet she could see the other side of the coin, and was briefly thankful that physicians were trained to be objective. If only a little of her objectivity had rubbed off on Chris, she thought dismally.

The moderator rapped the gavel for silence and, still absorbed in her own thoughts, Madeline heard him say, "If there is no further business to be brought before us..."

Without pausing to consider the consequences of her actions, Madeline shot her hand up in the air and caught the moderator's attention.

He looked down at her questioningly. "Yes?" he queried politely.

Madeline stood, feeling almost as conspicuous as if she'd been stripped naked in a room full of strangers.

"I'd like to say something, if I may."

"Your name please, miss?" the moderator inquired.

Madeline thought her throat was going to close completely. "Madeline Clarke," she said. And added, automatically, "Dr. Madeline Clarke. I'm a staff physician at Lakeport General Hospital."

She was only vaguely aware of the interested hum that filled the auditorium following this announcement. She was concentrating on the moderator's face, knowing that if she didn't, she'd literally fall on her own.

"Yes, Dr. Clarke," the moderator said. Then he encouraged, "Why don't you step up here and use the microphone?"

CHAPTER SIXTEEN

MADELINE WAS FLABBERGASTED. She'd not expected to be asked up on stage and invited to address the whole assembly. That idea had never entered her mind. But the moderator was waiting expectantly, and she was painfully aware that all eyes in the auditorium were upon her—including Chris's.

King whispered encouragingly, "Go for it!"

Madeline looked down at him, momentarily incapable of moving an inch. Briefly, she didn't think she'd have the fortitude to stand in front of everyone and tell them how much Lakeport needed an outpatient clinic, but Claire's firm nudge gave her the needed impetus.

She walked forward slowly, feeling like a zombie, and she desperately hoped that she wouldn't sound like a zombie once she opened her mouth. Now that she'd come this far, though, she not only had to see it through, she had to accomplish something valid. Otherwise, Chris would never understand her move.

The moderator helped her up the steps to the stage, then bestowed a fatherly smile on her. "We'll all be interested to hear what you have to say, Dr. Clarke," he said, which didn't help her situation in the least.

Madeline tried to adjust the microphone, but her hands were too icy and numb.

"Let me help you," the moderator beamed, lowering the mike slightly. "That should do it," he approved.

With considerable effort, Madeline got a grip on herself. Chris was sitting to her right, and it took every last ounce of willpower not to glance toward him. She felt his strong vibes, and knew he was hoping she'd look him in the face. But she wasn't about to. She was clutching for courage as it was, and knew it would be much too easy to falter.

Chris, of course, had no idea what she was about to say. Nor was Madeline entirely sure, herself. She knew only that it had better be good!

She cleared her throat and began, slowly. "I'm a newcomer to Lakeport. But because I'm on the staff of your hospital, I already feel I'm a part of this community."

She drew a deep breath, then continued. "Lakeport needs industries like the plastics factory Chris Talmadge was planning to rebuild. The town also needs a park and recreational complex, like several of the people here tonight proposed so eloquently. But there's another need—an even greater one—that I think many of you are unaware of."

She began to feel more sure of herself and decided to come on more strongly. She said, her voice steady now, "In the relatively short time I've been at Lakeport General, I've become increasingly aware of the crowded conditions that exist in certain departments there. The situation is very serious, and it will get worse, unless something is done about it . . . and soon. There's an urgent need for more space, especially in the emergency room. If any of you have had the occasion to seek care in the emergency room lately, particularly on weekends, you know without my having to tell you that patients wait much longer than they should to receive treatment. This is because we simply don't have any place to put people once the examining rooms are filled. We've even had to resort to treating people in the corridor—many, many times.

"The staff physicians at Lakeport General are deeply concerned about this. Believe me, we don't like to see people—often people who are in pain—being forced to wait on the sidelines until we can find a free room in which to care for them."

Here and there in the audience, Madeline noticed heads nodding and people whispering back and forth. She wished she could see Chris's reaction to what she was going to say next, but she still didn't dare look at him.

"Among ourselves," she continued seriously, "we've discussed the need for expansion. Not expansion of the entire hospital, mind you...just certain departments—the emergency room in particular."

She paused, quickly forming a strategy for her argument. Then she said, "I'm aware that several years ago—actually about a dozen years ago, I believe—there was a successful fund-raising drive for the new wing. And thank God that wing was built," she added fervently.

"What we need now," she went on carefully, "is a satellite clinic to augment the services of Lakeport General. Again, let me stress that I'm not talking about another *hospital*. I'm talking about an outpatient clinic that could offer not only emergency care around the clock, but also handle walk-in patients during daytime hours. You can imagine the amount of time, effort and energy that would save many of you, especially those of you who live on the opposite side of town from the hospital.

"Perhaps, if you've traveled around in other areas recently, you've observed that walk-in medical clinics are springing up in communities everywhere. I've heard that a lot of you go South for winter vacations. If you've been in Florida, I'm sure you've noticed, maybe even used, the excellent walk-in clinics they have down there.

"Some of you may raise the question of how we'd staff such a clinic, when the hospital itself, from time to time, suffers a shortage of physicians. I can assure you that, with proper advertising, and the dissemination of pertinent facts to the medical community, there would be no problem attracting qualified job applicants."

Madeline managed a smile. "I can say from personal experience, now, that Lakeport is a very attractive town in which to live and work. I would happily recommend settling here to many of my colleagues."

An enthusiastic round of applause followed this well-timed compliment, and Madeline felt a warm flush suffuse her. But she *still* didn't dare glance at Chris.

"Speaking of Lakeport," she went on carefully, "I understand that, before I came here, several of the physicians at Lakeport General undertook a study of available land in this region, with a view toward finding a site that might be suitable for the kind of facility we feel is so desperately needed. Perhaps it will surprise you to learn that very few sites were found. In fact, the parcel of land that had the best potential for what I'm advocating is...part of the property owned by Chris Talmadge."

As she said this, Madeline would have sworn she heard the man in question mutter something under his breath. And though she realized her imagination was probably playing tricks on her, she couldn't avoid looking at Chris any longer.

Immediately she wished she hadn't. Chris was staring at her as if she'd just stabbed him in the back. His hazel eyes blazed with fury, and his mouth was set in a tight line.

Madeline couldn't blame him. She knew how she'd feel if their positions were reversed, but she'd gone too far now to retreat.

"I know that Mr. Talmadge has not been approached about this," she said, her voice quavering slightly. "And that's unfortunate. He should have been consulted first, before this subject was brought up in a public forum. But as I listened to what many of you have been saying here tonight, I thought it foolish to wait any longer in making the desperate need for a clinic known both to you, and to Chris."

Madeline felt herself perspiring and, summoning the last of her resolve, finished, "I regret this need wasn't brought to your attention sooner. And I ask that you, and he, consider it now."

The applause was thunderous. It rang in Madeline's ears as she stepped down from the podium and quickly rejoined Claire and King.

King whispered to her, "Gutsy lady." And Claire pressed her hand hard. But as much as she welcomed their support, Madeline was thinking only of Chris. And she was terrified.

She wondered what he'd do. She wondered if he'd turn his back on her as the meeting broke up, and stalk out. She steeled herself for the worst scenario, but as she stood numbly by King and Claire, Chris slowly approached them. He was leaning heavily on his cane, as he did when he was tired, and there was a bleakness in his eyes that Madeline hated to see.

He said quietly, addressing King and Claire, as well as Madeline, "Let's get out of here."

Fortunately they were near a side door, so they were able to make a quick exit. Clouds had been gathering earlier in the evening, and now a light rain was falling.

King said, "Why don't you guys wait? I'll bring my car around. No need for everyone to get wet."

"I don't mind getting wet," Chris said tersely. "I need some fresh air." As he moved off with King, he called back over his shoulder, "You wait with Claire, Madeline."

She cringed at his tone, and muttered helplessly, "Oh, God, Claire. He hates me for this."

"He won't, once he comes to his senses," Claire stated. "I'm proud of you, King is proud of you, and Chris will be, too—once he can see clearly again. Right now he's in a funk!"

"I've never seen him like this," Madeline managed to say.

"I know," Claire said. "But don't forget...this is Chris's home town. He cares a lot about Lakeport, and the people here. Once he gets his mind straight he'll see that there's a real opportunity to do something terrific."

Madeline wished Claire's optimism was contagious, but when Chris pulled up in front of them, her heart sank even more. In the dim light, his expression blended anger and disgust. It made her want to bypass him and go with King and Claire, but that would only further aggravate an already dismal situation.

She climbed into the seat beside him, and his stony silence was a shock. She hadn't expected casual conversation from him, but this was like finding herself suddenly surrounded by a rock wall.

Chris didn't speak on the drive home, and neither did she. Madeline's nerves were shrieking by the time they reached the house. Once inside, she faced him, her voice breaking as she pleaded, "Get it off your chest, will you please? Say whatever you have to say to me and get it over with!"

"I don't have anything to say to you."

She'd never heard a voice more flat, more totally devoid of expression. Worse, his face matched it. He was looking at her as if she was invisible. That hurt more than it would have if he'd slapped her.

"Chris, everyone was going to walk out of there thinking park-recreation center and nothing else," she told him bluntly.

"You're saying I did a lousy job of stating my case, is that it?"

Madeline wasn't about to dissemble with him. "What you told those people just didn't come across," she said frankly. "Not because they were against *you*, necessarily, but because they were united by a common interest."

"And my interest in them, which I at least *tried* to express, didn't register?"

"No, damn it, it did not!" She drew a long breath. "I don't know whether you can actually be forced to give up your land," she persisted, "but it's obvious people are going to look for legal ways to pressure you. There could be long delays—"

"I told you that myself, Madeline," he cut in sharply, "so you're hardly giving me any news. Well, the hell with them! Too bad the town doesn't need a new disposal area. I'd be tempted to donate my land for *that*, believe me. That's all I heard tonight—a lot of garbage."

Madeline faced him squarely. "What I said was *not* garbage!"

"I know," Chris admitted grudgingly. There was a dangerous edge to his voice, but at least this show of emotion was better than his previous nothingness. "Of course, you were parroting King," he accused.

"What!"

"You heard me," Chris retorted impatiently.

That did it. "I don't need King, or anyone else, to open my eyes to the inadequate situation that exists in the emergency room at Lakeport General!" Madeline shot back. "What the hell do you think I've been doing there, playing? Why don't you come out and see for yourself the next time I'm working on Saturday night!"

"Thanks, but I'll pass on that. I'd only be in your way."

The statement dripped cynicism, and Madeline resented Chris for saying it. Claire had pointed out that Chris wasn't thinking straight just now. Well, he wasn't seeing straight, either. Or hearing straight.

"There's no point in talking to you if you're going to stick your head in the sand," she flared.

"So now I'm an ostrich, is that the latest accusation?" he drawled.

Madeline was brimming with anger, discouragement and fatigue. She chided herself for raising her hand in the first place, but she also wondered how Chris would be acting if King, instead, had made a speech advocating a clinic. Would he be more tolerant of his lifelong friend, the surgeon who'd saved his life?

Suddenly the room just wasn't big enough to hold two people at such drastic odds with each other. The *house* wasn't big enough! Madeline could feel Chris's stubbornness assaulting her like a tidal wave. She could feel herself drowning, and she no longer had the strength to fight back.

She mumbled helplessly, "I should never have given up that hotel room."

There was dead silence. Then Chris asked ominously, "What did you say?"

She brushed back a lock of straying hair. "It doesn't matter."

"It matters very much. Did I hear you correctly? Did you say that you shouldn't have given up your room at the Château Champlain?"

"Chris, please—"

"Is that what you said?"

She gritted her teeth. "Yes, damn it! That's what I said."

His eyes were icy, his voice deadly calm. "You don't have to worry. You'll have this house entirely to yourself tonight."

Without another word, Chris turned and limped out of the room. A moment later Madeline heard the outside door thud closed.

She moved in a daze toward the front parlor, then lowered herself onto the couch, overwhelmed by his rejection. The dimensions of time and space had no meaning as she stared bleakly into the darkness.

Time passed. She didn't know how much time. Then slowly her thoughts began to focus again, and with alertness came fear.

Madeline began pacing the floor. She told herself Chris wouldn't get very far down the road before he'd realize what damn fools both of them had been. He, especially, she thought, her mouth tight at the memory.

He'd acted like she'd betrayed him, like she'd shot him without remorse. That, certainly, had not been her intention. Still, though grudgingly, she could see his viewpoint, could understand why he felt the way he did. But it was up to him to show her a little understanding, too. He was too intelligent and logical a person not to eventually realize that she'd never have spoken out as she had, unless she'd believed totally in what she was saying.

The sun was sending out advance messages, streaking bands of rosy color across the eastern sky when Madeline finally went upstairs and fell onto the four-poster without bothering to undress. She had to be at the hospital by eight, so it was imperative that she give her body some rest. She only wished she could divorce herself from her emotions. Their turmoil was not so easily resolved.

At work that morning, she was reminded of the days when she'd done her residency in Boston. For long periods of time, sleep had virtually been a stranger. She functioned now as she had then, primarily because she'd been trained to do so under such conditions. But by early afternoon she knew that if she didn't get away from the hospital for at least an hour she'd be totally ineffective. And that wasn't fair to her patients.

She dialed the house again, as she'd done every time she'd had the chance to get to a phone. Again there was no answer. Anger surfaced, anger directed toward Chris. But Madeline was also worried to death about him, so worried she was tempted to hurry down the hall to King's office and solicit his help.

Reminding herself that this impasse between Chris and herself was highly personal, she left word that she'd be out of the building for an hour. Then, avoiding the elevator where she'd likely run into people she'd rather not see at the moment, she scampered down the back stairs.

She drove directly to Chris's house, praying that she'd see his car in the driveway. The driveway was empty. She went inside, hoping that maybe he'd stopped by and had left her a note. She checked the kitchen table, which was where they always left notes for each other. There was no message there.

She went back to the hospital, and used the main entrance this time, not caring at this point whom she might confront. And she was passing the front desk when she suddenly heard her name called.

The receptionist, a pretty young French-Canadian woman, said, "That man's been waiting to see you for quite a while, Dr. Clarke."

Madeline turned to see a tall, dark-haired young man slowly approaching her, looking with every step he took as if he'd rather be backtracking.

Perhaps it was because she wanted so much to backtrack herself that Madeline empathized with him. She managed a smile. "You wanted to see me?"

"Dr. Clarke?"

"That's right."

"I'm Tim O'Brien, Lorna Henderson's fiancé."

Madeline was surprised, and hoped she didn't show it. She'd realized she'd not seen Lorna all day. Then she remembered that Thursday was Lorna's day off.

"Nothing's wrong with Lorna, is there?" she demanded.

Tim O'Brien's jaw tightened. Then he said, "No. I'd just like to talk to you—if you have a minute, that is. It's kind of personal."

Madeline glanced at her wristwatch. She had a few patients she wanted to check up on, but none were critical. It wouldn't matter if she postponed her duties for ten or fifteen minutes.

"There's a small waiting room right over there," she suggested. "It looks empty."

Madeline led the way and Tim O'Brien followed, so obviously ill at ease that she felt sorry for him. She sat down in a padded leatherette chair and motioned him to take a seat, all the while noticing that he was attractive, but still very young looking. He'd be Lorna's age, she remembered, as they'd been in high school together but he could have passed as a teenager. He had a shock of dark brown hair, light blue eyes, a sprinkling of freckles across his nose, and the rather appealing awkwardness of youth.

Wondering what he could want with her, she asked, "Does this concern Lorna?"

He nodded unhappily, then admitted, "I don't know how to put this to you."

Madeline smiled encouragingly. "Well, the best place to start is usually at the beginning."

He clasped his hands together. They were long, slim hands with bony fingers. Like the rest of him, they looked young. He said, "Okay, what it comes down to is that... well, I know that you and Chris Talmadge are..."

Madeline took pity on him. "Are you trying to say that we live together?" she asked gently.

He flushed slightly, but he nodded. "I guess what I was trying to say is that I know you have a relationship."

"And how do you know that, Tim?"

"From Lorna. Last night we were at that hearing at the high school. She dragged me there because it involved Mr. Talmadge's property."

Madeline shifted uncomfortably. She wanted to remain cool, calm and collected about this, but he wasn't making it easy.

Tim coughed, then said, "When you got up and suggested that a clinic might be built out on Mr. Talmadge's land, I thought Lorna'd go straight into orbit. She got very mad."

"Mad?" Madeline asked curiously. "Why?"

"She said you and Chris Talmadge are supposed to be...um, pretty special together. But you didn't hesitate to get up and stab him in the back. That's something like what she said."

"I wasn't stabbing him in the back, Tim."

"No, I'm sure you weren't. I know what you mean about the situation in the emergency room here. My father fell down the cellar stairs last Christmas when I was home on leave. We had to bring him over here to have him checked out, and I felt like we waited forever."

"Yes, tell me about it!"

"I tried to point that out to Lorna, but I didn't get anywhere. That's after we left—we were on the way back to her apartment." Tim paused again, then looked across at Madeline almost desperately. "I've wondered for a long time about Lorna and Mr. Talmadge," he said. "She took care of him when he was a patient here."

"Yes, I know."

"Well, the fact is, Lorna and I had a helluva fight last night, mostly about that. She ended up throwing her ring at me like it was nothing."

"Because of Chris?" Madeline asked, genuinely shocked.

"I guess you could say so. Look, I don't know what his feelings are about Lorna, but Lorna acts like he's some kind of god."

"I thought she'd gotten over it," Madeline murmured.

"Excuse me, Dr. Clarke?"

Tim was being painfully honest with her. Madeline appreciated that. The least she could do was to be equally honest with him.

"I thought Lorna had gotten over her infatuation with Chris," she said levelly. "I mean, I know she developed a crush on him when he was her patient, but things like that happen. Usually, though, they don't last very long. Once the episode itself is over, the people involved—whether patient, nurse or doctor—most often come to their senses."

Tim nodded dully, and Madeline added, "I thought Lorna had come to her senses when she accepted your ring. I hope you won't take this too personally but, as I understand it, a lot of the problem in your relationship with her has been that your career requires travel. Evidently, Lorna's a young lady who wants to stay put—"

"Only because of Chris Talmadge," Tim interjected. "Not because she's so crazy about Lakeport."

Madeline saw real pain in his eyes, and it made her flinch. She knew how he felt. She'd just had someone she loved walk out on her, too.

He went on, "I told her I'd quit the air force, if that's what she wanted."

"But you like what you're doing, don't you?"

"Yes, very much. I'm into electronics. I'm young enough to put twenty years into the service, take my retirement, and still have a career, or even start a business of my own."

"So you'd be giving up a lot if you were to resign now?"

"Yes," he said soberly, "I would. Lorna means that much to me. But if she really cares about Talmadge..."

"I doubt she does," Madeline said dryly. "Lorna's in love with a vision, not reality. She doesn't even know Chris, really. Do you follow me, Tim?"

"Yes, I think I do."

"He's much older than she is, and...I admit he makes a romantic fantasy figure," Madeline said wryly. "But there's no more place in Lorna's life for Chris than there is in Chris's life for her, believe me."

Tim smiled slightly, giving Madeline a glimmer of just how attractive he'd be one of these years, when he'd added a few layers of maturity.

"I'd like to believe you," he admitted.

"What Lorna needs," Madeline told him firmly, "is a good jolt from you! Whatever you do, don't resign from the air force! You've always been there when Lorna's wanted you, haven't you? So don't let her take you too much for granted."

Madeline glanced at her watch, then got up. "I'm sorry," she said. "I wish we could talk longer, but I've been keeping a couple of patients waiting."

Tim O'Brien stood also, tall and military straight. He faced Madeline squarely and offered her his hand.

"Thanks a lot, Dr. Clarke," he said. "I appreciate what you said. Believe me, I'll follow your advice."

As she left Tim in the lobby, Madeline was aware that being with him made her feel downright middle-aged. It was a funny feeling.

It wasn't until later in the day that she thought back to her conversation with him, and wished she'd voiced a few things differently. If he managed to jolt Lorna, as she'd suggested, but ended up losing her, it would certainly prove out the adage about fools rushing in where angels fear to tread. Last night and today, Madeline reflected whimsically, she'd surely proved she was no angel!

It was dusk when she got back to the Talmadge house, hoping against hope that she'd see a light on in one of the windows. But the dark panes stared back vacantly.

Upstairs, Madeline foraged in the closet for something comfortable and warm to slip on because the house felt cool. As she pulled out a sheer wool robe, her hand brushed a blue silk dress she'd worn one night in Aruba—the night when she and Chris had gone out with Arthur Taylor and Theda von Storch, the outrageous platinum blonde.

She'd sent each of them a postcard with her address when she'd moved from Bangor to Lakeport, but thus far they hadn't answered. Heaven only knew where Theda might be at this point. But Arthur, she surmised, would be in Pennsylvania, busy giving out advice on land planning, his lifelong career specialty.

Land planning. Madeline stood stock-still, as the import of Arthur Taylor's area of expertise swept over her. A moment later she was on the telephone, tracking down his number.

CHAPTER SEVENTEEN

ARTHUR TAYLOR ARRIVED in Lakeport three days later. Madeline had arranged to take the afternoon off and met him at the airport. Over the phone she'd told him something of what had been happening and, as they drove into town, she filled him in further.

He glanced at her as she finished her narrative, his blue eyes twinkling, and said succinctly, "The path of true love never runs smooth, my dear. Chris will get over this."

"I hope so," Madeline answered fervently.

She and Chris were still at loggerheads. He'd come home a couple of hours after she placed her phone call to Arthur. But he'd been sleeping on the cot in the makeshift bedroom downstairs, which she personally considered a childish gesture.

He was scrupulously polite every time they encountered each other—and since they were "sharing" the same house space, such encounters couldn't be avoided. In turn, Madeline went out of her way *not* to avoid him. Rather stubbornly, she made herself as evident as possible whenever they were home at the same time.

With Arthur's consent, she hadn't told Chris that they'd be having a houseguest. She was sure that Chris's innate good manners would triumph when he met Arthur again, but as an ace up the sleeve, she invited Claire and King over for dinner. It was the first real meal she'd prepared in a long time, and she was nervous enough as it was.

Her menu worked out well, though. And afterward everyone seemed happy and replete as they moved into the front parlor for coffee and liqueurs. Everyone, that was, except Chris.

Chris had been polite throughout dinner, but remote, taciturn—Madeline conjured up a whole bevy of adjectives to describe him, and came to the conclusion that she wanted to throttle him. She told herself yet again that if she didn't love him so damned much she would have walked out on him a hundred times over these past few days.

He'd offered no explanation for his absence of more than twenty-four hours, and Madeline was equally determined not to ask him where he'd been. The big mirror in the hall told her she was holding up extremely well under this strain, yet she knew full well there was a limit to her tolerance. And the ice man Chris had turned into was fast pushing her past the point of no return.

There was a fire blazing on the hearth, the mantle was decorated with Indian corn and bittersweet, and polished apples filled a wooden bowl on the coffee table. These things, and the crisp autumn air, made Madeline keenly aware that soon it would be Thanksgiving and, shortly thereafter, Christmas. The holidays would have been especially wonderful for Chris and her, had the events of the past few days never occurred. As it was, she couldn't imagine facing him on Christmas morning if the atmosphere between them was even a fraction as tense as it was now.

She was counting heavily on Arthur to save the situation concerning Chris and his property. She was literally holding her breath, hoping Arthur could help with the impasse that threatened the relationship she wanted so badly.

Arthur was convinced, from what little she'd told him, that everything everyone wanted could be accomplished on a large tract of land like Chris's—and he'd yet to see the site! "There are all kinds of ways to get a goose to lay golden eggs," he'd said enigmatically over the phone.

Madeline was glad when King, as if on cue, steered the conversation toward the subject of Arthur's new career, and Arthur enthusiastically launched into the interesting story of what he was doing in his "retired" life.

"I wasn't ready to be put out to pasture," he announced firmly as he accepted a glass of apricot brandy from the tray Madeline was passing around. "It's really a shame, I think, that people stop using their talents when they've put in so many years to be the best at what they do."

Madeline pretended to be listening to Arthur intently, but all the while she was sneaking glances at Chris, hoping he wouldn't notice. To her distress, she saw that he was mirroring more and more suspicion.

There *was* a certain subterfuge involved in Arthur's visit, and she began to wish that she'd come right out and told Chris exactly why he was here. As it was, she and Arthur had cooked up a story about Arthur's going to visit an old college classmate in Montreal. Then, supposedly, he'd remembered that she and Chris lived not too far from there, and had phoned on the chance they'd be around. One thing led to the next, and here he was. Their alibi had sounded plausible enough at the time of invention, but now the holes in it were much too discernible.

It was a relief when the evening came to an end and King and Claire took off for the Parmeter mansion next door. Arthur, after bidding his hosts a hasty good-night, headed upstairs to the guestroom Madeline had prepared for him. Chris vanished into the library, firmly shutting the door.

Claire had insisted on helping with the cleanup after dinner, so once Madeline had carried the few remaining glasses and cups out to the kitchen and washed them, there really wasn't anything left to do. Reluctantly she turned off most of the downstairs lights and went up to the room that, until so recently, she'd shared with Chris, but was now hers alone.

She was in her nightgown, brushing her hair, when there was a knock on the door. Thinking it must be Arthur, and that he probably needed something, she slipped on her robe. But when she opened the door it was a decided shock to find Chris standing on the threshold.

He looked so tired and harried that Madeline's heart went out to him. But the cold glint in his eyes was enough to dissuade her from making any physical approach toward him, even though she yearned to do exactly that.

"May I speak to you?" he asked abruptly.

Under other circumstances, Madeline would have gladly welcomed this suggestion from him, thinking it might provide a breakthrough in this stalemate between them. But his tone was enough to convince her otherwise.

"Of course," she told him quietly, then retreated to the bed and sat down on its edge.

Chris stood a careful distance away from her, very much on guard. His gaze raked her briefly, and the look he gave her was anything but flattering. "You invited Arthur Taylor here, didn't you?" he asked pointedly.

"Yes, I did," Madeline said, glad to be honest.

"Your scheme is to have him advise me as to what I should do with my land, isn't it?"

"Scheme?" Madeline echoed, her eyebrows arching defiantly. "I don't think I like your word choice," she added, matching Chris in abruptness.

"What would you call it, then?"

"Plan, suggestion, thought, idea—" Madeline broke off, then allowed, "It suddenly occurred to me that Arthur could be very helpful to you. If you'll listen to him, that is."

"Do you think I'm capable of that, Madeline? Or do you think I'm too pigheaded to listen to anybody?"

This admission, if she could call it that, was not what Madeline was expecting. She'd been truly afraid that Chris was apt to be the last person on earth to recognize his own stubbornness.

She met his eyes and wearily confessed, "I don't know."

Chris tugged a straight-backed chair out from the wall, placed it near the bed and sat down. "I've been doing a lot of thinking," he said then, not unpleasantly.

"About . . . your factory?"

"About my factory, about us, about everything."

Madeline waited, her heart beginning to pound. She almost didn't want to hear what he might say next.

Sensing her apprehension, Chris said softly, "Maybe I just don't understand you, Maddie. Maybe you think differently than I do. I don't know. But loyalty has always ranked high in my book."

"Loyalty ranks high with me, too," she managed to say.

"Does it? I would say you were as disloyal as hell to me at that meeting the other night."

His scorn stung, and she actually flinched. Crazy, but she felt as if she were growing smaller, sitting there on the side of the bed, huddled up into a miserable little mass. But Madeline *was* miserable. Chris's disapproval hurt worse than a raw wound.

Patching her voice together, she said, "The last thing I intended was to be disloyal to you, Chris. And...I still don't think that I was. What I did the other night— getting up in front of a crowded auditorium—was an impetuous move on my part. Can you see that?"

"Maybe that's part of the problem, Maddie," Chris answered. "I've never considered you an impetuous type. To me, you've always been a cool and logical woman of science."

Madeline stared at him, and her mouth fell open. Remembering their many mutual moments of unbridled passion, she didn't see how he could say such a thing. But those special together times were a rare commodity of late, Madeline thought sadly.

Summoning her professional objectivity to the best of her ability, she had to admit Chris was right—to a point. Even King had observed she was "cool," she recalled. As for being a "logical woman of science," she supposed that was true. But what was so wrong with that, damn it? She was also flesh and blood...and right now every cell in her head was in total confusion.

Madeline yearned to slap Chris's handsome face, and yet she also wanted to go to bed with him so badly she could hardly stand it!

Trying to rein in that maddening thought, she conceded, "You're right, Chris. I suppose I'm not usually impetuous. But that night at the meeting I could sense the way the wind was blowing, and I didn't like it. It seemed pretty obvious to me that public opinion was not on your side. But just because I feared you were going to be in for a lot of grief..."

"Yes?"

"I wish you'd stop looking at me that way! Now I know how a microbe laid out on a microscopic slide would feel—if it had any feelings."

"That's very funny," Chris told her sarcastically.

Madeline ignored that, and continued, "I brought up the issue of the clinic because I sincerely felt it needed to be brought up."

"And you decided that I'd never appreciate being consulted on this idea first?" Chris demanded, his tone again glacial.

"I didn't really decide *that* either way," she told him honestly. "King and I planned to talk to you about the concept of a clinic, but then the fire happened and... well, the moment was never right. There was nothing deliberate about it, though. Please believe me when I say that the opportunity simply didn't arise."

"Sometimes you have to create the opportunity."

"I couldn't agree more," Madeline murmured. "We didn't, and we should have. I'm just saying there wasn't any malice involved, that's all. I wasn't trying to hide anything from you and neither was your best friend."

Madeline had no doubt that Chris was hearing and listening to what she was telling him. But he still looked skeptical.

"At the meeting," she went on, "I admit I had the sudden compulsion to snatch the moment because I didn't think there'd be another chance."

"Snatch the moment," Chris repeated dryly. "I'd say you grabbed it and hung on for dear life."

"Perhaps, in your mind, I did. I can only say that, whether you believe it or not, I was thinking of you."

"The hell you were," he scoffed, glowering at her. "You were thinking of the damned clinic, Madeline, not of me. You were thinking of medicine—the force that rules your life."

Madeline could see the black hole gaping between them. It would be so easy for both of them to fall in and become lost to the point where they'd never be able to climb out and stand on common ground again.

She said, very carefully, "If it's a career conflict between us you're bringing up, then this is a very different ball game, Chris."

"I don't think so. I think what we're bringing up is an honest assessment of where your priorities lie. I should have gotten the message when you insisted on moving into the Château Champlain. It seems obvious, in retrospect, that you were afraid of jeopardizing your medical reputation."

Madeline shook her head in frustration. "I thought it was wiser not to move in with you immediately, and I still think it was the right course to follow," she said steadily. "I was thinking of your reputation, too."

"Were you? You could have shared that idea with me. I wasn't in the least worried about my reputation. I'm an adult, damn it! The way I live my life is nobody's business but my own."

"You haven't been behaving like an adult lately, Chris," Madeline whispered, making Chris lean forward to catch her words. "If you'd stop acting like a spoiled child who's had his candy taken away from him, you'd realize I love you far too much to ever deliberately do anything that might hurt you."

Chris folded his arms across the top of the chair, nestled his chin against his wrist, and closed his eyes. Then he exhaled heavily, and his whole body seemed to shudder. After a long moment, he slowly raised his head and met Madeline's anxious eyes. He said huskily, "I needed so badly to hear you say that."

They met halfway across the bedroom, and fell into a passionate embrace. When their mouths came together, their kiss was filled with more wanting and desire than Madeline had ever experienced. Chris caressed her tenderly one moment, feverishly the next and, as her emotions spilled over the edge, tears welled in Madeline's eyes.

"This has been such hell," Chris murmured finally, holding her as if he'd never let her go. "Nothing is worth going on like this...absolutely nothing!"

Madeline clung to Chris desperately, her love for him surmounting everything else. Suddenly they were in bed, and it was so natural, so right. Blissfully they released their tensions in the oldest and most wonderful of ways. And it was also natural when the sleep they both badly needed finally overtook them as they nestled together.

MADELINE AWAKENED FIRST. She gazed lovingly at Chris, still asleep, and thought he looked ten years younger than he had last night. His sandy hair was tousled and he needed a shave, but he'd never looked more marvelously alive.

She wanted to awaken him with a kiss, but thought better of it. There wasn't time to start this day with lovemaking because she was due at the hospital in another hour. Also, she and Chris still needed to talk, on a rational, practical level.

She slipped downstairs and made coffee. Then she returned to the bed, carefully carrying two cups of the aromatic eye-opener. Leaning over the bed, she kissed him awake.

His smile was incredibly tender as Madeline sat down beside him. She hated to erase that smile and was very much afraid she would, with what she was about to say.

If only time weren't always of the essence!

"Chris," she began uncertainly, "I hate to bring anything up, but . . ."

"Anything's a rather vague term," he stated cautiously.

"Yes, I know. I . . . well, the thing is, I need to ask something of you."

His smile faded slightly. "Ask away," he said.

"Chris . . . look, will you at least talk to Arthur?"

He feigned surprise. "Of course I'll talk to Arthur. He's our guest, after all."

The "our," at least, was encouraging.

Madeline took another plunge. "You know what I'm saying," she told him. "I wish I didn't have to go to work today, but I do. Otherwise I'd suggest the three of us drive out to the factory site . . ."

She both sensed and saw Chris back away. Nevertheless she continued. "I wish, more than I can possibly tell you, that you'd drive Arthur out to the site yourself. That's all I'm asking. Drive him out there, let him look at it, and listen to what he has to say. Is that too much to ask?"

"No," he said slowly, "it's not. But I'm not going to do it, Maddie. I'm not ready for it—it's as simple as that. Something else has come up..." He ran a hand through his hair, mussing it even more. "At this point," he added, staring toward the far side of the room, "I don't know what I'm going to do."

Madeline surveyed his face anxiously, dismayed and discouraged to think Chris might actually have kept something really important from her. "What's the problem?" she asked, feeling almost weak.

"The problem is a woman who was killed at the plant when lightning caused the explosion, almost a year and a half ago," Chris said heavily. "The police finally tracked down the right orange pickup. It belongs to her husband. To make a long story short, he's confessed to setting the second fire."

"Oh, my God," Madeline murmured.

"To tell you the truth," Chris continued hoarsely, "I don't want to prefer charges against him. He's gone through such hell that he's built up an admittedly crazy idea that the whole thing happened because of negligence on my part. I don't think any court in the land would find him guilty. Probably it'd be a verdict of temporary insanity. Whatever... it's made me think, Maddie. I've had nightmares over this. I've come close to the point of believing I actually was responsible for the deaths and injuries of my employees and..."

Madeline placed two fingers against his lips. "Shush," she cautioned. "That's wrong and you know it. It won't do you, me or anyone else any good to start off on that kind of guilt trip. It wasn't your fault, Chris, and you know it."

"Logically, yes. But..."

"I don't imagine you can stop the police bringing charges against this man whether or not you want to," she said. "Arson's a felony, after all. But even if that happens, even if he *is* convicted, Chris, you can't blame yourself."

"Sometimes it's a lot easier to blame yourself, than not to."

"I know, but whatever happens in regard to this man, it should have no bearing on whether or not you rebuild your plant, if that's what you've been thinking about."

"That's exactly what I've been thinking about," he admitted, "and driving myself crazy over. That . . . and you."

Madeline took his hand and held it. Then she said shakily, "Chris, you have to rebuild. Whether you stick to your original plan or go by Arthur's suggestions isn't the issue here. You need to rebuild your factory. Even more, you need a research lab where you can work on your designs. I've heard King talk about the current device you've been working on. He has such great hopes for it. Think what this may mean to a lot of people someday."

Chris didn't answer, and Madeline had the feeling he'd been so lost in his own thoughts he hadn't even heard what she'd said. She gently disentangled their fingers, got up and, with a backward glance at him, headed for the shower. He didn't even move.

It was very difficult to leave the house that morning. Arthur was still asleep, so Madeline suggested to Chris that maybe he and Arthur could go out to breakfast together a little later in the morning. Chris only nodded dully.

She put in a long and difficult day at the hospital. Again, Lorna Henderson was working with her, which didn't make things any easier. Lorna appeared to be deeply preoccupied. Several times Madeline had to repeat a question or an order.

Then, as she was about to leave late that afternoon, Madeline was called in for consultation by a neurologist who wanted her opinion concerning a stomach problem one of his patients had developed. It was an important matter, and something she couldn't sidestep or defer to someone else.

Claire had invited Madeline, Chris and Arthur for drinks, and they'd all planned to go out to a popular local spot for dinner afterward. Knowing that she'd be late, Madeline tried to reach Chris by phone, but there wasn't any answer at the house. So she called Claire and told her to urge the men to come over by themselves. She'd join them as soon as she could.

It was nearly seven by the time she got home. She showered quickly, chose a jersey dress in a gorgeous burnt orange shade, and then went across to the Faradays.

King insisted on fixing her one of his fantastic martinis, but Madeline sipped it cautiously. She was tired and still emotionally drained from last night. She knew the gin would quickly go to her head.

Actually, Chris and Arthur seemed to be getting along very well together. Arthur was relating some of the incidents that had happened in Aruba and it was fun to listen and let some happy memories take over.

"Ever hear from Theda?" Chris asked as he reached for another of the delicious hors d'oeuvres Claire was serving.

Arthur chuckled. "Somehow she found out my birthday was in August and sent me a birthday card," he recalled. "She's married again. To an Englishman this time."

"This time?" Claire queried.

"This is Theda's fourth," Chris reported. "That's right, isn't it, Arthur?"

"Unless she's lost count," Arthur chuckled. "But from the way she writes, it just may be her last. She's living in London, and she sounds ecstatically happy."

"I hope so," Madeline said. She was remembering the vulnerable Theda—that lonely, frightened woman beneath the glossy exterior. She hoped she'd finally found the right life partner.

"Remember that night in the casino?" Arthur began, but was interrupted by the steady pealing of the doorbell.

King glanced at Claire. "You expecting anyone else?" he queried.

"No, are you?"

King shook his head and rose rather reluctantly. "Okay," he said, "I'll get it. Gad, it must be someone who's really eager to get in. They don't want to let up."

The doorbell kept ringing steadily as King made his way toward the front of the house, and Claire said, frowning, "Whoever it is, you'd think they might realize—" She broke off as King came into the room with Lorna Henderson.

Lorna was still wearing her nurse's uniform, complete with white stockings and sturdy white shoes. But her dark hair was in disarray, her makeup smudged, and her eyes wild.

King said, "Sit down, Lorna. Look...sit down!" He literally pushed her into the nearest chair. "I'm going to get you a drink."

She tossed her head negatively. "I don't need a drink, Dr. Faraday," she gasped, breathing as if she'd just run a marathon.

Madeline surveyed the girl anxiously. "Lorna, what's happened?"

"It's Tim," Lorna quavered and suddenly tears filled her eyes. "I got home and there was this note from him pushed under the door of my apartment," she cried. "He told me he's going A.W.O.L."

"Absent without leave," Chris muttered automatically.

"Are you saying he's running off without letting the air force know what he's doing?" Madeline demanded.

"Yes," Lorna moaned and added before anyone else could speak, "He could be shot when they catch him! That's what they do to deserters, isn't it?"

"Maybe in the middle of a war," Chris admitted. "But certainly not in these times—provided he has some pretty good explanation of his actions."

"He says all I've ever done is take him for granted," Lorna sobbed. "I—I broke our engagement the other day. I gave him back his ring. I haven't seen him since. But I didn't have any idea he'd do something like this."

Madeline froze as the memory of her conversation with Tim O'Brien returned to her vividly. She'd urged Tim to give Lorna a jolt. She'd convinced him that he'd become too predictable where Lorna was concerned. Well...he'd taken her advice.

She swallowed hard. *Fools rush in?* She'd never felt more of a fool!

King was handing Lorna a small glass half-filled with amber liquid. "Bourbon," he said. "Go ahead, drink some of it. You need a jolt right now."

His choice of words made Madeline wince. Then she felt Chris's eyes upon her. They could have been twin magnets, compelling her to meet them. She did, and saw a strange expression on Chris's face. It gave her the weird feeling that he knew she had something to do with Tim O'Brien's disappearance.

She sighed, wishing she could sink through the floor. Turning to Lorna, she said slowly, "Lorna, try to calm down, try to think clearly. You know more about Tim and his habits than any of us. If you'll comb your memory, maybe we can find him."

Meeting Chris's demanding gaze again Madeline added, "I've a feeling he's not too far away from here."

CHAPTER EIGHTEEN

AS SOON AS SHE SPOKE, Madeline knew that later on she'd have to do some explaining to Chris. He was much too perceptive.

"*Think*, Lorna," she urged. "Where would Tim be apt to go if he wanted to get away from it all?"

Or, she added silently, *if he wanted to give you the scare of your young life!*

"I don't know," Lorna said dully.

"Well, have you checked with Tim's family? He does have family here in Lakeport, doesn't he?"

Lorna shook her head. "Tim's father died a couple of years ago. His mother's remarried and lives over in Watertown. I don't think Tim would go there. He can't stand his stepfather. He has a couple of brothers and sisters, but they're scattered all over the place. They were a lot older than Tim anyway. He's never been close to any of them."

Lorna sighed. Tears brimming, she said, "I guess Tim has always been a loner. He's always said I'm the only person in his life who really meant anything to him. I guess I never took that seriously enough. Tim was just *there*. I guess I thought I could do whatever I wanted to do and he'd always be there." The tears spilled over and Lorna wailed, "Oh, I feel awful!"

Claire found a linen napkin and handed it to Lorna. Lorna wiped at her eyes. "What do you mean, Dr. Clarke, by a place where Tim might go?"

"Exactly that. A lot of us have escape hatches. Sometimes it might be a park bench, or a corner booth in a café, or the attic in our own house. Sometimes it's a place where we might have gone on vacation a long time ago, or—"

"There's a cabin up in the mountains!" Lorna interrupted. "Tim's father had a little cabin over toward Bremerville, about thirty miles from here. It's on the slope of Mount Candy, right on a little lake. Tim's father left it to him. I don't think his mother ever knew anything about it. Mr. O'Brien used to use it as a... what did you call it? As an escape hatch sometimes. He used to take Tim up there hunting and fishing."

Lorna flushed. "Tim and I spent a few days there while I was on vacation recently," she admitted.

Madeline stood. "Well," she asked, "what are we waiting for?"

She and Chris opted to make the drive up into the mountains with Lorna. The night air was nippy and Madeline shivered as she slid into the front seat next to Chris. From time to time she glanced back at Lorna, who had lapsed into total silence. For that matter, neither she nor Chris said very much during the drive, which took the better part of an hour because of the winding mountain roads.

Lorna was somewhat vague in her directions. Twice they took the wrong turn and had to backtrack, losing still more time. The tension mounted, and Madeline began to wonder what they'd do if they got to the cabin and Tim wasn't there.

Finally they hit the right road and pulled up alongside the small lakeside structure. It was a relief to see candlelight flickering in the window and smoke wisping out of the chimney.

Madeline asked, "Do you want us to come in with you, Lorna? Or would you rather do this on your own?"

Lorna's hesitation was brief. Then she said, "I'd like to go in by myself. But... will you two please wait around?"

"You can count on it," Chris promised.

Lorna mounted the cabin steps and they heard the echoing thud as she knocked on the front door. It seemed forever before the door finally opened, and another eternity before Lorna went inside and the door closed behind her.

Only then did Chris slant a knowing glance at Madeline. "So where do you fit into this?" he asked.

Not daring to look at him, she said, "I guess once again I rushed into a situation an angel would avoid at all costs. Tim came to the hospital to see me and I told him the problem was that Lorna took him too much for granted. I said he should give her a real jolt." She added fervently, "Believe me, I'll never again try to play Cupid, or meddle in anyone else's business."

"Even at public hearings?" Chris said wickedly.

Madeline swung around to face him and saw love in his eyes and laughter on his lips. She let him laugh, and nothing had ever sounded better, even though she knew his mirth was directed at her. It was tender mirth, though, and her love for Chris overflowed as she listened to him.

He reached out for her, muttering, "Damn bucket seats!"

"Yes, I think it's time you got a more comfortable car."

"Maybe a bedroom on wheels?" Chris suggested.

"Maybe."

"Maddie..."

"Yes?"

"This business about rushing in where angels fear to tread?"

"Yes?"

"Never change, darling. I admit you raise a lot of havoc, but I'd never doubt that your intentions are as good as anyone's could ever be."

"You know what the road to hell is paved with, don't you?" Madeline asked darkly. "Good intentions!"

"I don't believe that," Chris said. "I..."

He didn't finish what he was going to say because at that moment the cabin door opened. He and Madeline held their collective breaths until they saw *both* Tim and Lorna emerge.

Arm in arm they walked down the steps and toward the car. Chris rolled down the window as they came abreast of it. Tim greeted Chris, but his eyes were for Madeline.

She caught his message. He might as well have said aloud to her, "It worked!"

"Will the two of you come in?" Tim asked politely. "I can put a pot of coffee on."

"Thanks," Chris said, "but I think we'd better get back to Lakeport."

"This was very decent of you, Mr. Talmadge," Tim said sincerely, his eyes still on Madeline.

"I take it Lorna's going to stay here with you?" Chris asked.

"Yes," Lorna answered for herself. "Forever," she added. She still looked teary, but her smile was radiant as she gazed at Tim. "From now on," she said, "wherever Tim goes, I go. After all, I can get a job as a nurse anywhere."

"You certainly can," Madeline agreed.

"I'm going to be stationed at Plattsburg for at least two more years, so we can get to that later," Tim said confidently. "Meanwhile, thank you again."

With farewells ringing in the air, Madeline and Chris drove off. But their exit soon proved to be anything but simple. Almost at once Chris took a wrong turn and they found themselves heading up Mount Candy.

"Damn, if Lorna hadn't gotten so mixed up coming over here I'd have had the route memorized," Chris complained, backtracking.

From then on they both had to concentrate completely on directions. There was no time for conversation until they were on the last lap of the road to Lakeport and the aftereffects of Lorna's emotional crisis were setting in.

Madeline felt tired all the way through—body, mind and soul. And Chris had retreated into a tight-lipped silence. She guessed he was once again absorbed with the problems she wished they could both put on the shelf.

Claire, King, and Arthur met them at the door of the Parmeter mansion. A round of drinks were made, and Chris and Madeline filled the others in about Tim and Lorna's reunion. Madeline was thankful when Chris refrained from bringing up anything about her part in that particular episode.

Arthur left the next morning. He actually did have a friend in Montreal, and was going up to visit him for a few days. Chris volunteered to drive him to the bus station since Madeline had to be at the hospital early in the morning.

She shared a breakfast cup of coffee with Arthur, then said goodbye to him. Chris was in the library, attending to some paperwork, so Madeline was able to say, "I can't thank you enough for coming. And... I can't say how sorry I am that it didn't work out. Chris can be terribly stubborn."

"I don't think I'd call it stubbornness," Arthur corrected gently. "I think Chris has a lot on his mind. He has to think things through for himself. Give him a little more time, Madeline."

Her laugh was shaky. "I'm willing to give him all the time in the world," she confessed. "I just hate to see him doing this to himself, that's all."

"We always hate to see someone we love struggling, and suffering in the process," Arthur said wisely. "But life deals out brickbats, as well as bouquets. You do your own thing for a while, Madeline, and let Chris work this out himself."

Arthur was suggesting a hands-off policy, at least temporarily, and Madeline knew he was right. She reminded herself that she'd sworn not to rush into other people's business anymore. That promise applied to Chris, too.

It wasn't an easy vow to keep. Though she and Chris shared the same bed again, there was still a dark chasm between them.

Halloween came, and Chris chuckled when Madeline spent the afternoon candying apples, and making little packets of sweets with which she filled a big plastic pumpkin.

"I think you're going to enjoy trick or treat night more than the kids will," he teased.

She did. She loved doling out her largess to the bevy of goblins, witches and fairy princesses who came trooping to the front door that night.

"I think the word's out that the pickings are good here," Chris observed as Madeline refilled the plastic pumpkin for the second time. "Next Halloween we'll probably have such a mob we'll have to call out the cops to keep the peace."

Next Halloween. To Madeline, carefully wrapping some additional candied apples in waxed paper, next Halloween seemed an awfully long way away.

With the advent of November, the last of the bronze, red and amber leaves drifted off the trees, and the wind blowing in from Lake Champlain was chilly and raw. Madeline went to a ski shop on Main Street and bought herself a pair of flannel winter underwear, about which Chris teased her unmercifully.

She was having an exceptionally busy time at the hospital. People's ailments seemed to peak with the onset of winter. Many days she had to start too early and work too late. She'd be so tired when she got home she would fall asleep at the drop of a hat.

An added problem was that this wasn't a good period for Chris. The police had been adamant about charging the perpetrator of the fire with arson. There'd been nothing he could do to forestall that. There'd been a preliminary hearing, and now the man was undergoing psychiatric evaluation. Chances were, Chris said one night, that he would be pronounced fit to stand trial. But it still seemed fairly certain that, in the end, he'd probably be found not guilty by reason of insanity.

"Which'll mean he'll have to spend a lot of time with a shrink, in the hope he can be straightened out," Chris opined.

It was Thanksgiving morning when he said that. He and Madeline were having a late breakfast, which they decided would be their only meal until dinner. They'd been invited to King and Claire's for "the feast."

Madeline said, "Frankly, I think that's the best thing that could happen, Chris. No matter how sympathetic you feel toward this man, you can't let him go scot-free when he's done something as serious as setting fire to a factory. Suppose there'd been someone inside that night?"

"I've thought about that many times," Chris said heavily.

Remembering her vow about not rushing in, Madeline had avoided pinning him down about anything these past few weeks. But now she couldn't resist asking, "Have you decided about rebuilding, Chris?"

He shook his head. "No, I still don't know what I want to do."

"What about your invention?"

"The plans for it are finished. I need to translate the plans into a working model."

"For which you need your lab?"

"Not necessarily," he hedged. "I think I can rig up space in the basement that will be adequate for the time being. I've done some preliminary testing, and King agrees there's little doubt that it's going to work."

"Assuming you're right, you'd want to go into production with it, wouldn't you?" Madeline persisted. "And you'd want to produce it in your own plant, wouldn't you?"

"I haven't gotten that far," Chris said abruptly. He picked up a section of the morning paper and started reading it, effectively shutting her off.

Madeline had insisted on doing her share toward the Thanksgiving dinner. She'd baked cranberry nut bread, made pumpkin pies and a molded salad. Late in the afternoon she took the food across to Claire's kitchen, walking through the back door just as Claire was basting the turkey.

The aromas wafting through the house and the sight of the big brown bird brought back long ago memories of Thanksgivings at the house in Scranton, when Madeline's father was still alive. For the first time since then, this holiday was having a real meaning for her. During the years of her marriage to Jeffrey, they'd rarely celebrated Thanksgiving and most other holidays together. Usually one of them had been working.

She smiled at Claire, swept by a sweet nostalgia—a feeling that persisted all day. She was in a happy, mellow frame of mind as she slipped into the deep gold dress she'd chosen to wear to dinner.

Chris looked very handsome in dark brown slacks and a fawn-colored jacket. As they were about to leave the house, he deliberately laid his cane aside.

"I'm going to make it without this tonight," he told Madeline, then added with a laugh, "If I fall on my face, you guys'll have to pick me up."

She doubted Chris would fall on his face. His leg was stronger and he'd learned to balance better. As they walked next door to the Faradays, she felt very proud of him.

They were sitting in front of the living room fireplace, enjoying pre-dinner mugs of mulled cider when the telephone rang.

Madeline wasn't much of a believer in intuition, but she had the uncanny feeling that her holiday was about to be ruined. When King returned and she saw his face, she knew she was right.

"That was the hospital," he told her. "The call was for you, actually. It's Mrs. Abbott. She appears to be having some rather severe problems."

Madeline rose reluctantly. "Sorry, folks, I'll have to go out there." She sighed.

Claire, who'd gone to the kitchen to make a final check on the turkey, appeared in the doorway just in time to hear this. "Must you, Madeline?" she pleaded. "Isn't there someone else who could fill in for you?"

King answered first. "Not really," he said. "This woman has been a patient of Madeline's for several weeks now. She's been in and out of the hospital, and it's been difficult to pinpoint her problems. Madeline's done a terrific diagnostic job, but evidently whatever's flared up now is something relatively new. There's not much doubt that it would be best to have someone who knows her history handle it."

Madeline forced a smile. "I'm on my way, King," she assured him.

"We'll wait dinner for you," Claire decided. "I'll fix a few snacks for the boys."

"No," Madeline replied quickly. "You'd better not do that. Anyway, I love cold turkey. I'll be ready to pick away the moment I get back."

All this time Chris had not said a single word. Now he volunteered, "Would you like me to drive you to the hospital?"

"There'd be no point, Chris," she answered, wishing he'd injected just a little warmth into his tone. "I mean, I might as well go myself because there's no telling how long I'll be."

Chris nodded, and let it go at that. But as Madeline turned away and headed for the door with King accompanying her, he was sorely tempted to either go after her or call her back.

He knew he'd handled matters badly, once again. But so damned often she'd had to defer plans they'd made because of her work. He realized only too well that this wasn't something that was ever going to end. Madeline was first and foremost a doctor. She'd be forever subject to the demands of her career. She was, after all, dealing with human lives, so it could not be otherwise. And he supposed he was being a selfish bastard to resent it.

King came back, and Claire asked, "Don't you think we should wait for Madeline?"

He shook his head. "There's no telling how long she'll be tied up." He turned to Chris and added, "It's rotten luck having this happen on Thanksgiving. I'm sure Madeline will make it back as soon as she can. She doesn't want to work today any more than you want her to."

"Well," Claire said unhappily, "how about lighting the candles on the dining room table, King? I'll bring in the bird."

The three of them sat down to the feast Claire had prepared, but they were hard put to maintain a festive spirit. Claire and King did their best to entertain Chris and he was very much aware that that's exactly what they were trying to do—entertain him.

King was carving the turkey when the phone rang again. Claire slipped out to the kitchen to answer it, but he'd instinctively put the carving knife down and was getting up when she returned to say the call was for him.

A minute later he reluctantly explained, "That was Madeline. She's run into a problem—an abdominal obstruction that's going to require emergency surgery. Otherwise, we're apt to lose Mrs. Abbott."

"Get on your horse, King," Claire said softly and actually smiled. She went over and threw her arms around him, then kissed him fully on the lips. "There's nothing better than cold turkey sandwiches," she reminded him.

Once King had left, Claire's smile faded. She came back to the table, sat down opposite Chris, and said, "It's all part of the deal, Chris. Better for you to find that out now than later."

She surveyed the table, laden with food. "Why don't we put this stuff away," she suggested. "We'll all have turkey sandwiches when they get back. Meanwhile, how about you and I fixing a couple of good, strong drinks and spending a little time in front of the fireplace."

Chris helped Claire clear the table, moving very carefully without the cane as a prop, but managing nevertheless. It felt good, once they'd finished, to stretch out before the hearth, drink in hand.

He glanced at Claire, and saw she was staring at the flames, her lovely face thoughtful but serene. He felt a real stirring of admiration for her and said, "You handle your life awfully well, Claire."

She laughed wryly. "It took me a while," she admitted. "But you know that better than anyone else, except King. All those years King and I were apart. Then we got together again and it didn't look as if we'd make it. So...I wouldn't give up what I have with King for all the missed Thanksgiving dinners in the world." She turned her gaze upon Chris. "You have to weigh the bitter and the sweet, assess your priorities, and decide where you stand," she told him. "I did that. Now it's your turn."

"I know where my priorities are," Chris said, his voice low. "I've been doing a lousy job of juggling them, that's all."

"It takes time, Chris. And you've had a lot on your plate. When I think of everything you've handled in the past year and a half, I'd give you straight A's."

"Sure about that?" He smiled as he said it, but her answer was important to him. He'd known Claire a long time and valued her friendship, just as he valued King's.

"Well, maybe I'd sneak in a couple of B's," she allowed, smiling back at him. "You're not always a very good actor, but you'll learn. You'll get to the point where you can send Madeline off with a kiss and a smile just as I do King. Because you know she'll always be coming back to you. That's what counts."

Claire's remark echoed in Chris's head when King and Madeline returned from the hospital, almost three hours later. There was every indication that the surgery King performed was successful. Both doctors were very tired, but satisfied with their work. They ate cold turkey sandwiches, drank hot chocolate and, at the end of it all, King said, "Say what you like...but it's still been a great Thanksgiving."

"I second that," Chris nodded.

His eyes caressed Madeline as he spoke, and he hoped she was listening. He wanted her to know this represented a quantum leap on his part.

That night Chris gently tucked Madeline into bed. Then he went back downstairs to the library and, sitting at his desk, did some heavy thinking.

Madeline had to be at the hospital at nine the next morning. Chris waited until she'd left the house, then tracked Arthur Taylor down by telephone.

Their conversation began with an apology. "This is something I should have had the sense to take up with you when you were here," Chris admitted frankly.

"Stuff and nonsense," Arthur rejoined. "To tell you the truth, I thought I'd be hearing from you. So I took the liberty of getting a plan of your property at the town office while I was in Lakeport. I thought it would save us both a little time."

Chris chuckled. "Was I so predictable, Arthur?"

"I wouldn't say 'predictable.' I just knew that sooner or later you'd want to know what the score really can be."

When he finished talking with Arthur Taylor, Chris leaned back, dazed by the possibilities Arthur had dangled before him. Arthur had one job to do in Trenton, then another in Connecticut. But he promised that before Christmas he'd return to Lakeport and get down to the nitty-gritty.

Chris was tempted to page Madeline at the hospital and share the good news with her. He was fired with hope and an excitement he'd not felt in ages.

Arthur was positive that the swamp could be converted into a man-made lake—the focal point of a park and recreational area. On one side of the park the woods could be judiciously cleared, leaving plenty of room for construction of the clinic. The factory would be situated well back of the park. And a research lab where Chris could have the privacy to concentrate on his inventions would be built a short distance away.

Chris worked through the day, losing all track of time in his absorption. It was late in the afternoon when

Claire called, urging him to bring Madeline over for a day-after Thanksgiving feast.

He accepted for both of them and, during the course of the evening, fought off the temptation to tell them about Arthur Taylor's vision. Now that he'd waited this long, he wanted to hold off until Arthur himself came back. That would make the surprise even more exciting for Madeline.

ONE AFTERNOON, during the week before Christmas, Chris drove out to Lakeport General Hospital and sought Madeline out. He found her sipping coffee in the doctors' lounge, scanning a stack of patient histories.

She'd been on call the night before and one look at her was enough to show Chris that she hadn't gotten much sleep. Circles of fatigue smudged her eyes and her whole body telegraphed weariness. But surprise and delight mingled when she saw him, bringing new life to her face.

Chris was relieved by her reaction. He wanted to wrap his arms around her and put all the emotions he was feeling into a single kiss. Then he would take her home and make her get some rest. But instead of yielding to impulse, he held out a long narrow package and said, "Here's an early Christmas present for you."

Madeline looked at the vaguely familiar foreign stamps glued to the brown paper wrapping, then slowly met Chris's eyes. "What is it?" she asked curiously.

"Open it and find out," Chris suggested.

Madeline tore away the paper, opened the box, and stared down at a mass of spindly branches and scraggly leaves. She looked perplexed, and Chris laughed.

"Think of Aruba," he suggested.

"Aruba?"

"Remember the divi-divi trees?" Chris asked softly. Madeline nodded. Her pulse began to throb.

"Remember the story about them?"

She nodded again. She said, her voice almost a whisper, "The trade wind always blows the divi-divi leaves in one direction. So if you follow the way they're pointing, you can never get lost."

"That's right," Chris murmured huskily. He took a deep breath and added, "We've been losing our way with each other much too often, Maddie—mainly because of me. I promise you that's going to change. But I thought perhaps if we kept a few divi-divi branches around it would always remind us—"

He broke off, watching the play of emotions on her lovely face. Tears began to fill her eyes and a flush of color tinged her cheeks. "I love you, you know," he told her quietly.

The tears spilled over. "Oh, Chris," Madeline whispered brokenly, "I love you, too."

"Then I wonder..." He paused and, his voice steadying, asked, "How would you feel about marrying me?"

The tears spilled over, but with them came a tremulous smile. "I thought you'd never ask."

She set the box aside and went to Chris, her arms outstretched. He clasped her and, as their lips met, they lost track of time and place. Finally Chris pulled back and looked at his watch.

"What is it, darling?" Madeline asked.

"I'm supposed to meet Arthur's plane at the airport," he said, "and if I don't get out of here, I'm going to be late."

"Arthur?"

"Arthur Taylor. He's going to be our houseguest for a while—right through Christmas, if it's okay with you." Chris's eyes sparkled. "Oh, Maddie," he told her, "there's so much to tell you. It's going to work out, everything's going to work out..."

Chris's excitement was contagious, and Madeline's laugh rang out. She loved seeing him like this, brimming with enthusiasm, vibrantly alive. He was everything she wanted in life—tall, handsome, healthy and wonderful.

She reached for a divi-divi branch, broke off a small piece, and placed it in his hand.

"Just to make sure," she told him.

Chris grinned. "I'll take it to make you happy, but I don't need it," he said. And added, before kissing her again, "Wherever I am, wherever I may be, I'll always find my way back to you."

IT'S NEVER TOO LATE FOR LOVE....

A SEASON FOR ROSES

A VERY SPECIAL SUPERROMANCE
BY A VERY SPECIAL AUTHOR

Ashley Harte is an elegant fifty-year-old widow whose fondest desire is someday to have grandchildren. But from the moment the handsome and distinguished Ryan McKay sets eyes on Ashley, he courts her with the fervor and determination of a man half his age. Ashley had always thought that romantic love was for her children's generation. Ryan McKay is about to prove her wrong....

A SEASON FOR ROSES is a heartwarming story, filled with the intensity that well-loved Superromance author Barbara Kaye always brings to romance.

Coming in April 1987

Harlequin
Superromance

COMING NEXT MONTH

#254 DRIVE THE NIGHT AWAY • Jocelyn Haley
Sara Deane thinks she's found love at last in the
arms of Cal Mathieson. But she's a teacher, he's a
woodworker, and Cal is adamant their relationship
won't work. Sensing that Cal's hiding the real
reason for his reluctance, Sara devises a plan to
uncover the truth....

#255 TANGLED DREAMS • Lynn Erickson
When financial consultant Margery Lundstrom
meets Dr. Warren Yeager, a brilliant scientist, she
finds her emotions soaring. But she soon decides
he's beyond help in matters of romance. It's up to
him to prove her wrong....

#256 CHANCES • Janice Kaiser
Blaine Kidwell is a professional poker player.
Caleb Rutledge is a man of the cloth. They've got
as much in common as a church and a gambling hall.
So why are they falling in love?

#257 A SEASON FOR ROSES • Barbara Kaye
Fifty-year-old widow Ashley Harte thinks romantic
love is for her children's generation. But the
handsome and distinguished Ryan McKay sets out
to change her mind.

Can you keep a secret?

You can keep this one plus 4 free novels